"HEY THERE, GORGEOUS."

Sydney swung around in surprise. He was about eight feet away, between her and her car. His Harley was parked up the dirt road, near the bend.

"I didn't hear you ride up."

"Yeah," he said, "I walked that big son of a bitch all the way from the main road."

"Why'd you do that?"

He grinned, and tucked his thumbs in the front belt loops of his jeans. "Guess."

"So I wouldn't hear you. What about the bar? Friday's a busy night . . . won't you be missed?"

"The guys'll cover for me. Besides, this won't take long. Unless, of course, you want it to."

Sydney felt her pulse quicken; out here passersby were few and far between . . . it was getting dark quickly. "What is it exactly that you have in mind?"

"Well, I thought we'd get better acquainted . . . for starters. . . ."

PATRICIA WALLACE

DEADLY DEVOTION

ZEBRA BOOKS
KENSINGTON PUBLISHING CORP.

ZEBRA BOOKS are published by

Kensington Publishing Corp.
850 Third Avenue
New York, NY 10022

Zebra and the Z logo Reg. U.S. Pat. & TM Off.

First Printing: August, 1994

Printed in the United States of America

For Maxine O'Callaghan,
who as usual beat me to it;
And for Andy,
for laughing in the right places.

With Thanks To
Jean Jenkins, my San Diego eyes,
and to
Eugene S. Gini, Jr.
of the Lake Tahoe District Attorney's Office
for letting me pick his brain.

With devotion's visage
And pious action do we sugar o'er
The devil himself
—Shakespeare

Prologue

April

The courtroom was hushed as he rose to speak, and Deputy District Attorney Jake Scott felt the cumulative weight of the jury's—and indeed his own—expectations. Satisfying those expectations was undeniably a challenge, but one he welcomed, even savored.

In a criminal trial, the State of California reserved the last word for the prosecution, which bore the heavy burden of overcoming the presumption of innocence guaranteed to the accused by the Constitution.

Jake alone was responsible for making the final summation strike a responsive nerve. Even though the judge might warn the jury that neither opening or closing arguments were to be considered as evidence, the jurors were only human. Chances were they couldn't help but give added weight to the State's final words.

As was his practice, Jake began to pace. He cleared his throat and spoke quietly, forcing them to concentrate on listening to the sound of his voice.

"You've heard the defense's contention that Keith Reilly, although far from perfect, was a satisfactory husband to Denise. An interesting word, satisfactory . . . except, what is it they say about damning with faint praise?

"By all accounts, however, Mr. Reilly has been shown to be a devoted father to little Daniel. And Miriam Reilly testified that Keith was always a good boy, very much the loving son."

In the first row of seats behind the wood gate, Miriam Reilly raised an immaculate white handkerchief to dab at her eyes.

Right on cue, Jake thought cynically, averting his gaze. Several of the jurors had also seen her, judging by their doleful expressions, and Jake felt a flash of irritation, which he knew better than to show.

"Defense counsel would have you believe that being one or all of these things means that Keith Reilly is innocent. That he couldn't have done what he is accused of, because only a heartless monster would kill a beautiful young woman while her child slept a short distance away in another room. But we . . . *you* know better."

He looked directly at the defendant. "Husbands kill their wives. Fathers murder the mothers of their children. Sons can and do commit homicide."

Reilly didn't blink, but a corner of his mouth twitched fractionally.

"And Keith Reilly shot and killed both his wife, Denise, and her best friend, Gayle Honeywell, in cold, calculating blood. He murdered his wife because he feared she would take their son and leave him as a result of learning of his numerous affairs. He killed Gayle Honeywell simply because she was there."

In the gallery, Miriam Reilly pressed the handkerchief to her trembling mouth.

"In his initial statement to the police, Keith Reilly stated unequivocally that at the time the murders occurred, he was working at The Quick Gold Fox, his place of business, preparing for an upcoming—and vitally important—inventory. He also indicated that his partner, Nigel Fox, who the police had rather conveniently 'just missed' could and would confirm this."

Jake Scott paused as he turned toward the jury, and looked thoughtfully from face to face.

"What Keith Reilly didn't know was that Nigel Fox, his presumed alibi, had been in police custody since two A.M., and Fox was at that very moment sleeping it off in the drunk tank at the San Diego County Jail.

"But right out of the gate, what the police *knew* was that Keith Reilly was not telling the truth. Keith Reilly had something to hide.

"The *evidence* has shown that on the night of the murders, Keith Reilly left his business at around one A.M. He did not return until approximately two-thirty.

"You heard the security guard testify that Mr. Reilly's car was not in the parking lot at a quarter past one when he came through on patrol. That, in fact, upon seeing the lights on in The Quick Gold Fox, he tried the door and found it secured, and that no one responded when he, and I quote, 'knocked loud enough to wake the dead.' "

One of the jurors gave a slight nod.

"Keith Reilly would have you believe that he'd just slipped out for a breath of night air and a fresh cup of coffee, never mind that there was and is a coffee maker in the back office."

The same juror cast a sideways glance at Reilly, who sat with bowed head.

"You heard Lieutenant Mitchell Travis testify that the police were unable to find a waitress or convenience store clerk in the surrounding area who'd served or sold Keith Reilly a cup of coffee. And no one has come forward, in all these many months, to say that they did."

The defense attorney, Wade Cooper, stifled a yawn, feigning nonchalance.

"The evidence further shows that there were no signs of forced entry at the Reilly home, that the doors and windows were securely locked when the police arrived at five fifty-seven A.M., which indicates the killer either had a key, or was admitted by Denise Reilly or Gayle Honeywell."

He stood and crossed to the easel, which displayed a floor plan of the house. He directed the jury's attention to the living room, where body-shaped outlines represented the slain women.

"We can estimate from the crime scene evidence—the trajectory of the bullets and blood distribution patterns—that the killer stood about here." A black X marked the spot. "Denise Reilly was shot in the back with, according to ballistics, a nine-millimeter automatic as she started for the nursery—" he indicated a nearby room "—where baby Daniel slept."

A low murmur passed through the courtroom.

"The first shot was not instantly fatal, because she managed to drag herself, bleeding profusely, another few feet toward the baby's room." He paused, letting them consider the desperation that

Denise must have felt, so horribly wounded, trying in vain to get to her child.

"Then Denise was shot again, at the base of the skull. And that stopped her, although it too failed to kill her outright."

He contemplated the pros and cons of repeating the precise medical descriptions of her wounds from the autopsy—the requisite gory details—but decided against it. There came a point of saturation, when detail numbed instead of outraged, and he preferred not to chance diluting anyone's rage. Besides, the jury had seen the lurid color photographs from the crime scene and the autopsy. And they'd sat, white-faced, as the pathologist testified at length.

More to the point, a couple of the female jurors now appeared to be on the verge of tears; it would serve his purpose better if they saved their emotions for the jury room.

"Gayle Honeywell was shot at close range in the chest," he went on dispassionately. "The police surmise that she put up her hands in a futile attempt to ward off attack, which explains the grazing wound to her left index finger. Gayle probably was backing away when she was shot."

He raised his own hands to illustrate how inadequate a shield mere flesh and bone would provide against an automatic weapon, and then lowered them to his sides.

"The murder weapon has never been found. But you heard sworn testimony that Keith Reilly, who collected guns as a consequence of his occupation as a dealer in gold and rare coins, had purchased a nine-millimeter Beretta automatic in 1989. That weapon is also missing, presumed to be stolen. No police report regarding the theft was ever filed.

"Is the missing Beretta the murder weapon? I can't answer that, and we may never know. It is curious, however, that of all Mr. Reilly's guns, it was the Beretta that came up missing."

He frowned and shook his head. "Regardless. Gayle Honeywell didn't want to die. She didn't deserve to die. And even if, in the hurt and confusion of her failing marriage, she threatened to punish her husband by running away with their child, neither did Denise Reilly."

His throat felt dry and he stopped briefly at the prosecution table to take a sip of water.

"The State contends that on the night in question, Keith Reilly left his place of business and went to his home, where he'd been banished to a guest room. He let himself in with his key and confronted Denise.

"Perhaps it was his intention simply to persuade Denise not to act rashly, not to run off, but there came a point in their confrontation when something went horribly wrong. It may well be that Denise threatened, as she'd done before, that Keith would never see his son again. In the heat of the moment, he abandoned reason and embraced force.

"He shot her as she turned to run to her child, quickly shot Gayle Honeywell to keep her from interfering, and then, more deliberately, stepped forward and aimed at his wife's fallen body. That third shot eliminates any pretense of impulse. It was clearly Mr. Reilly's intent that his wife die."

Reilly's jaw was tight, his eyes angry.

Finally rising to the bait, Jake Scott thought.

Good; the timing couldn't be better. Let everyone see that hot Irish temper.

"It is likely that Keith Reilly remained in the house for a time, waiting to make certain both women would die. The pathologist testified that Miss Honeywell might have lived up to thirty minutes after being shot; Denise . . . less than that. Both were in a terminal condition, in end-stage agonal breathing. Gasping for air."

He pressed his fingertips together and brought his steepled hands to rest under his chin in an attitude of prayer.

"Then, when it was over, Keith Reilly left the silent house in the dark of night, disposed of the 'stolen' Beretta, and returned to work to await the police, who would arrive several hours later to tell him what he already knew, that Denise and Gayle were dead."

At the defense table, Wade Cooper made notes on a yellow legal pad.

"The defense has charged that much of the State's case against Mr. Reilly is circumstantial. I would remind you that few murders occur in public view. Camcorders can't witness every brutal act. But the verifiable facts are like signposts, pointing in his direction, and his direction only. Keith Reilly had the opportunity, the means, and the motive to kill.

"Husbands kill their wives," he repeated. "Fathers murder the mothers of their children. Sons can and do commit homicide. Don't let him get away with it."

* * *

Jake Scott smiled, listening absently to his co-counsel describe an encounter in the public restroom with one of the courthouse regulars, an elderly homeless man who thought nothing of stripping down to his skivvies and "bathing" by way of the sink.

His attention, however, was riveted on the muffled sound of voices behind the door that led to the jury room. The call advising him to return to the court was hardly a guarantee that a verdict was in—it might be another request to have testimony reread, or it could be that the jurors wished the judge to clarify again his complex instructions to them—but gut instinct told him this was something else entirely.

Something he wouldn't like.

It was too late in the deliberation process for a down-and-dirty guilty vote, and yet far too early for a by-the-book conviction.

As much as he prided himself on the accuracy of his instincts, this time he prayed he was wrong. And in any case, why was it taking so damned long for them to enter the courtroom?

At the defense table, Keith Reilly sat, his face pale but otherwise devoid of emotion. So expressionless was he that a casual observer might conclude it was a touch of the flu that made him appear ashen, rather than the actuality: that twelve jurors were all that stood between him and death row.

Jake Scott had been a prosecutor for seven years, during which he'd helped convict a handful of cold-blooded killers, sending them on to await execution in California's apple-green gas chamber, but he still found it curious the way some men hid their emotions—assuming they had any—even when their lives were on the line.

Of course, the word going around was that Reilly insisted he was innocent, and thus felt there was nothing to worry about.

Where had Jake heard *that* before?

Glancing around the courtroom, he noticed a couple of underlings from the D.A.'s office were huddled near the double doors in conference with a reporter from the *San Diego Union-Tribune*. One of the two had stood in to file a minor motion in the Reilly case a few months back, and now he was probably lobbying to get his name mentioned in the press coverage.

Ambitious toad.

Lieutenant Mitch Travis was also in attendance, along with his betrothed, Sydney Bryant. A bright and competent private investigator, Sydney was undeniably an up-and-comer in town, as well as being a nice bit of work—

The door opened behind him just then and all else was forgotten as he turned to watch the jury file silently in. One of them, a heavyset woman in her fifties, wouldn't meet his eyes.

Not a good sign.

A few anxious moments later came the verdict: the jury was hung.

Jake Scott swallowed his frustration long enough to determine that the vote had been deadlocked at eleven to one for convicting Keith Reilly of two counts of first degree murder.

One lousy vote.

The judge declared a mistrial.

"Your Honor," he shouted over the din of voices from the gallery, "the State intends to refile against Mr. Reilly, *today*. We request a hearing to set a new trial date, and we further request that Mr. Reilly's bail be revoked since he is now a substantial flight risk."

One

After thanking the jury for their diligence, the judge dismissed them, and scheduled a hearing to set a date for retrial. Then, without comment, he summarily revoked the defendant's bail. Virtually at the same instant, bailiffs appeared on either side of Keith Reilly to take him into custody.

An impressive display of efficiency, Sydney Bryant thought. Here at least—and for now—law and order reigned . . . whether or not justice had prevailed.

Wielding the gavel, the judge announced, "Court is adjourned," and left the bench, disappearing into chambers with a swirl of his black robe.

"I'll be back in a minute," Mitch said.

Caught off guard, Sydney could only watch as he maneuvered his way to the prosecution table, where Jake Scott was jamming files into a leather briefcase with barely contained fury.

Evidently Jake wasn't satisfied with fighting to a draw. Not that she blamed him; from what she'd heard and read about the Reilly case, a guilty verdict should have been a foregone conclusion.

Then, too, Jake had never been known to be a

gracious loser, which probably accounted for his
rapid ascendance through the ranks to assume the
role of heir apparent to the District Attorney.

If he didn't blow a gasket first.

Stepping into the aisle, Sydney narrowly avoided
being caught in the tangle of reporters elbowing a
path through the crowded courtroom, presumably
in a hurry to file their respective stories.

"Pardon me," one of them kept saying, even as he
all but trampled those too slow to get out of his
way.

Two rows in front of her, the defendant's mother
had leaned awkwardly over the wooden divider that
separated the gallery from the court proper, and
was fiercely embracing her son. Bracketed by stern-
faced bailiffs, each holding an arm, Keith Reilly
appeared to be the unfortunate prize in a tug-of-
war.

Wade Cooper was doing his best to pry his client
loose. "It'll be all right, Miriam. Let him go. He has
to go with them."

"Why? Why are they taking him back to that
awful jail? My boy is innocent, do you hear?"

One of Cooper's assistants, a striking young
black woman, came through the gate and gently
disengaged Miriam Reilly from her son. "You can
see Keith in a little while, I promise. But he has to
go with them now."

As if her strength had deserted her, Mrs. Reilly
sank into her seat, covering her face with her hands.

The bailiffs spirited Reilly away, taking him out
through a side exit into the secured holding area
behind thick bullet-proof glass. There they paused
for a moment to handcuff him before hustling him
out a second door. Reilly did not look back.

Wade Cooper sighed as he ran a hand through his white-silver hair.

Meeting his eyes briefly, Sydney sensed his frustration. It surprised her a little: Cooper was a seasoned pro, thirty years into a distinguished law career, during which he'd never hesitated to take on the most challenging, high-profile cases.

Certainly he'd lost before, many times. If a hung jury even counted as a loss. Unless. Unless Cooper truly believed his client to be innocent and had sincerely expected an acquittal?

"None of my business," Sydney said under her breath, turning to leave the courtroom. She'd wait for Mitch in the hall, but if he didn't hurry, they'd have to forget about lunch.

Mitch was off duty—he was working swing shift this month—but she had to get back to the office to assist her partner, Xavier Walker, in interviewing job applicants. The newly incorporated Bryant and Walker Investigations was sorely in need of a secretary, and they had appointments scheduled throughout the afternoon.

She had reached the double doors when a hand tapped her on the shoulder. "Excuse me," said a female voice. "Are you Sydney Bryant?"

Against her better judgment, she answered "Yes."

"You understand, Ms. Bryant, that this isn't the way I normally handle a case," Wade Cooper said.

"I imagine not." Her words echoed faintly. They'd found refuge in a stairwell. The cement floor was littered with cigarette butts, and a fine blue haze of smoke hung languidly in the air.

"I have, of course, an in-house investigator."

"Of course," Sydney murmured.

"He's been with the firm since 1973, but he under-went a triple bypass last year, so I contracted with an outside agency to conduct interviews, gather background information, review evidence, and the like."

Sydney nodded in what she hoped was a noncom-mittal way. "I see."

"I have to admit I was satisfied with their work initially, but as the trial has progressed, I've become uncomfortably aware that there are *gaps,* quite pos-sibly fatal gaps, in what we know and don't know. Which brings me to you, Ms. Bryant."

"I prefer Sydney."

"Sydney then. From the beginning I believed that the District Attorney's office hadn't a chance in hell of making their case. Maybe old age has addled my brain, but in retrospect, I realize that I was relying on the weakness of their case instead of the strength of my own."

Sydney doubted that age had anything to do with it; Cooper's eyes held a look of keen intelligence, that of someone who had seen it all and could be counted on to never miss a trick.

"Notwithstanding my own shortcomings in strat-egy, I have been inexcusably lax."

Through the wire-reinforced glass window of the stairwell door, Sydney saw Mitch enter the hall. With his dark good looks, dressed casually in a black shirt and tan chinos, he captured the attention of more than one female bystander.

Forever the cop, he instinctively scanned the crowd. Within seconds he'd located Sydney and their eyes met. From twenty yards away, his smile felt like a caress.

"I'd like to hire you to work on Reilly's defense," Wade Cooper continued, with a glance of his own through the window.

"Why me? Wouldn't it be easier—"

"—if the original investigators took up where they left off? Perhaps, but I feel strongly that what we need at this point is a fresh perspective. A year into it, I'm concerned that it becomes ever more difficult for anyone—myself included—to disregard preconceptions."

"I can't argue with that, but why me?"

"Ayanna, my paralegal, has been following your career for some time now—"

"My career?"

"—and I trust her insight." Almost in contradiction, Cooper gave her a thoughtful, measuring look. "You were the investigator in the Blood Bride murder?"

Blood Bride. The media had a curious fondness for tagging names on prominent cases—if nothing else, it made for tidy headlines. In this instance the tag referred to the brutal stabbing death of Martina Saxon. The blood was Martina's, but the bride had been the one wearing it.

There were still nights when her dreams were haunted by the memory of having found Martina, floating lifeless in a courtyard pool . . .

"Yes," she said, turning the thought aside. "That was mine."

"Then you're not a novice." Cooper reached into his inside coat pocket and withdrew a small gold case, from which he extracted a business card. He held the card between his index and middle fingers, offering it to her with an elegant economy of motion. "I'd like you to come by my office this afternoon."

Sydney ignored the proffered card. "My schedule is tight—"

"Tomorrow will do. I have a morning court date, but Ayanna can give you an overview of the details, enough to get started with."

"I appreciate the offer but—" she shook her head regretfully "—I'll have to pass."

He regarded her for a moment. "Why is that?"

A simple question, for which there was no single easy answer. "There are a number of reasons. For one, I'm in the process of setting up a new office with my partner—"

"Xavier Walker; yes, I'd heard."

"—and we agreed not to accept any new cases until after we're settled in."

"You could make an exception."

"Theoretically, but I would have to consult with Xavier before doing so."

The defense attorney smiled, reextending his business card. "Consult with him, by all means. Then give my office a call."

Sydney got the impression that Cooper believed he'd outmaneuvered her, although it wasn't clear how. Feeling stubborn, she continued to ignore the card. "Even if Xavier is willing to make an exception, there's a potential conflict of interest."

"I assume you're referring to your relationship with Lieutenant Travis."

Despite the incestuous nature of the legal community, it never ceased to amaze her how much those in power knew about other people's private lives, never mind that in her line of work she knew that in an age of computers, privacy was little more than an illusion.

"The lieutenant isn't an issue as far as my client and I are concerned," Cooper went on. "The prosecution has a legal obligation to share information with the defense. I trust the San Diego Police Department *and* Lieutenant Travis to act accordingly."

"What about the fact that I think your client is probably guilty?"

"You said 'probably,' which I take to mean you're not sure. That's good enough for me. I know I can rely on your professional integrity, that you'll keep an open mind."

Wade Cooper would have made a great snake-oil salesman, Sydney thought wryly.

"More to the point, I'm confident that no matter what you might think now, when you take a closer look, you're going to conclude that the D.A.'s case doesn't fit the facts."

An intriguing premise. Sydney hesitated, considering the various demands upon her time—her mother wanted her to start shopping for a trousseau, although no wedding date had been set. She reached for the business card.

"I'll let you know," she said, tucking the card into her shoulder bag.

Wade Cooper smiled and held the door.

"What was that all about?" Mitch asked as they walked down the hall.

"He wants me to work for him."

"On Reilly?"

Sydney nodded.

"Avoiding a conviction by one vote must have put the fear of God into them."

"I noticed Jake Scott didn't look all that happy, either," she observed.

"Now there's an understatement if ever I've heard one," he laughed. "Speak of the devil . . ."

They were nearing the bank of elevators where a couple of camera crews from local stations had cornered the deputy D.A. The bright wash of television lights made everyone look pale and bereft of blood, as though they'd been carved from wax.

Mitch did a smooth about-face, guiding her toward the stairwell, his hand on the small of her back. "I'm not in the mood to play media fodder," he said.

When they were out of earshot, she asked, "Is Reilly guilty?"

"I think he is. But if you're inclined to work with Wade Cooper on his defense, have at it."

"The thing is," she said, "I'm not at all sure I want to take this case."

Two

"Are you crazy?" Xavier Walker asked, swinging his feet off the desk. "Of course we should take the case."

Sydney picked up a paper airplane from where it had crash-landed near the waste basket and handed it to him, then sat on the corner of his desk. "I don't think we have the time—"

"Then we'll *make* time. We'd be fools to pass up the publicity this'll bring us. And we both know that publicity equals profits."

"Xavier—"

"Sydney—" he imitated her tone perfectly, then grinned. "Remember, darlin' we've got overhead to worry about."

"You had to remind me."

In fact, she wasn't likely to forget; the suite they'd leased in the heart of San Diego's Golden Triangle had a price tag every bit as upscale as the address. Granted, the place had everything—a private office for each of them, connected by glass pocket doors; a stylish reception area; a secure computer and file room; a recently converted darkroom; and even a small lounge, complete with kitchenette and a bathroom that included a shower stall. But the cost was breathtaking.

Were it not for the surplus of office space due to that curious California propensity for over-building and the recessionary ceiling on commercial rents, they'd be way out of their league, never mind what they were saving by pooling their resources.

"Anyway," Xavier said, running his thumbnail along a crease in the paper airplane, "you and I both know you've been aching to return to those sixteen-hour days in the field."

"Aching isn't the word."

When he glanced up, the light reflected off of his glasses, obscuring his eyes. "Isn't it?"

It was more like an itch, really, but she wasn't about to admit it. Instead she said, "I'm just not overly fond of the administrative side of the business. But there's no avoiding the fact that we have at least another ten days worth of scut work ahead of us. Not to mention we've got to hire a secretary, and soon."

"I'll handle that." He sailed the plane toward the tinted window, which overlooked University Towne Centre, the open-air mall across La Jolla Village Drive.

"You will?"

"Absolutely." The plane hit the window and dropped to the floor. "I swear I won't rest until I find the perfect secretary."

"Right." Sydney made no attempt to disguise her skepticism. "Define 'perfect' for me."

"Well, first and foremost, she—"

"Or *he.*" There were male names on the appointment calendar.

"—would have to be willing to work a little un-

compensated overtime now and then without filing
a complaint with the Labor Board. Otherwise, the
usual attributes . . . experienced, competent, reliable, prompt, and pleasant."

"You forgot thrifty, brave, clean, and reverent."

"That too."

Although they'd only known each other since December and worked together for less than six weeks,
she had a notion of what type of woman appealed
to Xavier. Nearing fifty, short and balding, gleefully
happy at being divorced for the fifth time, he virtually hummed like a tuning fork when in the vicinity
of any female wearing spike heels, a leather skirt, or
faux animal print.

None of which qualified as front-office apparel.

"I don't know," Sydney said.

Xavier held up a hand. "Word of honor, I won't
hire anyone who snaps their gum, chews tobacco,
wears a nose-ring, or engages in otherwise unto-
ward behavior."

"Why am I not reassured?" she laughed.

"Trust me."

"Ah, famous last words."

He waved a dismissive hand. "Run along now,
before I come to regret my generosity."

Wade Cooper's law practice occupied an entire
three-story building near Old Town. Its wood exterior contrasted nicely with the lush green land-
scaping surrounding it. The interior was even more
impressive, with an open floor plan which revealed
the wood beam ceiling and the circular walkway
accessing the upper floors.

A waterfall in the lobby added to the feeling of

spaciousness; the sound of splashing water no doubt was soothing to the tender psyches of both the firm's lawyers and clientele.

Crossing to the reception desk, Sydney briefly regretted that she was wearing mocassins. Although she preferred to dress for comfort and utility, she admired the smart tap of heels on a stone floor.

The receptionist was straight out of a Norman Rockwell painting, dressed in a simple white blouse and a straight navy skirt. As far as Sydney could tell, she wore only a touch of pale pink lipstick. Her brown hair was drawn up in a neat, old-fashioned bun, and her horn-rimmed glasses were perched on a lightly freckled nose.

The ideal front office look. It would be bad form, she supposed, to try to hire away Cooper's personnel, but it certainly was tempting . . .

"May I help you?"

"I'm here to see Ayanna Parke. She's expecting me," she added, having called from her cellular phone on the drive down.

The receptionist picked up the phone. "And your name, please?"

"Sydney Bryant."

"An unusual name," the receptionist noted as she rang what was presumably Ayanna Parke's extension. "You certainly don't look like a Sydney."

People were always saying that.

"I'm glad you decided to work with us on this," Ayanna Parke said as she led the way to her office on the second floor. "Mr. Cooper was certain that you would. Then again, this is a man who is accustomed to getting what he wants, period."

"Is he now?"

"What lawyer isn't?" Ayanna asked *sotto voce,* nodding to a passing colleague. "Although hiring you was my idea in the first place."

"Then I have you to thank—"

"Or blame."

They left the walkway, turning into a narrow corridor between floor-to-ceiling shelves, densely packed with bulging case files. The smell of paper dust was oppressive, and for a moment, Sydney fought back a sneeze.

"Here we are. Excuse the mess."

Any mess was in the eye of the beholder: the office, while small and windowless, was as organized as Sydney's own. Files were stacked neatly on one side of an L-shaped table, legal forms were stored in an open cabinet designed for that purpose, and law books—their spines precisely aligned—filled the built-in shelf. An IBM 486sx computer and a Hewlett-Packard Laser Jet Series II printer dominated the desk.

A gold-framed photograph of a little boy dressed in shorts and a purple-and-gold Lakers T-shirt adorned the wall. A charmer, his mischievous grin showed dimples and a space for missing teeth.

"Yours?"

"That's Denzel, my other boss." Ayanna kissed her fingertips and pressed them to the photograph. "Also used to having his way."

Sydney laughed.

"Now . . . these—" Ayanna manhandled a cardboard box from a back corner of the table "—are copies I made of the Reilly files."

Looking into the box, Sydney estimated there were twenty-odd classification folders of varying thickness. She picked one off the top, marked *Statements,* and began to page through it.

"All of this is for you," Ayanna went on, patting the box.

"Great, a little light reading."

"Exactly. And I've arranged for you to get a look at the crime scene."

Sydney glanced up from the file. "The Reilly house? When?"

"First thing tomorrow morning, preferably. And Mr. Cooper wants you to go with him to meet with Keith later in the day, if you can."

"I definitely can," she said without hesitation. "On both counts."

There was nothing that would give her a quicker feel for the case than to look in Keith Reilly's eyes and ask him, point blank, if he'd murdered his wife.

Three

Somehow it had gotten to be late afternoon. The sun was only minutes from setting, and the fading light softened the focus, blurring the edges of the city and disguising its flaws.

At the horizon, the sky was the color of lemon butter. Above that were striations of pink and a soft lilac, finally deepening to a clear indigo blue.

Traffic on Interstate 5 had slowed to a crawl near Mission Bay, where the kite flyers accessorized the twilight with their brilliantly-colored crafts. Taking advantage of the downtime, Sydney dialed the office. Listening to the line ring, she wondered how the interviews had gone, and if even at this moment, some lucky applicant was celebrating her—or his—good fortune at landing the job.

Five rings, six, and then a gruff, "Yeah?"

Which was how Xavier answered the phone, yet another incentive for filling the secretarial position. "It's me," she said. "How'd it go?"

"Sydney! I was about to put out an A.P.B. for you, call up the National Guard."

"I know it's late—"

"No shit it's late. I was beginning to wonder if

maybe Wade found himself unexpectedly short of cash, and sold you into white slavery across the border."

"I'm glad," she said, "that you're not the type whose imagination gets the better of him."

Xavier chuckled. "Never happen. Anyway, what's up? I assume we're hired?"

"We're hired."

"Damn! You just made my day."

Although traffic was inching along at less than five miles per hour, she had to brake for a decrepit Volkswagon bus making an unsignaled lane change. "Speaking of being hired, how did the interviews go?"

"You know, I never realized the multiplicity of skills required to be a secretary."

"Multiplicity?"

"Exactly. Do you know how many computer illiterates there are out there applying for these jobs?"

"All I'm interested in is *this* job, Xavier. Our job. Do we have a secretary or not?"

"Right now . . . not."

"Not." She sighed. "That complicates things; I'd planned on both of us being available for the Reilly case, starting tomorrow."

"Well, you're available for now. I'll do what I can to assist you from the office, and at the same time I'll hunt for a top-notch secretary. By Friday at the latest, we'll have one signed on."

Today was Tuesday. "Is that a promise?"

"It is, I swear. Listen, I hate to cut this short, but I've got a date and—"

"Tell me you didn't make a date with one of the applicants."

"Sydney, I'd never lie to you. *Ciao.*"

"There are times," she said to the dial tone, "when I wish you would."

There was no point in going to the office, so she took the San Clemente Canyon Road exit and headed for home. On the way she made a brief detour, stopping at the store to construct her dinner from the salad bar.

At the apartment complex, she parked the Mustang in its assigned space, squeezing between a rusting Dodge Dart and a Chevrolet Suburban that she thought of, none too fondly, as the Behemoth. Seen out of the corner of her eye, shrouded in shadows and offering ample opportunity for concealment, the Suburban seemed vaguely menacing.

Then again, so did a lot of things ever since her apartment had been broken into last December. A couple of thugs-in-training had trashed the apartment as retribution for her having had the nerve to question their leader in the Blood Bride murder case. The damage had been extensive; they hadn't overlooked a single drawer, closet, or cupboard in their rampage.

Ever since, she'd been increasingly security conscious. She now had two dead bolts and a cross-bar lock on her front door, motion alarms on every window—her bedroom window had been the point of entry. She'd also set up timers throughout the apartment, which turned lights and a radio off and on at selected intervals to mimic occupancy.

And if anyone were to break in while she was home, she had provided for her protection with a collection of Mace canisters, hidden in virtually every room. As a P.I., she was licensed to carry a

concealed weapon and owned a Smith & Wesson
.38 Special, but most of the time she left it in the
Mustang in the locked strong box that she'd recently had welded inside the trunk.

Rational or not, she felt safer without a gun in the
apartment, probably because of the crime statistics
that demonstrated how often intruders had turned
a weapon on its owner.

There were better ways to die; she'd be damned if
she'd supply the instrument of her own demise.

After dinner, she settled down to read, pulling
several thick folders from the box Ayanna Parke
had given her. Her intention was to spend a quiet
evening going over the files to prepare for tomorrow. At the very least, she wanted to scrutinize the
crime scene photographs and evidence reports, and
she needed to carefully analyze the statements Keith
Reilly had given to the police.

Plus she wanted to review the witness statements
and, if time allowed, draw up a time or flow chart
for the night of the murders in order to track the
purported movements of each of the witnesses.

All work and no play . . . her mother's voice gently
scolded.

". . . is sometimes what it takes," Sydney finished
the saying aloud.

Her mother maintained that Sydney was obses-
sive about her work, but if so, the cause was genetic.
Her father, who'd died a month to the day after
she'd graduated from college, had been an invete-
rate amateur detective; a bum knee had kept him
from pursuing his avocation after World War II. He

had taught her the value of critical thinking, and instilled in her a passion for the truth.

Growing up, she'd spent countless hours sitting on the arm of his overstuffed chair, looking over his shoulder at detective magazines and puzzling out the who, how, and why of notorious crimes that had caught her father's fancy.

"Think about it, Sydney," Jonathan Bryant would say, "who stood to gain from this heinous act? Find the logic, and you'll have the answer."

Sydney smiled, remembering. If she closed her eyes, she could feel the soft warmth of his favorite cardigan and smell the sweet cherry smoke from his pipe.

The best times were long, stormy weekends, when they could devote days to solving a case. Hours would pass with the only sounds that of rain beating against the windows and the hiss of tires on wet pavement as cars passed by on the street. At some point her father would look up from his notes and say, "I think I know . . ."

Rainy days weren't the same anymore.

Work beckoned.

She looked for and found the police report filed by Mitch in his capacity as the supervising investigator on the case. Skimming through it, she admired the conciseness of the details he presented, and even more, the clarity of thought. The tone was neutral—"Just the facts, ma'am"—and yet somehow he had managed to communicate the awful finality and senselessness of sudden, brutal death.

And it had been brutal; as eloquent as Jake Scott had been, the deputy district attorney's summation didn't begin to convey what Denise Reilly and Gayle Honeywell must have gone through during the final, frantic moments of their lives.

The proof of that was in the crime-scene photographs.

Included among them was a close-up of Denise Reilly's hands, her bloodied fingers digging into the carpet as she tried to drag herself toward the nursery. Several of her fingernails were broken down to the quick, the skin abraded from rug burns.

Death had frozen her fingers in stricture, one encircled by a plain gold wedding band.

Another photograph, this of Denise's face. She'd died with her eyes open, her pupils fixed and dilated. Blood had bubbled from her nose and out of her mouth. Her lips were parted slightly. Her hair, which had been stylishly short and blond, was matted with blood from the head wound.

Head wounds always bled profusely.

There were several similar shots, taken from different angles, including one in which her eyes, reflecting the camera flash, glowed red.

A common photographic phenomena, but it sent a chill up Sydney's spine.

She shuffled through the prints until she came to those taken of Gayle Honeywell. After the murders and throughout the trial, the *Union-Tribune* had published always the same picture of Gayle. It showed an attractive, slender young woman at the beach, barefoot, dressed in jeans—wet to the knees—and a halter top, her shoulder-length hair windblown. She was laughing, preparing to throw a Frisbee, and very much alive.

The contrast between that image and what Sydney now held in her hands was almost incomprehensible.

In death, Gayle Honeywell had been diminished to little more than a bloodied, contorted form, laid out face up on the floor. Her back was arched, her neck hyperextended, and her mouth was open wider than seemed humanly possible. One hand was braced against the floor while the other grasped at her chest, as though in a futile attempt to stop the bleeding. A copious amount of blood had pooled around her body.

There could be no doubt that Gayle Honeywell had been in complete and total agony when she died.

Sydney felt a flush of anger; no one should have to die that way.

Was it possible that Jake Scott's theory was right, and the killer had waited in the house until both women were dead? What kind of a person could do that? Stand by and watch and wait?

Had it been Keith?

Disturbed, she put aside the photographs, got up and went into the kitchen. Caffeine wasn't a calming influence, but she had a low tolerance for anything much stronger than Pepsi. She pulled the lift-tab more emphatically than usual, and it came off in her hand.

She took a sip, relishing the way it burned her throat, leaned against the counter and simply stood there, her mind racing with questions for which, as of yet, there were no answers.

"Look for the logic," she said aloud.

Four

Sydney eased the Mustang to the curb, verified the address, then switched off the ignition. Her watch read twenty till eight; she was early for her appointment with Ayanna. But that had been the plan, since she wanted to get an overall sense of the place—house *and* neighborhood—before going inside.

She got out of the car and retrieved the camera bags from the trunk. After locking up and slipping the keys into the back pocket of her jeans, she walked to the foot of the driveway, where she paused to survey the property.

A weeping willow dominated the front yard, its melancholy branches stirring gently in the morning breeze, making a sound very much like a human sigh.

The Reilly home was a sprawling ranch-style, with an attached three-car garage. Painted dark gray and accented with a brick facade to window height, the house looked solid and substantial, a safe haven from the random violence of big city life.

Except that it hadn't been. Nothing ever was.

To the right of the garage was a covered entry—

where darkness collected, even in the light of day—
and beyond that along the front of the house were
three multi-pane windows. According to the floor
plan she'd been given, the nursery was to the right,
the guest room on the left, with a shared bathroom
between them.

All three of the front-facing windows were closed
off by miniblinds. A six-foot high wrought-iron
fence graced with wicked, gothic spikes effectively
blocked access to the back of the house.

Which meant the morbidly curious, drawn to the
murder scene by the aura and notoriety of death,
would not have been able to see inside.

"Tough luck, sports fans," she mused aloud,
turning to look at the other houses on the cul-de-
sac.

Like many hillside neighborhoods in San Diego,
this one overlooked a canyon, and to take advantage of the spectacular view, the houses had been
built in a cozy half-circle on the gentle slope. The
individual lots were narrow at the front and wide at
the back to accommodate the terraces, covered
decks, pools, and spas that were *de rigueur* in the
California lifestyle.

There were six houses including the Reilly's, and
four of the others were similar in design: sleek, modern, and undoubtedly expensive. The fifth, outer-
most house appeared to be a throw-back to an earlier time, with a clapboard exterior and twin gables
upstairs beneath the double-pitched roof. There was
a screened veranda in the front, through which she
could see an old-fashioned wicker porch swing.
Painted white with dark green trim, the house presented a prim and tidy appearance.

As did its occupant, who emerged from a cluster

of carefully-tended rosebushes, gardening shears in her hand. Silver-haired, slightly bowed, and slender to the point of seeming frail, the elderly woman cast a sharp-eyed glance in Sydney's direction before disappearing around the far corner of the house.

The angle between the old woman's house and this one offered a perfect, unobstructed view.

A witness, possibly? If so, the woman had kept her own counsel; according to the list she'd been given, the only neighbor who had testified at Keith Reilly's trial had been Talia Sorvino, age twenty, who often baby-sat with little Daniel.

The police would have canvassed the neighborhood, and knocked on every door within hours after the bodies had been found—and again in the weeks that followed—looking for anyone who might have seen anything. Reason held that the old woman had been interviewed and had nothing pertinent to contribute to the investigation.

No doubt there was a copy of the initial and follow-up field investigation reports among the files she hadn't gotten to yet.

Even so, Sydney made a mental note to pay the neighbors a call. As supervisor of the homicide team, Mitch would have demanded thoroughness and objectivity, but the police had focused on Keith Reilly as their primary suspect very early in the case, and it was only natural under the circumstances to develop tunnel vision, seeing only what they expected—and wanted—to find.

Which meant there was a distinct possibility that they had overlooked something . . . or someone. Granted, a lot of time had passed since the murders, and memories of the night in question would not be as vivid, but so too would the shock have worn away.

Sometimes the truth could only be seen in retrospect, through a careful reexamination of circumstances and events.

For now that would have to wait: a car had turned into the cul-de-sac and was coming down the hill.

"Am I late?" Ayanna Parke asked with a glance at her watch.

"I'm early. I've been told," she said, thinking of Ethan Ross, "that being habitually early is one of my more annoying traits."

"That hardly qualifies as a character flaw." Ayanna's arm disappeared into the huge shoulder bag she was carrying as they walked toward the front door. "The keys are in here somewhere. Nice house, isn't it?"

"Very."

"You'd think folks who had it this good would find better things to do than fuss with each other." Ayanna brought out a tangle of keys. "You'd think they'd be, I don't know . . . content."

"If anyone ever *is* content."

"Maybe not, human nature being what it is. Even so, it's a damned shame."

At the door, Ayanna selected a key tagged *Reilly* and inserted it into the deadbolt. As she turned the key, her demeanor changed, the smile fading from her face. Her hands, Sydney noticed, shook ever so slightly.

Murder and its aftermath affected people that way.

Ayanna gave the door a little push and it swung open, releasing a waft of stale air. Dust motes danced in the sunlight that slanted past them into the entry.

Beyond the entry, Sydney could see partway into both the living room—where the murders had occurred—and the formal dining room. A floral bouquet on the dining-room table had dried up, its browned petals littering the dusty tabletop. On one corner of the table sat a messy collection of envelopes and magazines.

Sydney wondered who'd brought in the mail that day. Not that it made any real difference, except that she had always felt there was a kind of poignancy associated with the last events of ordinary life to have taken place in any house where a murder occurred.

Then again, there was an equal chance that it had been one of the police who'd collected, examined, inventoried and possibly confiscated items of the mail, after the bodies were found.

So much for poignancy.

The living room—what she could see of it—likewise appeared normal. There were two wing chairs with a small table between them, and what had to be a fake ficus tree in front of a tri-sectional Oriental screen in one corner. The couch opposite looked like something out of a harem scene, with tasseled arms and a mountainous collection of large ruby and gold brocaded pillows.

Unseen but remembered from the crime-scene photographs was the area just beyond the couch, where irregular sections of bloodied carpet and padding had been removed by the evidence technicians.

Sydney stepped into the tiled entry—and an oppressive, unnerving silence. The common household background noises—the hum of the refrigerator, the sound of running water, the whir of a fan, or the ticking of a clock—were notably absent.

The quiet was so intense and had such substance that it felt like she'd gone suddenly deaf. She cleared her throat for little more than the sound of it, and glanced over her shoulder at Ayanna Parke.

"Are you coming in?"

"I've *been* in before," Ayanna said, looking grim. "I'll wait in my car."

Sydney nodded, at the same time noticing a white Miata cruising by the house. Her view was partially obstructed by the willow tree, but she caught a glimpse of the dark-haired young woman at the wheel, an avid expression on her pretty face.

Two houses to the right, the garage door was lowering. Another neighbor, it would seem, curious at the goings-on at the Reilly's.

Ayanna had noticed, too. "Maybe someone should sell tickets."

"God forbid." Sydney watched the Miata complete its circle and speed up the hill, tires squealing as it rounded the corner and disappeared from sight.

"What's *her* hurry, I wonder?"

"No telling," Sydney said, and frowned. "But I'd better get to work."

Five

Sydney started with the master suite, which included the bedroom, a combination walk-in closet and dressing room, and private bath. Using a Panasonic VHS camcorder—Xavier's idea—with a ten-watt color-enhancement light, she walked through the rooms, opening doors, drawers and cabinets along the way.

She knew from newspaper accounts that following a particularly venomous argument, Keith had been "moved out" by Denise to a spare room at the opposite end of the house. His banishment was remarkably complete: his half of the closet had been stripped bare, and six of the built-in drawers were empty. There wasn't a hint of his presence left behind, not as much as a mislaid tie tack.

Which gave her an inkling of how furious Denise Reilly had been at Keith's infidelities. Then again, why not kick him out of the house entirely?

During her first year of training as a private investigator at Dunn Security and Investigations in Los Angeles, Sydney had been required to work almost exclusively on divorce cases—the primary reason she hated to take them on now—and she'd seen firsthand a legion of betrayed wives changing the locks and throwing their errant spouses' clothes into the street.

Occasionally, when emotions were running particularly high, the hubby's belongings might be doused with lighter fluid and set afire. In one instance, bags of fertilizer were dumped into a snazzy midlife-crisis Porsche convertible that had aided and abetted the unfaithful wretch in luring younger, status-conscious prey.

She'd even conducted surveillance for one woman who, when her suspicions were confirmed, bought her children not a puppy but a hundred fifty-pound Rottweiler with a spiked collar and a reputed taste for male flesh.

Any and all of which was taking matters to the extreme, but underlying the dramatics was a message that was clear and generally final: Happy Trails, you bottom-dwelling, scum-sucking bastard.

The ambiguity of Denise's response troubled her. Had Denise meant to remove Keith from her life in degrees, one step at a time? If so, why? If not, was there a reason that she'd let him stay in the house?

As much as it rankled, Sydney had to accept that she might never know what Denise had been thinking. The police hadn't come across a diary or journal, nor had they unearthed any personal letters—or, at least, none that Sydney was aware of.

If Denise had poured out her heart to anyone, it most likely would have been to her closest friend, Gayle. Which meant that in all probability Denise's secrets, and Gayle's own, had died with them.

* * *

The nursery had an air of abandonment about it. A mobile with an assortment of smiling, cartoon dinosaurs hung motionless above the crib. A white blanket with green trim was draped over the railing.

Daniel had been taken into protective custody that morning by Social Services. Presumably, the social worker had packed a diaper bag for nine-month-old Daniel, but whatever was taken, much more had been left behind. There were drawers full of infant clothes, many brand new, in sizes Daniel was meant to grow into . . . and now, of course, would have outgrown.

A tray on a shelf above the changing table held the usual baby oils, powders, and ointments, as well as cotton swabs. A cluster of diaper pins were stuck into a dried cake of soap.

Denise had obviously come down on the cloth side of the great diaper debate: six paper-wrapped bundles of diapers from a local service were stacked in a zippered storage unit, which was suspended from heavy-duty hooks in the ceiling. The top bundle was torn open, the diapers in disarray, as though Denise had grabbed too many in a rush to change the baby.

A white toy chest painted with ivy growing up its sides served as a bench for an eclectic assortment of stuffed animals. Included among the teddy and koala bears, Easter bunnies, and baby lambs were a black-and-white killer whale, a toothy Tyrannosaurus rex, a mascot anteater from the University of California at Irvine, a big-beaked toucan, and what was clearly a handmade clown.

A clear plastic baby bottle sat between the clown's legs. The murky remains of a brownish liquid—sugar water?—remained inside.

Finally, there was a deep, cushioned window seat, lined with a colorful array of geometric-shaped pillows. The miniblinds were closed now, but on a sunny day, what better place to sit and feed the baby, then sing him back to sleep?

In her mind, she heard a lullaby:

Hush, little baby, don't say a word,
Poppa's gonna buy you a mockingbird . . .

Sydney lowered the camcorder; there was nothing else to see here.

In the guest room, where Gayle Honeywell was to have spent the night a year ago, Sydney found the bed still turned down, a blue cotton nightgown folded neatly on the pillow. Presumably the gown had belonged to Denise, since a notation in the files indicated that Gayle's few personal effects—a sisal bag and a Levi's jacket—had been returned to her family by the police.

As might be expected in guest quarters, the room was sparsely furnished, offering only a bed, bedside table, and a chair. One side of the closet was open, revealing a couple of extra towels, a spare pillow, and a thermal blanket on a shelf.

There was a phone, though, with an automatic redial feature which stored the last number called. Sydney turned off the camcorder, picked up the receiver and pressed the button, listening to a rapid series of tones.

The line rang.

"Harvey's," a gruff male voice answered after the second ring. There were other voices in the background, as well as the throbbing bass of an unidentifiable rock song.

"I'm sorry," Sydney said. "What number have I reached?"

"Damned if I know, I just work here."

"Where is here?" she tried again.

"Harvey's. It's a bar, lady."

"In San Diego?"

"Nah, out near Borrego Springs. Listen, I ain't got time to play twenty questions, so why don't you tell me who you're trying to reach?"

"Never mind. Thank you anyway." Sydney hung up the phone. Why would Gayle have called a bar way out in the Anza-Borrego Desert? *If* Gayle had.

Theoretically, anyone who'd been in the house over the past year could have called Harvey's. One of the cops, an evidence tech, the District Attorney's investigator, even the P.I. who'd preceded her.

Or the killer.

Sydney sat on her heels in front of the bedside table, squinting at the phone, looking for any residue of the fine powder used to develop fingerprints. Surely Mitch had ordered every phone in the house to be dusted; that was standard operating procedure.

And in fact there was a fine line of black powder in the recesses of the handset.

"Thank God," Sydney breathed.

The last thing she needed was to have carelessly smudged fingerprints on a forgotten phone. That kind of an amateur mistake could exact a heavy price.

Shaking her head at her own lapse of technique, she grabbed the camcorder and headed for the other side of the house.

* * *

Thoroughness required that she make a pass through the formal dining room, kitchen, breakfast nook, and family room. There was also a service area—with pantry, laundry, and wet bar—that led into the garage.

She didn't expect to find much of anything, really, and so was surprised to discover a shallow cabinet in the service area, the inside of which was fitted with a dozen pegs. The pegs were empty, but neatly printed labels above them left little doubt that this had been a key cabinet. Keys to the front door, the side garage door, both cars—a Lexus and a Jeep Cherokee—and Keith's business had hung here, accessible to anyone who knew where to look.

It was early in her investigation, but there wasn't a doubt in her mind that there had to be at least a few people who'd known the keys were there.

The defense only needed one.

Keith Reilly had been exiled to what the developer's floor plan identified as a "bonus" room. It was crammed in a back corner of the house with one bunker-style window, and it probably felt like a solitary confinement cell.

Keith evidently had slept on a brass daybed, which was all of five feet long and three feet wide. A digital clock sat on the floor next to the bed. Next to the clock, a metal lap tray held the remnants of what had been—judging by the bones—a chicken TV dinner.

The room had no closet, and Keith had been forced to improvise, hanging clothes over the door as well as on door knobs. There were even a couple of suits hanging from the curtain rod, which bowed from the weight. Folded clothes were piled in laundry baskets lined up along one wall. A travel bag on the bed held a razor, shaving cream, Fahrenheit cologne, and assorted other necessities.

There was a half-bath adjacent to the room, but it was small to the point of inducing claustrophobia, the kind of space in which you needed to make an appointment just to turn around.

Keith had been living like an outcast in his own home. In spite of her intention to remain impartial and objective, Sydney felt a twinge of sympathy for him.

Finally, she did a walk-through of the living room. Detailed both in diagrams and photographs, the crime scene was hauntingly familiar to her: she had the uncanny feeling that she could make her way through this room in the absolute dark.

Near the couch was a pentagonal end table, on which sat the family Bible. Sydney paused for a moment, her fingertips resting on the worn leather cover. She wondered if Denise's name was inscribed inside, but didn't look.

When she came to the exposed sections of plywood where the bloodied carpet had been removed, she stood in the approximate center of each space and turned slowly in a tight circle, watching through the viewfinder as she taped her surroundings from those perspectives. Or rather, from *their* perspectives, Denise's and Gayle's—

—and for a split second, it seemed as though she could hear the shots, and taste the acrid smoke of gunpowder. The sensation was vivid enough to send a cold rush of adrenaline through her veins.

Behind her, a gust of wind blew the front door fully open, so that the doorknob hit the wall. The sound—or the echo of gunfire? —made her jump.

"Damn it," she swore. What was it about this place that was getting to her?

Irritated at her display of nerves, Sydney went to pack the camcorder into the camera bag. Zipping it shut, her gaze wandered to the French doors, which opened onto the covered patio, overlooking the downward-sloping yard.

Curiosity drew her.

Enough time had passed that the once carefully-tended yard had become overgrown, and it was beginning to resemble the wild canyon below. Weeds triumphed over the grass, which had yellowed and died.

A trio of apple trees littered the ground beneath them with unpicked fruit. She could almost smell the ripe cider scent of rotting apples.

Nature never hesitated to reclaim its own.

The canyon faced north, and the morning sunlight slanted in from her right. She stepped close to the doors and pressed her hands against the glass, letting the sun warm them.

Keith Reilly would be waiting.

Six

"I'm going to make myself scarce," Wade Cooper said, standing in the doorway, "so you two can talk. And Keith . . . keep the faith."

Sydney waited until the door closed, then met Keith Reilly's eyes. Sitting across a narrow table from him in one of the small, private rooms used for attorney-client meetings, she studied his face. Although it had been less than twenty-four hours since she'd seen him in court, he had changed in a not-so subtle way.

It was as if, overnight, his facial features had set, becoming better delineated, the angles hard and squared. He seemed mentally sharper and in total focus, as though nothing existed beyond the here and now.

Judging by the sheen of perspiration on his forehead, he was also more than a little nervous.

"Did you kill them?" she spoke quietly, so that the question would not be overheard by the guard who stood watch beyond the door.

"No."

It was both an answer and not; what he hadn't said—*I loved Denise, I could never hurt her*—seemed under the circumstances almost to constitute a crime of omission. Was he aware of the danger of appearing to protest too little? Or had he simply been worn down by the process, by the unrelenting disbelief of others?

"Did you hire someone to shoot your wife?"

"No, I did not."

"Can you think of anyone who might have wanted Denise or Gayle dead?"

"If I had even the slightest idea, believe me, I'd be naming names."

"Have you thought about it?"

"I haven't had the time." Reilly used his shirt-sleeve to wipe his face. "Being charged with two counts of murder is a major distraction, you know?"

"I imagine it is. Where did you go when you left your office that night?"

"Shit," he said. "You *are* on my side, right?"

"I am. But I need to know what really happened, or I won't be able to do you any good."

He chewed on his lower lip for a moment before nodding. "Okay, I got nothing to hide. What really happened is I went out for coffee, but my stomach felt queasy, so I changed my mind. Instead I drove around for a while with the window down. The fresh air helped."

Which sounded feasible, although it didn't explain why he hadn't told the police that, instead of letting them look for someone who'd sold him coffee. Unless he'd felt that changing his story would do more harm than good.

"How long were you gone?"

"Half an hour, maybe forty-five minutes at the

most. I must have just missed that jerk-off security guard when he came by—"

"At a quarter past one." Sydney consulted the flow chart she'd drawn up. "So you think you were back by two?"

"No later than," he agreed.

The police had timed how long it took to drive from The Quick Gold Fox to the Reilly house at approximately fifteen minutes. If in fact he had returned to the office at two, the thirty minutes necessarily spent in transit would have left him only fifteen minutes in which to confront and shoot both women, wait for them to die—although that might be only the D.A.'s pet theory—then coolly dispose of the gun.

"Forty-five minutes," she said. "Not a lot of time."

"Not enough to do what they said I did."

"Except there's no one who can verify that it was two and not two-thirty." At two-thirty, the baker, whose business was in the same U-shaped complex, had arrived to begin his day's work, and had noticed Keith Reilly across the way. "That thirty minute discrepancy hurts. Badly."

"You're telling me. It hurts even more knowing that if Nigel hadn't gotten cheap and cancelled the alarm service, there'd be an electronic record of when I left and came back."

Sydney nodded thoughtfully. "Speaking of Nigel, why did you lie in your statement about him? I mean, you swore he was with you."

"That—" Reilly ran a hand through his hair "—was a mistake."

"It certainly was."

"No, you don't understand. When the police first

spoke to me, I had no idea that they were there about Denise. I thought that after Nigel left, he'd gone and done something stupid again—"

"Like what?"

"I don't know. *Something.* He has a knack for finding trouble, and like a fool, I was trying to alibi *him.* I didn't know that what I was saying would later be so badly . . . misconstrued."

"It was a lie," she pointed out, not at all sure she bought his explanation.

"But not for my sake." Reilly's brown eyes were insistent. "Don't you see? I wasn't lying to save my own ass, I was trying to help a friend."

"The distinction might be obvious to you, but to the police and the D.A., a liar is a liar is a liar."

"And a liar is a killer? Is that it?"

He'd raised his voice, and Sydney made a motion to keep it down. "Not exactly, but people who lie usually have something to hide."

"Damn it, it wasn't like that."

"Then tell me, Mr. Reilly, what it was like. Let's talk about you and Denise. What went wrong between you? How did it end up . . . that way."

Reilly sat back in his chair. A minute passed in silence, while he stared blankly at his hands, which were clenched into fists. Slowly, deliberately, he straightened his fingers until his hands lay flat on the table. Letting go of the anger?

"I did love her—"

Better late than never.

"—in my way."

"Which was?"

"Inadequate, I suppose. Shit, I don't know."

"How did you meet?"

"I picked her up at a teen club in Solana Beach. I know that's not very romantic . . ."

Like many men, he used 'romantic' as if it were an off-color word. "It happens."

"Anyway, I saw her come in with a bunch of her girlfriends. It was somebody's birthday, if I remember right, and they were out celebrating being legal." His expression turned wistful. "Denise looked so fresh, so damned *young.*"

It took an effort for Sydney not to say what she was thinking, that Denise, at the tender age of twenty-three, had been too damned young when she died. Instead she asked, "Was Denise legal?"

"Just shy of it."

Sydney knew from Reilly's booking sheet that he was thirty-eight, which would have made him fourteen years older than his wife. "That didn't stop you?"

He hesitated, digging a thumbnail into the soft wood of the table where someone had carved the scales of justice in outrageous imbalance, then looked up. "You don't like me, do you Ms. Bryant?"

"I haven't made up my mind. But I give points for being candid and direct."

"Then I'll be honest. Denise was only seventeen when I met her. She was a sweet kid, maybe a touch naive. And for the record I prefer younger women; they're not nearly as demanding and critical as women my age."

"How very nice for you." The words were out before she realized how sarcastic it sounded.

Reilly surprised her by laughing, albeit ruefully. "Kind of direct yourself, aren't you?"

"I'm sorry, that was—" she frowned "—unprofessional and uncalled for."

"You're entitled to your opinion. My mother didn't approve of my marriage, either—because of the difference in our ages. I can't say she didn't warn me."

"Warn you about what?"

"That Denise and I were a disaster in the making. Mom thinks I'm perfect, of course, but she'd convinced herself that Denise was too immature to be a good wife. Much less a mother."

"Was your mother right?"

"Denise was wonderful with Danny. She was a better mother than even I gave her credit for."

"You're avoiding the question."

"Just the part I don't want to answer." His smile was engagingly boyish.

"If you want me to help you, I have to know."

His smile faded and he looked away. Wade Cooper had left an engraved gold lighter and an open pack of Marlboros behind. Reilly extracted a cigarette and tapped it, filter-side down, on the table. "Do you mind?"

"Go ahead." Maybe it would relax him. "Listen, the D.A. has constructed a strong case against you based on the disintegration of your marriage. On a personal level, I detest the practice of vilifying victims to justify the crimes against them, but there are only two people who ever really know what's going on inside a marriage, and in this instance—"

"—one of them is dead." His voice sounded flat. "What happened between us wasn't Denise's fault."

"Tell me."

"I was fooling around. If anyone was too imma-ture to be married, it was me." He shrugged. "I'm not used to self-denial."

"How did Denise find out?"

"Don't women always know?" He blew smoke at the ceiling and sighed. "Somebody told her. One of the neighbors, I think."

"You brought someone to the house?" Sydney asked, openly incredulous.

"Well. We were *at* the house. I didn't bring her."

"What was she doing there, then? Who was she?" But even as she asked, she knew.

"The baby-sitter."

"Talia Sorvino."

"One and the same."

"Damn." There hadn't been time to read Talia Sorvino's statement and testimony, but Sydney couldn't recall any news coverage naming the baby-sitter as Reilly's lover. "I'm at a loss here. I wasn't aware—"

"Talia was a witness for the prosecution, testify-ing against me." His smile was caustic. "There's no way they'd smear her lily-white reputation by bring-ing up that petty detail."

"And the defense couldn't ask questions that went beyond the scope of what she'd testified to on direct." Nor, she supposed, would they want to. "How long had it been going on?"

"With Talia? Sexually only a few months, but she'd been chasing me since the day we met."

"Which was?"

Reilly had the grace to look embarrassed. "When Denise and I moved into the house after our honey-moon."

Sydney did the math in her head. "She was seventeen."

"Seventeen, too, you mean. I know what you're thinking, but it wasn't the same at all because—"

"Talia was chasing you."

"I guess you find that hard to believe," he said, squinting through the smoke.

"Anything's possible."

"It's true, though. I never meant to rob that cradle, believe me. Not with a father like hers."

"What do you mean?"

"The guy's one of those survivalist nutcases. And he's armed to the teeth, preparing for Armageddon." Reilly stubbed his cigarette out. "Hell, he's looking forward to it."

"Does he own a nine-millimeter automatic?" Sydney asked, thinking of the missing murder weapon.

"I doubt if that would pack enough firepower for this guy's purposes. We're talking an assault weapon mentality here—"

"Except when the purpose is murder," Sydney interrupted, "a nine-millimeter would be less . . . emphatic. And a good deal quieter."

Reilly frowned. "You're right about that. Only I'm not sure Denise would've even recognized Sorvino if he showed up at the door, never mind invited him in. He does a lot of traveling."

"I wasn't talking about Mr. Sorvino."

It took a moment, and then his eyes widened. "You mean Talia? You think Talia did it?"

"At this point, I obviously don't know. But it's a possibility, something to consider."

Evidently dumbfounded, Reilly said nothing.

"Because if you didn't do it," Sydney went on, stating the obvious, "someone else did."

"How'd it go?" Wade Cooper asked as they walked down the hall.

"Better than I thought it would." She reached the inner double doors a step before he did, and held the door open for him. "Which isn't to say I have much to go on."

"I'm sorry to hear that."

At the locked exit they paused and waited for the guard who monitored the closed-circuit cameras to buzz them through. Once in the waiting area, they turned in their visitors badges to a uniformed officer at the desk who didn't bother to look up from the *Tribune* sports page.

"Then again, I haven't finished reviewing the files yet—"

"Of course not. Not in one day."

"And," Sydney said, thinking of Talia Sorvino and Nigel Fox, "there are people I'd like to talk to. Plus, I may have a lead out near Borrego Springs."

"As far as I'm concerned, you have carte blanche to go wherever and talk to whomever you want." As they left the jail, the attorney glanced at his watch. "If you'll excuse me, I'm due in court in five minutes."

"No problem."

Cooper took one step and then turned, his expression mildly troubled. "He is innocent, you know."

"I hope you're right."

"He is. You'll see."

Sydney watched him hurry down C Street toward

the courthouse, weaving his way through the foot traffic like a skier on a downhill run.

Distracted by her thoughts, it took a moment before she realized that Ethan Ross was walking in her direction. And that he'd seen her.

Seven

"Ethan, hello." The wind had blown her hair across her face and she brushed it back. Dressed in a navy pinstripe, his sandy hair cut shorter than normal, Ethan looked almost corporate.

He motioned with his briefcase toward the building behind her. "Just get out of jail?"

Sydney smiled. "I wish it were that simple. No, I'm working."

"As usual."

"As usual. But what are you doing here?" As a rule, Ethan's law practice was limited to civil cases, although on occasion he might be persuaded—or coerced—into handling a criminal matter for a favored client. He was remarkably good at both.

"Bailing out a D.U.I."

"Sure you want to do that? Anyone who drives under the influence—"

"—should sober up in jail."

"—should *rot* in jail," she said under her breath, watching a van from the local independent TV station park illegally down the street.

"I heard that."

"I figured you would." An ex-cop, he didn't miss much.

"Besides, as crowded as the jails are, there isn't room for nonfelons."

"Wait until he tags somebody, you mean. Let him *prove* he's a menace to society."

"That isn't what I mean, and you know it."

It was downright cold standing in the building's shadow with the wind whipping by, and she tucked her hands in her jacket pockets. "Sorry."

"I'm not the enemy," Ethan said, as if he hadn't heard. "And I don't condone what he did."

"I know that, and I'm sorry," she repeated. "I don't usually foam at the mouth. I must be overdue for my rabies booster."

Ethan looked away, unsuccessfully hiding a smile. A smile that filled her with a sense of longing that came very close to pain.

She'd known him all of her life, having grown up across the street from him. Eight years her senior, he'd always looked out for her. He was the big brother she'd never had . . . and more. But he made no secret of how he felt about her engagement to Mitch Travis—a former partner from his police days—and that had come between them.

"Let's start over," she said, touching his arm. "Hello, Ethan. How have you been? I haven't seen you in awhile."

"Keeping busy. And you?" The man could be maddeningly polite. "Still working eighteen-hour days?"

"I'm trying to cut back." She hated how awkward it felt to be making small talk.

"Well." His smile didn't quite reach his gray eyes. "I'd better get going. Duty calls."

"As usual."

"As usual. See you later."

"One of these days," Sydney said on impulse as he turned away, "we're going to have to talk about it."

He hesitated, glancing back at her. "I doubt that there's anything else to say."

Knowing this wasn't the time or place, she waited until he was out of hearing distance before whispering, "You might try listening."

"Lord have mercy," a voice said from behind her at the same instant a hand closed around her right wrist, pulling it free of her pocket. "Lawyers. They're the ones who ought to be locked away."

Sydney looked at the bony fingers encircling her wrist and then at him. "Victor, damn it . . ."

"I know," Victor Griffith said, pulling her along with him, "you could drop me with a well-aimed kick, if you could get your leg up that high." A shade under six-foot-six, he towered over her five-foot-four.

"Want me to try?"

"Some other time." When they'd reached the corner of the building, after a quick glance in all directions, he let her go. "I need to talk to you, off the record. You know, hush-hush."

"Don't you get tired of this cloak-and-dagger stuff?"

Victor grinned. "Never."

Which figured. Still in his early twenties, Victor had attained a certain notoriety as a hot-shot journalist whose heart beat in time with the city's pulse. If he had a heart; Sydney often imagined he was powered by some kind of internal Geiger counter that detected waves of human misery instead of radiation.

Never without his pawn-shop camera, he had captured on film drive-by shootings in Southeast San Diego; illegal aliens being struck by cars while trying to cross Interstate 5; suicidal jumpers taking the plunge off the Coronado Bridge; and a horrendous three-car collision with multiple fatalities involving—or caused by—a police vehicle in hot pursuit.

Initially a per diem stringer for a wire service, he'd been lured into working for the *Union-Tribune* after the local paper got tired of being scooped. And recently, she'd heard, he'd signed to host a weekly half-hour show profiling San Diego's Most Wanted.

Ergo the illegally parked TV van.

"What do you want?"

"I've been told by an impeccable source that you're going to reinvestigate the Reilly case."

Sydney sighed. "I guess there's nothing to be gained by denying it."

Victor waggled a finger at her. "Shame on you for not calling me."

"It must have slipped my mind."

"Don't toy with me, Sydney. We both know the protocol. A: Get a case. B: Call Victor."

She laughed at the absurdity of it. "C: Get your head examined."

"I'm not kidding. If the case is hopelessly dull and boring, as I suspect most of them are, I'll tell you as much. But if it's juicy, hey! We can hit the ground running, and never look back."

"Hasn't it ever occurred to you that the 'private'

in private investigator might refer to the confiden-
tial nature of what I do?"

"Be real. Keith Reilly's best bet for avoiding
being fricasseed by the State of California is to get
the right kind of press coverage. Whip up enough
public support and he might walk."

"It's odd, but I never thought of you as delu-
sional until just now. Outrageous, yes—"

"Hold on, let me finish. Are you aware that
there's a growing movement out there of men
who've had it up to their eyebrows with the little
woman always getting custody of the kiddies?"

"This isn't about custody, Victor. This is about
murder."

"Ah! But you're only considering one side of the
coin. Assuming that he killed her—"

"Which I'm not."

"—he can argue that he was driven to it by the
prospect of never setting eyes on his bouncing baby
boy ever again. Get it? Maybe it's not politically
correct, but who gives a damn? This is the male
equivalent of the abused-wife defense."

"Why am I listening to you?" Sydney muttered.
With a shake of her head, she side-stepped him and
started off down the street toward the pay lot where
she'd parked the Mustang.

Victor trailed after her. "You know, wherein the
brutish husband slaps the old lady around until one
night when she's had enough, she sneaks up on him
with a .357 while he's sleeping and ventilates his
brain?"

A woman passing on the street gasped and gave
them both a dirty look.

"Victor," Sydney said warningly.

But he seemed oblivious. "To hear the feminists

talk, you'd think all it amounted to was a new kind of do-it-yourself, high-caliber divorce."

They'd reached the traffic light at the corner, and she pushed the pedestrian crossing button urgently. "I don't see the parallel."

"How could you miss it? Women feel the system turns a blind eye to wife abuse; men are frustrated by a pro-mommy bias in custodial orders. I'm talking virtual mirror images, my love."

"Except it hadn't gotten that far. They hadn't been to court, nothing had been filed. If you're arguing that Keith shot her in *anticipation* of bias—"

"Yeah, yeah, yeah." He waved off her objections as they crossed the street. "I'll concede there was no imminent danger or perceived threat, but if you'd gone to the trouble of reading the series of articles I wrote after the murders, you might remember that Denise Reilly was an army brat—and I quote that brilliant and humble journalist, yours truly—'the indulged youngest child and only daughter of a career military man.'"

"What does that have to do with anything?"

"Denise had friends in countries all over the world, and a valid passport. She could have taken the kid and vanished into thin air."

Sydney frowned. "It galls me to say it, but you might have something there. Although just because the fear of losing his son was a real one, doesn't mean Keith Reilly acted on it."

"Whatever." Victor followed her onto the lot, maneuvering his lanky body between the closely-parked cars. "The point is, none of these issues have been raised by the defense—"

"Wade Cooper insists Reilly's innocent."

"Hell, what else could he say? On the other hand,

I am offering my assistance in your pursuit of justice. Work with me, share a little inside info, and I can help you."

"I don't think so."

"Really, I can get you *air* time."

Sydney unlocked the car door. "I appreciate the offer, but no thanks."

"You're being very shortsighted. This could be the hottest defense since the Twinkie. And you heard it here first."

"Maybe, but I'm looking for answers, not excuses. Not . . . justification."

As she started to open the car door, Victor straight-armed it shut. "Are you sure the answers you find will set him free?"

"I'm not sure of anything yet, but that's the way it works. There are no guarantees."

"A man's life is at risk, hon."

"And two women are dead."

"Funny," Victor scratched his head, "that I keep forgetting the other one. Gayle. Hmm. Why is that, I wonder?"

"I haven't a clue."

"Some detective *you* are."

"Now if you don't mind, I've got places to go and—"

"—promises to keep." He made a show of opening the car door and ushering her in. "Call me if you come to your senses."

"You'll be the first."

Victor shut the door for her, but a moment later rapped on the glass with his knuckles. She had to turn the key in the ignition to operate the power window.

"Yes?"

"This *is* a limited-time offer," he said, "and certain restrictions may apply."

In spite of herself, she laughed. "Thanks for the warning."

On the way out of the parking lot, as she waited for the attendant to make change for a ten, she watched in the rearview mirror as Victor walk away.

Victor had been the one who'd brought her into the Blood Bride case, calling in a favor she owed him. He'd asked her to do a so-called Lover's Profile on Martina Saxon, with whom he was seriously smitten.

Her death hit him hard—it had been the first and only time she ever saw him take a drink—but even so, Sydney found it odd that, in the months since, they never talked about Martina.

Love, she thought, hurts.

Eight

The Quick Gold Fox registered on the elegant end of the coin-shop scale. Once beyond the customary safeguards—which included barred windows and a secured door not unlike that at the jail—the surroundings were determinedly plush, featuring pristine white carpeting accented by pale blue walls.

The gleaming glass cases were lit from within, displaying—on black velvet—what had to be a fortune in gold and silver coins, many of mint quality and all quite beautiful.

Having access to such extremely liquid assets had no doubt played a critical part in the revocation of Keith Reilly's bail.

Beyond the display area were the offices and vault, protected by a wall of what most likely was bullet-proof glass. The glass had a pink-gold tint, giving the man standing behind it a rose-colored glow—a marked contrast to the scowl on his face.

He looked to be in his midforties, perhaps five-foot-six and slightly overweight. That pudginess did not extend to his features: his nose was narrow and long, with dimples on either side of the tip, while his lips were thinner than a Yankee blue blood's. Dark roots showed in his bristly blond hair.

He'd buzzed her in and was staring directly at her—there were no customers in the shop—but seemed frozen in his tracks.

"Nigel Fox?" she inquired, uncertain whether he could hear her behind the glass.

Evidently he could. He blinked twice, gave his head a quick ear-to-shoulder jerk, and shuddered. Then he rolled his shoulders, bounced on the balls of his feet, and opened the inner office door.

What was that about, she wondered? Then asked again, "Are you Nigel Fox?"

"Yeesss," he drew the word out into a hiss. "May I help you?" Although his arrest record—which had been included in the files—indicated that he was a native of Oklahoma, he had a slight British accent. An affectation?

"I'm Sydney Bryant." She crossed the room and extended her hand. "I'm a private investigator and I've been hired by Wade Cooper to—"

Fox put his hands behind his back. "I know who you are; I saw you in court the other day with that cop. But what in the world would bring you here?"

"I have a few questions I need to ask."

"Me?" It came out as a croak, and he cleared his throat. "Ask me?"

Sydney nodded, frankly perplexed at his reaction. "Yes. About the night Denise Reilly and Gayle Honeywell were killed."

"I, uh, I know nothing about that."

"But you do. You gave a statement to the police and testified at the trial—"

"Whatever I said, that's all I know."

"You don't recall what you said?"

"No. It's been a year since I gave that statement, and if I hadn't looked at it before I testified, I wouldn't have remembered a thing."

"That's difficult to believe."

Nigel Fox glared at her. "Oh? What were *you* doing that day?"

Sydney shook her head. "I wasn't a party to murder."

"Neither was I. I simply had the misfortune—" he lowered his voice "—to have as my partner a man who shot his wife. I am not responsible for his troubles."

"You think Keith Reilly shot them?"

Fox made a face. "That is not what I said."

There was, she realized, no point in arguing. "Let me rephrase the question: *Do* you think that Keith Reilly shot them?"

"He might have," Fox said with a shrug. "He was very angry with Denise. And he had cause . . . she was being most unreasonable. Piss her off and she became Mary, Mary, quite contrary, with a vengeance."

"How?"

He jerked his head sideways again, in both directions, accompanied by the unsettling sound of cracking vertebrae. "I'm not sure I should answer that. It distresses me to speak ill of the dead."

Sydney resisted pointing out that he just had. "How did you get along with Denise?" she asked, changing tactics. "I mean personally."

"I didn't know her all that well, but we had a pleasant social relationship."

"When was the last time you saw her?"

"The last time?" he echoed weakly.

"Yes." Watching him, she had the distinct impression of gears turning behind his impossibly blue eyes.

"That's a difficult question."

The man was stalling, most likely trying to recall what was public knowledge, while second-guessing what information she might have obtained from other sources. She decided to bluff. "Maybe I can help refresh your memory. The murders occurred early in the morning on Monday, April fifth. I've been told that—"

"It was the Friday before," Fox said. "She came by to sign some papers."

Sydney nodded as though he'd confirmed what she already knew. "Go on."

"Keith was out. With all the running around we were doing trying to get the bank loan, we'd missed our UPS delivery the day before. He had to go down to pick up the portable display cases we'd ordered from New Jersey for an upcoming coin show."

"You were here alone when Denise came in?"

"I think I had a customer but—" he squinted in concentration "—not a regular. The guy couldn't make up his mind, should he buy Pandas or Eagles. In the end he didn't buy either."

"Was Denise alone?"

"Yes and no. She came in by herself, but I could see the other one—"

"Gayle?"

"Right, Gayle stayed in the Jeep to watch the baby, I guess. Denise went into the office, and when the customer left, I joined her."

"How long was she here?"

"I couldn't say. Not long, though."

"What did you talk about?"

"Well, the papers, of course. I went through them with her to make sure she signed by all the Xs. The rest was idle chatter. Wasn't it a nice day, would it rain over the weekend, that kind of thing."

"Keith wasn't mentioned?"

"Not by me."

"Did she—"

"She may have muttered something, but I can't tell you what she said, because I didn't listen. I wanted to stay out of it. I still want to."

His withering glance left little doubt that he held her responsible for dragging him in. "What were these papers that she came in to sign?"

"You know that Denise was a silent partner in the business—"

In fact, she didn't know, but Sydney inclined her head in acknowledgment.

"—so she had to sign documents for the business loan we'd applied for."

"I can't imagine a bank granting a loan when two of the partners were on the brink of divorce."

"The bank wasn't to know. That's why Keith continued to live at home."

One question answered. One down, how many to go?

"It wasn't strictly kosher," Fox went on, matter-of-factly, as if he weren't tacitly admitting to conspiracy to defraud, "but business is business, and Denise had the good sense to understand that if we went under, she would go down, too."

Which didn't sound at all to her like a woman preparing to go into hiding with her child, as Jake Scott contended. "The business was failing?"

"Not failing, but gold hasn't performed well in the past few years. And there were a few mistakes made in operational matters." His smile was as acerbic as his manner. "Although not by me."

"All right. Denise signed the loan documents and then what?"

"She left."

"And that was the last time you saw or talked to her?"

Fox did another set of head jerks, and when he looked at her again, Sydney had the impression that a mental shield had come down.

"Yeesss," he said, "that was the last time."

His gaze reminded her of a cat with its inner eyelids closed, and she realized belatedly that it must be contact lenses which made his eyes so blue.

"I haven't asked you," she said, persisting, "about being arrested."

"For that, you'll have to consult the police report. I was hopelessly drunk."

"When they picked you up at two A.M., yes. But not when you left here. What time was that?"

"Midnight."

"Keith was here when you left?"

"Yes." Nigel Fox sighed. "We were doing an audit for the bank. And if I'd stayed all night to help him, as I should have, I'd be Keith's alibi, and he wouldn't be going through all of this. I'm reminded of that dismal fact every damned day."

"Why did you leave?"

"I wanted a drink," he enunciated the words clearly, stressing the hard consonants. "We'd already worked through the weekend and I was feeling put-upon."

His arrest record, peppered with drunk-and-disorderlies as well as D.U.I.s, suggested this was not a random event. "Did you go to a bar?"

"I had a bottle. I drove to Del Mar, parked on one of those dead-end roads overlooking the beach. Not that I could see much at that hour."

"Were there other people around?"

"I wasn't looking for company."

"Then you don't have an alibi, either."

Looking stricken, Fox all but stopped breathing. "The police stopped me at two A.M., and took me to jail."

"Yes, but the time of death was estimated at somewhere between one and three. Since neither Denise or Gayle died immediately, they could have been shot as early as twelve-thirty."

"But . . . but . . ."

"It works both ways, Mr. Fox. You're unable to provide an alibi for Keith Reilly, and he can't alibi you."

Nine

Sydney stepped off the elevator only to find Xavier locking the office door. His back to her, he was singing "The Way We Were" a trifle off-key, humming those lyrics he didn't know, which seemed to be most of them.

The air was redolent with the scent of peppermint—the man was addicted to breath mints—and Musk after-shave. The odd combination made her throat itch.

"Xavier?"

He mustn't have heard her, because when he turned, he gave a violent start. "Jesus, Sydney. You shouldn't sneak up on a person like that."

"I wasn't sneaking. Besides," she teased, "what happened to your nerves of steel?"

"Same as the old infrastructure, they rusted. What are you doing here, anyway? It's after five."

"I wanted to drop off the video equipment." She pulled a VHS tape from the outside pocket of the camera bag. "And make an extra copy of this."

"The Reilly walk-through?"

She nodded. "I'm glad I caught you before you left, you can give it a—"

"Ordinarily, there's nothing I'd rather do. But," he made a show out of consulting his watch, "I've got a date in forty-seven minutes, and it's not polite to keep the lady waiting."

"Another date, huh? That's two in as many nights."

"You're keeping track? Sydney my sweet, you need to get out more."

"Or you need to stay in. Is the lady another one of the applicants?"

Xavier favored her with his patented 'aw-shucks' grin. "Can I help it if so many unemployed secretaries find me fascinating?"

"You're sure it isn't vice versa?"

"She asked me, I swear to God."

"I hope so, or the Labor Board is going to be the least of our worries. There are entire law firms in this town getting rich off of sexual harassment lawsuits."

"Ah," Xavier sighed. "And they wonder why romance is dead."

"A shame, isn't it?" She moved past him to unlock the door. "Listen, if you've got to rush off, I'll leave a copy of the tape on your desk."

"I'll look at it tomorrow," he said, raising his hand to pledge as he walked backward to the elevator, "between interviews."

"Interviews, right. Don't forget, you promised to hire someone by Friday."

"Count on it." He pressed the call button, the doors opened, and he ducked inside. As the doors closed, he said, "Have a good night, Sydney."

Then, as she started inside she heard him calling up the elevator shaft, "Don't work too hard."

* * *

There were two VCRs in the computer room, and Sydney loaded the Reilly tape into one, a blank tape into the other. After pushing Play on the first, and Record on the second, she went in her office to make a few calls.

Wade Cooper had left for the night, according to his service. She declined to leave a message, since she would be unreachable most of the time, and telephone tag had never been her favorite game.

Do you ever play games? an annoying voice inside her head taunted. *Do you have time?*

She ignored it.

The next number she tried was picked up on the fourth ring by an answering machine. Sydney listened to a male voice declare, "You've reached the home of Cullen and Miriam Reilly. Sorry, we're not available right now." At first, she thought it might be Keith who'd recorded the message, but the man sounded older and phlegmy.

Cullen Reilly had died in 1990. Had his wife, like other widows, left his voice on the machine to hide the fact that she lived alone? Probably.

Sydney broke the connection, consulted her notes, and dialed the Honeywell residence. Gayle's parents lived in Mission Viejo, a bedroom community in southern Orange County. Frank and Betsy Honeywell had yet to grant an interview to anyone except the police.

Their attorney had released a statement shortly after the murders to the effect that they would have nothing to say until after their daughter's killer had been tried and convicted.

There was no answer at their number.

Finally, Sydney pressed the auto-dial button programmed with Mitch's direct number at the police department. It rang only once.

"Travis."

"What, no lieutenant?"

"Sydney. Hold on a minute. Hey guys—" he said, his voice muffled "—this is a private call. Find another place to sling your bullshit for a while."

"Private?" someone said. "Hell, does anyone know how to wiretap?"

"Try, and I'll bust you down to Traffic. You'll be stuffing tickets under windshield wipers till the day you retire. Out."

There were assorted grumblings in the background and then she heard a door close.

"I missed you today," Mitch said.

"I'll miss you tonight." Never mind that no one was around to overhear, Sydney felt the color rise in her face. "I think I'm beginning to hate the swing shift."

"Me too."

"Hmm. And you volunteered for it."

He laughed. "That won't happen again. Although there are advantages to working when the brass is home, tucked in their beds. Of course, when it gets dark the natives tend to get restless."

"Has it been busy?"

"Nothing major, but it's early. I think the perps plan all the heavy stuff for ten o'clock or later, so we'll have to pull overtime writing reports."

Overtime for homicide often ran into days. If doctors had a "golden hour" in trauma cases, during which they had the best chance of saving a life, cops had perhaps their best opportunity to close a case in the first forty-eight to seventy-two hours.

Golden days, marked by sleep deprivation, too much coffee, and a hint of desperation knowing that with each passing second, the killer's trail fades.

After a year, she wondered, would there be any trail left to follow?

"So how's your new case going?" Mitch asked, as if he'd read her mind.

"I'm not sure. I've got stacks of stuff I haven't read yet—"

"Sounds familiar."

"It's a little overwhelming. But I'm in deep enough to tell it's more complicated than I expected."

"Then you've got a shot at it."

"Excuse me?"

"As long as you remember that murder *is* complicated, you won't settle for the obvious answer."

"Like suspecting a husband when the wife is killed, Lieutenant?"

"Ouch. Go straight for the jugular, don't you, kid?"

Sydney smiled, leaned back and swiveled her chair to look out the window. To the west she could see a bank of fog moving inland. "I learned that from you."

"A likely story. Anyway, I'm not saying that we made a mistake in arresting Reilly, because I think the bastard did it."

"I'm not so sure. Was Nigel Fox ever a suspect?"

"Everyone starts out as a suspect. We eliminated Fox because he was picked up during the time frame we think the shooting occurred."

"When you *think* the shooting occurred."

"Right, based on the time of death—"

"Which is an estimate," she interrupted. "A rough estimate."

"Yes. Granted, the time of death can be tricky to determine, but, Perry Mason and Hollywood aside, you can't count on the victim's watch breaking during the commission of a crime."

"Still, there's some leeway in the time of death. And if they were shot earlier than one or later than two-thirty . . ." She left the rest unspoken.

"That's a big 'if.' Sounds like Cooper's converting you to the cause."

"Let's say that I'm trying to maintain an open mind."

"Just remember that you have to be willing to consider all of the facts, even those that implicate Reilly—"

"—or anyone else. I'll do my best."

"Your best is damned good." He lowered his voice to an intimate whisper. "Which reminds me, have I told you that I love you?"

"Once or twice."

There was silence on his end, and then he laughed again. "Are you going to make me beg?"

"I love you, Mitch," Sydney said, and hesitated, trying to decide whether or not to tell him that she'd run into Ethan. Discretion won out. "And now I've got to go. Mom's expecting me."

Ten

When she'd finished in the office, she headed for her mother's house for their customary Wednesday-night dinner. The thickening fog made driving treacherous, but it was, at least, a welcome distraction from thinking about the Reilly case.

Enveloped in the mist, which swallowed her headlights a mere ten feet beyond the front of the car, she relied on the reflective markers embedded in the road and her sense of direction. More than once she had to slow to a crawl, open the door, and look down at the pavement to make sure she hadn't crossed the center line.

Luckily, there wasn't much traffic, but every time she heard another vehicle approach, she braced herself and prayed that it wouldn't come hurdling out of the fog and crash into her head-on.

The ten-minute drive took at least three times that. When she pulled to the curb, the smell of home cooking greeted her, making her stomach growl. Lunch, grabbed on the run between the jail and The Quick Gold Fox, seemed a distant memory.

Her mother had opened the door before she

reached the porch. "Sydney, honey, is that you? I'd about given up on you. This horrible fog!"

"Hi, Mom." She kissed her mother's cheek.

"Come in, for heaven's sake. You must be chilled to the bone, that skimpy little jacket."

"There's a heater in the car, Mom." And the jacket was denim.

"Nevertheless."

Nevertheless was her mother's answer to almost everything. Spoken in a tone familiar from her childhood, the word forbade backtalk. Sydney gave her a hug. "Yes, ma'am."

"That's more like it," Kathryn Bryant nodded her approval. "Come and eat, and then we have some planning to do."

Dinner was comfort food, a chicken-vegetable-pasta soup with small crusty loaves of sourdough bread and real butter, cholesterol be damned. A blackberry cobbler sat cooling on the counter. Sydney had a Pepsi with dinner, shaking her head to the offer of red wine.

"It'll enrich your blood," her mom said. "The doctor says."

"Doctor?" She frowned, dipping a corner of bread into the thick chicken broth. Her mother was a young sixty-two, and as far as she knew, healthy. "When did you see the doctor?"

"On TV. You know, the nice one, with the mustache."

"Don't they all have mustaches?"

"Never mind, it's not important." Her mother took a sip of wine. "I heard you have a new case?"

The CIA had fewer sources than good old mom. "That's right."

"A murder case?"

Sydney nodded. "A double homicide, actually. Who told you?"

"Well," her mother smiled, lifting her glass, "it wasn't you."

"Mom . . ."

"Sydney, you are engaged to be married. You've been engaged since December—"

"January."

"Nevertheless. You haven't set a date yet, you won't look for a bride's dress, you won't sit still long enough to make any plans."

"Oh boy." She pretended to be busy with her soup, rounding up all of the carrots.

"And now you take on a double homicide? You're supposed to be taking a break from work to set up your new office."

"I am—"

"Sydney."

"I *was* taking a break," she amended, "but this case came along and I couldn't turn it down."

"Couldn't you?"

No matter that it had been twelve years since she'd last lived in this house, there were times when she felt like a child, uneasy with her mother's disapproval. But she shook her head. "No, I could not."

"Well."

How was it possible that a single word could speak volumes? "As for setting a date, there's plenty of time for that."

"There might be plenty of time, but why not do it now? I know Mitch wants to—"

"Mitch is busier than I am." She pressed the

spoon down on a pasta shell, flattening it. What
would a psychologist make of that, she wondered,
and ate the evidence. "Remember, he's been
through this before. I'm not sure he wants a *wedding*
with all the trimmings."

"It would seem to me," her mother said, "that
you should know what Mitch wants by now. Or is
it that you don't know what you want?"

"I do know."

"Are you sure this is it?"

Sydney had the odd impression that they were
talking about two different things. "What do you
mean by 'this'?" she asked heatedly. "Marrying
Mitch?"

"Honey—"

"Don't even start with that." She pushed her
soup bowl away. "I love him; he loves me. We're
going to get married. It's pretty simple."

"Honey, then why is it every time I want to talk
about making arrangements, you're too busy?"

"Because, Mother, I *am* busy."

"Forgive me if I'm wrong, but I think there's
another reason."

Even knowing she would regret it, she could not
help but ask, "Which is?"

"Ethan."

"Ethan." Sydney massaged her temples and
closed her eyes. "I saw Ethan today."

"I know you did."

Of course she knew. Ethan's mother Laura was
her mother's dearest friend. They had moved to this
neighborhood as young brides in 1949. They'd each
raised an only child—Ethan was eight when Sydney
was born—and lost their husbands within months
of each other. Shared joys and heartaches brought

them ever closer, and lightened the burdens that life handed out.

Of course she knew. Ethan must have mentioned it to Laura—although why would he do that?—and naturally Laura had called Kathryn.

"Then you probably also know," Sydney said, opening her eyes, "that we're still barely speaking. And he won't talk about it."

Her mother reached across the table and squeezed her hand. "That's because he loves you, baby."

"Mom . . ."

"Are you sure it's over between you?"

"How can something be over that never began?" she countered.

"Sydney, honey, it began before you were ever born. Ethan always wanted to touch my belly and feel you kick. He used to whisper to you. Telling you secrets, he said." Her mother smiled, remembering. "And you adored him growing up. Even when the other boys started hanging around, we all knew he was the one."

"*He* didn't know. I won't deny that I have feelings for Ethan, but we've never been in synch. He treats me like his little sister—"

"I don't think he can help it. He always was protective of you."

"I don't *need* protecting. Anyway, it's obvious that he wasn't in love with me—"

"Because he married Jennifer when you were living in Los Angeles?"

"That's right."

"The marriage lasted ten months, and he was miserable the whole time."

"Good." Restless, Sydney got up from the table

and went to the back door to look out. The fog had closed in, and she shivered unexpectedly. "Do you know he had the nerve to suggest that I started going out with Mitch again to get even with him for Jennifer?"

"Oh? That doesn't sound like Ethan."

"Well, it *was* Ethan." She rubbed her arms to warm them. "He shouldn't flatter himself. Getting even my ass."

Her mother laughed softly. "What language, Sydney. But tell me, is he wrong?"

"Very wrong. And when Mitch proposed, Ethan Ross was the furthest thing from my mind."

"You *are* angry," her mother said.

"Mom!" Sydney turned to face her. "Haven't you been listening?"

"I have. It seems to me that you and Ethan have a lot between you that needs to be resolved."

"Tell him that."

"Maybe I will."

"Don't you dare." She came back to the table and sat down. "If he wants to talk to me, he knows where I am. But I intend to marry Mitch."

"Then," her mother said, the voice of reason, "you'd better plan a wedding."

Sydney stared at her in amazement.

"Now, we could go to a consultant if you want; but, before we do, I think we should go to the bridal boutiques and look for a gown. I've always imagined you in white satin with just a hint of a train—"

"Like the one rolling over me?"

"Hush, now, let me think. White satin, sleek lines, seed pearls sewn into the bodice. As for the veil, I admit I'm a traditionalist. There was one I liked in those *Bride* magazines I gave you—"

"Magazines?" Her memory was a little hazy on the details, but she was almost certain that her young neighbor, Nicole Halpern, had taken the magazines—with her blessing—to the private high school she attended to share with her friends.

"—which would be stunning. And we probably have time to order it, since you haven't set a date. As for Mitch, he can go with a morning coat or a tuxedo, although if it's the latter, I hope he'll stick with basic black—"

"Mom?"

"Yes, dear?

"I've changed my mind about the wine."

Eleven

The wine was still a factor Thursday morning in the form of a Class A headache. As far as she could tell, her blood had not been enriched.

Sydney pulled into the carport at her apartment complex after having spent the night, fogged in, at her mother's. A shower, a change of clothes, maybe three or four aspirin, and she'd be ready to go.

Or so she hoped.

Waiting for her by the wrought-iron security gate was Trouble, the black-and-white cat who belonged to the lady in 129—in theory at least—and roamed the halls in search of a spare Pepperidge Farm cookie. He meowed plaintively as Sydney approached.

"What's the matter, Trouble?" she asked, turning her key in the lock. "Must be hard to be a cat with a sweet tooth when everybody is watching their weight."

When she came through, he rubbed up against her and began to purr.

"Know a soft touch when you see one, don't you?" She reached down and scratched behind his ears. "Come on, let's see what I can find for you to eat before you waste away to nothing."

The cat followed her to her apartment and sat patiently by as she unlocked both dead bolts. The moment she got the door open, Trouble darted inside, heading straight for the kitchen and the cookie jar.

Sydney tossed her purse and jacket on the couch and followed him. She crumbled an oatmeal-raisin cookie on a plate and put it on the floor. Trouble hunkered down, closed his eyes in contentment, and ate.

"Knock knock?" an unfamiliar voice called from the other room.

All those security measures, and she'd forgotten to shut the front door. "You're losing it," she said under her breath.

As she pushed open the swinging door to go into the living room, a flash of white ran by her and she turned to see a second cat sniffing at the cookie plate. Trouble, surprisingly, did not seem to mind.

"Oh, great," she said, "now you're telling your friends where the sucker with the cookies lives."

"Galaxie?" A nicely dressed, middle-aged woman appeared in the kitchen doorway. "There you are."

Nonplussed, Sydney said nothing, watching as the woman crossed the kitchen and picked up the cat.

"Where are your manners, Galaxie?"

Pure white Galaxie, who had a pink nose, one blue eye and one green, appeared blithely unconcerned at any lapse of etiquette.

"I'm sorry," the woman said then, extending her hand to Sydney, "for barging in like that. Galaxie thinks the world was invented for her amusement, which means she's entitled to go wherever she pleases. I'm Hannah, by the way. Apartment 120."

"Nice to meet you, I'm Sydney."

"Sydney. Now there's an unusual name." Hannah gave a thoughtful nod. "But it suits you. And your cat?"

"He's not mine. His name is Trouble and he does what he can to live up to it."

Trouble had finished his cookie and was licking his paw, which evidently had become soiled in the hunt. At the sound of his name, he stopped in mid-lick, got up, and stalked out, tail straight up in the air.

"I think we've offended him," Hannah said. She gently scratched Galaxie under the chin. "As for you, I always suspected you were the kind of girl who can't help looking for Trouble."

Sydney knew the type.

"Please accept my apologies again for intruding," Hannah said.

"No harm done."

"Well, I'd better go, I've got a job interview at eight-thirty and I don't want to be late."

"An interview, really. What do you do?"

"I'm a secretary slash office manager. You wouldn't think a position would be hard to come by, but this is my sixth interview this week."

Sydney gave her a closer look. Nicely dressed, very little makeup, pleasant smile, with the kind of voice that sounded good on the telephone, punctual, and affectionate to animals.

"Listen," Sydney said, "how are you with computers?"

* * *

After she'd showered, dressed, and washed three aspirin tablets down with skim milk, Sydney went down the hall to the Halpern apartment and rang the bell.

Nicole answered the door. Pretty, blond, and just turned sweet sixteen, Nicole had recently accessorized her school uniform—a white blouse and dark plaid skirt—with a flashy red beret. It was, Nicole had said when she bought the beret in violation of Hilyer High's dress code, her subtle form of youthful rebellion.

"Wow, what happened to you?" Nicole asked. "Your eyes are kind of bloodshot."

She discovered that it hurt to laugh. "I had a glass of wine last night."

"Oh."

The expression on Nicole's face suggested that she had struck a blow for temperance. "I'm glad you're home. Do you still have those magazines I gave you?"

"The bride ones? Sure."

"My mother spotted a veil in one of the issues that she thinks would look good on me—"

"Come on, *anything* would look good on you."

"As long as it covers my bloodshot eyes?"

"I didn't say that."

"You were thinking it. Anyway, she wants to order the damned thing. So I need them back."

"I can handle that, only . . ."

"You do have them?"

"I have them, but not here. They're at school. I can bring them to you this afternoon, or if it's real urgent, you could come by Hilyer."

"This afternoon will be fine, although I may not be home until after seven."

"Seven?" Nicole twisted a lock of her long blond hair around and between her index and middle fingers. "Okay. Will *he* be coming over?"

"He?"

"That gorgeous lieutenant. Because if he is, Amber and Velvet have *got* to come by. They don't believe he's as totally amazing as I say he is."

Sydney shook her head gingerly. "Sorry to disappoint you, but Mitch is working evenings this month."

"Doesn't he get a night off?"

"Not until Sunday."

"What about Ethan? I never see him anymore."

Sometimes Sydney forgot—perhaps conveniently—that over the past few years, Nicole and Ethan had gotten to be friends. "I don't think so, Nicole. Things between us are kind of difficult now . . ."

"I know you and Mitch are together, but does that mean Ethan has to stay away? You always said he was like an older brother, although—" Nicole gave her a knowing look "—I never really believed that."

"Why should you be any different than everyone else in my life?" Sydney asked with a sigh. "As my mother would say, nevertheless. I've got to get to work, and you're going to be late for school—"

"—like I care."

Sydney had already started down the hall, but she turned and, walking backward, gave Nicole a skeptical look. "That would be more convincing coming from someone with less than a 4.0 grade point average."

Nicole responded with an impish grin. "I'm trying to cultivate an attitude."

Aching head or not, Sydney laughed.

Twelve

Because in her experience it was often fruitless to try to canvass a neighborhood in the morning, Sydney made her first stop of the day the library at the University of California at San Diego.

The Central Library, which always begged the question, "central to what?" was located in relative isolation between the Third College and Warren College on the sprawling campus. Parking was atrocious, as always, but on her fifth go-round of the metered spaces, she lucked out and found a spot. She fed all of her change into the meter, which netted her an hour and a half.

Inside, she located a book on forensics without much difficulty—her reward for conducting frequent research—and found a quiet corner to read.

Her conversation with Mitch last night about determining the time of death had stayed with her, intruding even on her dreams. In one dream, she had knelt down in a dark alley to draw back the bloody sheet covering a murder victim, and was startled to discover that a broken clock had replaced the person's face.

In another dream, she was inexplicably in the

autopsy room as the coroner took a scalpel and cut into the mottled gray flesh of a young woman. The blade got stuck six inches above the pubis, and the coroner threw it aside, reaching into the cooling body with his gloved hands. A second later he pulled out—with a wet sucking sound—a black telephone handset, from which it was possible to hear a voice saying, "At the tone, the time will be twelve thirty-one and ten seconds. At the tone, the time will be twelve thirty-one and twenty seconds."

Obviously she was obsessing, and if she didn't settle the question one way or the other, it would continue to haunt her.

Her degree was in Criminal Justice, but since she hadn't gone into police work—as she'd first intended—the fine details of what she'd been taught about how the time of death was decided had faded from her mind.

"Time of death," she said quietly, turning to the index of *Scientific Evidence in Criminal Cases*. She found it as a subheading under Pathology, made a mental note of the page numbers since there were two references, and located the first.

There were, as she indeed remembered, five major factors: postmortem lividity; rigor mortis; putrefaction; loss of body heat; and the catch-all category of 'others'—which included stomach contents; potassium concentration of vitreous fluid in the eye; clouding of the cornea; and, in men, beard growth.

What she was most interested in was body temperature and rigor mortis.

She'd reviewed the autopsy reports for both young women, and she knew that, although the bodies had been discovered by the police at 5:57 A.M., the coroner had not arrived to take body temperatures until approximately 7:30. The temperatures obtained—by inserting a metal thermometer just under the ribcage, beneath or into the liver—were 90.8 degrees for Gayle and 90.4 for Denise.

Virtually the same, which indicated that they probably—and only probably—had died within thirty minutes of each other.

The common formula for heat loss into hours postmortem was normal body temperature minus current body temperature divided by 1.5 degrees equals time. With an average eight degrees of heat loss, that meant they had been dead for roughly five hours when their core body temperatures were taken.

And roughly was the operative word. There were too many variables pertaining to both the body and its environment to ever be precise. So make it four to six hours to be on the conservative side.

They could have died as early as one-thirty, or as late as three-thirty. Medical estimates of how long they might have lived after being shot varied from fifteen minutes to thirty to an hour. The last seemed unlikely.

All of which meant the D.A.'s time frame was right on target. And Keith Reilly, without an alibi, was directly in the line of fire.

"Damn," Sydney swore, and turned to the second reference to estimations of time of death, which dealt primarily with skeletal remains, and involved a time frame of years rather than hours.

Back to rigor mortis, which was only mildly interesting until she reached the final paragraph which described the morbid aspect of cadaveric spasm, or "instantaneous rigidity" after death. Attributed to the tension of the affected muscle groups and the chemical conversion of excess glycogen into lactic acid caused by straining muscles, this phenomenon very likely accounted for the contorted rigidity of Gayle Honeywell, who had been fighting with every fiber of her being to breathe.

Cadaveric spasm equals death throes, she thought, and closed the book. It must have been truly horrible to witness that struggle for life.

For a few minutes, she simply sat there, staring absently out the nearest window at the ubiquitous eucalyptus trees and wondering, once again, why Jake Scott had theorized that the killer had remained in the house until both women were dead.

It didn't seem logical.

Maybe the time had come to ask.

"Sydney, this is a pleasant surprise," Jake Scott said with a smile, ushering her into his private office. "I'm sorry if I kept you waiting."

"No problem."

"Make yourself comfortable." To the secretary in the outer office, he said, "Hold my calls unless it's urgent, okay?"

Sydney ignored the visitor's chair, positioned cozily next to the desk, and sat on the couch a good eight feet away. As a rule she kept her distance from the deputy D.A., who had a tendency to slip his arm around unwary females and whisper carefully ambiguous insinuations into their ears.

Jake "the Snake" had *earned* his nickname.

"So," he shut the office door, "to what do I owe this pleasure?"

"I'm here about the Reilly case."

"Reilly? Hmm, that's right. Wade mentioned

he'd brought you on-board." Jake sat on a corner of the desk. "I've often wondered why we don't use you here. You'd like being on the winning side."

"You haven't won yet," she noted archly.

"But we will." Jake intertwined his fingers around his knee and swung a loafered foot. "Forgive me, but I can't resist asking what it's like to work on an adversarial basis with your fiancé."

Sydney shook her head. "I don't think either of us considers it as being adversarial. We both want to uncover the truth."

"So do I. But if I were the lieutenant, I suspect I'd be irritated at having the woman I love devoting her . . . talents . . . to making me look like a fool."

"You aren't Mitch—"

"More's the pity." His eyes gave her the once-over, twice. "I imagine your talents go beyond investigative techniques."

"Are you hitting on me?"

Jake smirked. "Not at all. As a matter of fact, I have a strict policy never to flirt with any woman whose boyfriend wears a shoulder holster."

"You know," she said, keeping her expression neutral, "I could scarcely do a better job of making you look like a fool than you're doing right now all by yourself."

"It's a gift," he said, and laughed. Then his mood shifted from casual to serious. "I should warn you, however, never to underestimate my desire to win in court. And I will win next time."

If there was a next time.

"About the Reilly case . . . during your summation, you said that it was—" she referred to her notes "—'likely' that the killer remained in the house for an unspecified amount of time after the shootings."

"That's correct."

"On what do you base that assumption? There were no witnesses, no evidence—"

"Actually, there was."

"A witness?"

"Evidence. Of a sort."

Sydney felt a sense of frustration that she hadn't completed her review of the files. Tonight she would finish even if it meant staying up until dawn. "Could you be more specific? What kind of evidence?"

"Not what you might think." Jake stood up and walked over to the window where he stood with his back to her, gazing out. "It has to do with Daniel."

"Daniel?"

"His baby-sitter told us that Daniel wasn't a good sleeper. I've never spent much time around babies, so at first I didn't think much of it—"

"Back up a minute. By the baby-sitter, do you mean Talia Sorvino?"

"That's right." Jake returned to the desk, this time sitting behind it. "Ms. Sorvino also informed us that the kid startled easily. That he could be easily awakened by a loud noise."

Sydney considered that. "From which you've concluded that Daniel was awake—"

"—or woke up—"

"—when the shots were fired?"

Jake pantomimed firing a gun. "Exactly. And the noise made him—"

"—cry."

"Very good. Go to the head of the class."

"Of course," she said, "the baby was crying."

"Which probably explains why Denise was so desperate to get to him."

"And you think that the killer stayed to calm the baby down—"

"—before little Danny woke up the neighbors, who might have taken note of the time."

"Except these same neighbors presumably slept through three gunshots."

"That bothered me for a while," Jake admitted, "but then it came to me that the gunshots were fast, bam, bam . . . bam! Fifteen seconds, if that, and it's over. You wake up not knowing what the hell woke you up. A crying baby is a different matter entirely."

Sydney thought of what she'd seen in the nursery. If someone had stayed in the house to quiet Daniel, they very well might have changed his diaper and given him a bottle to lull him back to sleep. "Did the evidence technicians dust for prints in the nursery?"

"Of course. They didn't find anything."

"Then all you have is a very interesting theory."

"It's more than interesting. It's incriminating."

"You didn't present it in court."

"The baby can't talk." He had picked up a silver letter opener and was using it to clean his nails. "It would be all but impossible to prove. But that type of evidence functions as an internal check mark; it reaffirmed my belief that Keith Reilly is a double murderer."

"I don't follow." Sydney frowned. "If the child was quieted to keep him from disturbing the neighbors, wouldn't anyone have stayed?"

"Maybe, maybe not. Your typical stranger-killer is going to haul ass, figuring by the time anyone is annoyed enough by the baby's crying to get out of bed and look, he'll be on a freeway, putting miles of asphalt between him and his crime."

"What if the killer was the baby-sitter? I assume you know Talia Sorvino was—"

"—having it off with Reilly?" He shrugged. "We know. Only if she did it, why tell us that the kid would wake up at the drop of a pin?"

"It could be she believes the best defense is a good offense."

Jake shook his head. "Wait until you talk to this gal. She's not bright enough to figure that out. Not a chance she's laying a smoke screen."

"Even so, I don't see why any of this points exclusively to Keith Reilly's guilt."

"Because he was the one deliberately attempting to set up an alibi."

"If that's true, why wouldn't he object to Fox taking off? I can't believe he'd arrange for an alibi and then let Fox flake out on him. It defeats the purpose."

"What defeated the purpose was Fox getting arrested," Jake corrected. "If Fox had gone home and stayed there, Reilly probably could have coerced the little twerp into backing up his story."

"If he could trust Fox to do that." Sydney thought of the man's twitchy mannerisms and deliberate evasiveness. "I wouldn't trust him."

"Neither would I." The phone on the desk buzzed, and Jake picked it up. "Scott here. That's today? Okay, will do, but you owe me one." He dropped the receiver in the cradle and stood up. "This has been a lot of fun, but I've got to go."

Sydney rose. "I appreciate your time."

"Glad to help out, Sydney." His suggestive smile was back. "Say hello to the lieutenant for me."

"Oh, don't worry," she said. "I intend to."

Thirteen

When she arrived at the Sorvino residence—two houses to the right of the Reilly's—Sydney realized that it had almost certainly been Talia whom she'd seen driving the white Miata yesterday.

No wonder the curious look; witness-for-the-prosecution Talia had good reason to be interested in what was going on in the neighborhood.

Unfortunately, Ms. Sorvino wasn't home. Sydney rang the bell repeatedly, with no response. She considered sticking one of her business cards in the door with a request to call written on the back, but decided against it. Why surrender the element of surprise?

Instead she walked uphill to the next house on the cul-de-sac and rang that bell. Inside she could hear a TV blaring, and wondered if the doorbell could be heard over it, but as she raised her hand to knock in case it couldn't, the door was yanked open.

A woman of Rubenesque proportions dressed in a purple jogging outfit filled the doorway. An explosion of red hair framed her Kewpie doll face.

"Oh!" the woman said, and gave a startled laugh. "My goodness! You're not George."

"Sorry, no. I'm a private investigator." Sydney showed her a copy of her license issued by the State of California, Department of Consumer Affairs. "I wonder if I could ask you a few questions about Keith and Denise Reilly."

"About the murders?"

"Yes."

"Which side are you working on?"

"The defense."

"Well, it's about time. Come on in."

Sydney followed the woman into the living room where, mercifully, she turned off the television set.

"Sit anywhere that isn't sticky. Let me just pick the worst of this up," the woman said as she moved through the room grabbing toys and assorted items of children's clothing off the furniture. "It isn't this messy when my husband comes home—Mr. Quality Time would have a fit—but I don't usually have company during the day and it's kind of a relief to kiss it off."

Sydney smiled. "What about George?"

"George is our Irish setter. The kids taught him to ring the bell, don't ask me how." Her arms full to overflowing, the woman walked partway down a hall, used an ample hip to bump open a door, threw everything inside, and pulled the door shut. "I'm Rebecca Aiken, by the way. Mistress of the manor."

"Sydney Bryant. Am I to understand that no one has spoken with you yet?"

"No one from the defense. The police have been here twice." Rebecca settled into an overstuffed chair. "I didn't get the impression that they were really listening, though."

"I'll listen." Sydney pulled out a notebook; she'd forgotten her microcassette recorder.

"First of all, I want to make it clear that I didn't see or hear anything suspicious that night. No screams, no gunshots, nothing like that."

She drew a rough sketch of the neighborhood. "Yours is the house furthest from the Reilly's?"

"Mmm, we're about even with the Devlins, on the other side of the circle."

"That's the old-fashioned house?"

"Yes."

"Okay." She penciled in the name Devlin. "Would you normally hear it if, for instance, they were having a loud argument?"

"That depends. If my windows were open, I might. Sometimes—not always—there's like an echo in the canyon, and I can hear all kinds of things. Phones ringing, a vacuum cleaner, power tools . . . you know."

"A baby crying?"

"I suppose so." Rebecca paused and frowned. "Poor little Daniel, alone in that house with his mother and her friend dead."

"Was he crying that morning?"

"I believe he was. That's why the police were called to the house, you know. The poor little dear must have cried himself hoarse."

"You didn't hear him?"

Rebecca shook her head. "Not a whimper. But you know I've never understood why Talia called the police instead of just going over and checking herself."

"Talia Sorvino called the police?"

"That's right."

"Another unexpected little twist," Sydney said, thinking out loud and wondering what other petty details were buried among the masses of paperwork awaiting her.

"She is a twit," Rebecca agreed, "but I confess I've used her myself a couple of times."

Sydney did not bother correcting her. "As a baby-sitter?"

"Mmm. I figured it was safe, since she hasn't shown any interest in potbellied husbands. So far."

"Can I take it that you know about Talia and Keith Reilly?"

"I know about Talia. This is a small neighborhood, so everyone knows," Rebecca said. "As for Keith, I had my suspicions that if she kept after him, Talia would eventually see 'yes-yes' in his eyes."

A buzzer sounded from somewhere in the back of the house.

"Excuse me for a sec." She hoisted herself out of the chair and disappeared into the kitchen. A minute or two later she returned with a laundry basket filled with clothes. "I hope you don't mind if I fold while we talk, otherwise the wrinkles set in."

"Go right ahead. About Talia . . ."

"She's one of those girls who are all body and no brain. From the time she reached puberty, she chased after every good-looking male within a ten-mile radius." Rebecca laughed. "That's an exaggeration, of course, but not by much. Still, she can be sweet, and she's great with the kids."

"How did she get along with Denise Reilly?"

"Before or after?"

"Both."

"Actually, before Denise found out, she and Talia were thick as thieves. Denise was only a few years older than Talia, you know. Before the baby came along, they used to go out a lot—"

"Out? Do you mean to bars?" Sydney asked. Maybe it had been Talia who'd called Harvey's from the phone in the Reilly's guest room.

"More likely to the beach or a movie. Or to one of the malls. I remember Talia telling me they borrowed each other's clothes."

"What about after the baby was born?"

"Talia practically moved in. Of course, being around Keith so much probably aggravated *that* situation. The worm finally turned, if you get my meaning."

"And Denise found out."

Rebecca nodded. "I must say, she behaved more like a lady than I would have in her shoes. I have a whole set of Ginsu knives in the kitchen. My husband cheats on me and—" she smiled cheerfully "—he'll wake up one morning missing an essential part of his anatomy."

Sydney refrained from commenting, asking instead, "What did Talia do?"

"Talia? Not a lot. She stayed out of sight pretty much. Tony—that's her Neanderthal father—must have thought the neighborhood was ganging up on his little girl, so he went out and bought her a sports car to race around in, the better to thumb her nose at the rest of us. He rewarded her for misbehaving, the way I see it."

"That's one way of looking at it. Tell me . . . do you think Talia is the type to be vindictive?"

"I guess that depends on whether it runs in families. I know Tony Sorvino is a big fan of retribution, the kind of guy who's always keeping score so he can even it when the time is right."

"That's interesting."

"Actually, it's scary. He gets this look in his eyes, this measuring look, like he's wondering exactly how big of a hole he'd have to dig to bury you in the garden . . . ugh, he gives me the creeps."

"I understand he's a survivalist."

Rebecca made a derisive sound. "If that means he wants to be the last one left standing when all hell breaks loose, maybe he is."

"I can hardly wait to talk to Mr. Sorvino," Sydney said, underlining his name in her notes.

"But you'll have to. Wait, that is. Tony's out of town until the weekend."

That figured, the way her luck was running. "Back to Talia for a moment—"

"Oh, right, we got off the subject. You were asking if she's vindictive? I'd guess not. I mean, she's not the Amy Fisher type. I can't see her gunning for Denise because she wanted Keith all for her very own."

Sydney made note of that, too, although she would reserve judgment until she'd talked to Talia herself. "One last question. Earlier you said you didn't understand why Talia hadn't gone to the Reilly house to check on the baby instead of calling the police."

"That's right."

"Would you clarify that for me? Unless I'm mistaken, the police found the house locked."

Rebecca shook her head vigorously. "It wouldn't have mattered. Talia had a key."

Sydney felt a tingling, as if she'd received a mild electric shock. "Are you sure of that?"

"I am, unless Denise had the locks changed."

That would be easy to check. "How do you know she had a key?"

"She showed it to me," Rebecca said, folding a pint-sized pair of jeans. "The way it happened was, Denise found out in February, on Valentine's Day."

"Nice timing," Sydney said with a frown.

"Wasn't it? Anyway, maybe a month later, Denise was off somewhere with the other girl who got killed—"

"Gayle Honeywell," Sydney said automatically.

"—and Keith was at work. I saw Talia coming out of the house, and I went down there to confront her."

"What was she doing?"

"That's what I asked her, after I accused her of breaking in. She showed me the key, and said Keith had given it to her. She swore that she'd only gone into the house to try and find a cashmere sweater of hers that Denise had and wouldn't return."

"Did you tell anyone about this?"

"I told Keith. He said she'd had a key, but had given it back."

"You didn't believe him?"

"I believed he'd gotten *a* key from Talia. But I have a sneaking suspicion that Talia had copies of the key made before she returned it. And it hit me . . . what if her father found the key and decided to teach Keith a lesson?"

Anything was possible. "Did you mention your suspicions to the police?"

"Oh yes. At length."

"What was their response?"

"They thanked me and said they'd look into it. I assumed they were going to do just that. Then they arrested Keith, and for all I know, they filed my statement in the trash."

Sydney closed her notebook. "I have a source at the police department," she said, "I should be able to find out what happened."

"Really? I know it's none of my business, but if you find out—"

"I'll let you know."

Fourteen

After leaving Rebecca Aiken, Sydney tried the Sorvino residence again, but there was still no answer. Nor did she get a response at the house immediately to the right of the Reilly's.

At the house on the left, the door was answered by a Latina maid who managed to convey with broken English and a lot of head shaking that no one else was home. Something about the maid's wide-eyed watchfulness suggested that the woman might be undocumented, and Sydney, not wanting to alarm her, decided against showing her investigator's license or leaving a card.

"I'll come back another time," she said.

"Bueno," the maid responded with a shy smile, and shut the door.

Which left only the Devlin home, the last house on the cul-de-sac.

When she pushed the doorbell, she heard not the standard two-tone ring, but chimes playing a vaguely familiar melody. The door opened before the music stopped.

"Yes?" Dressed in a long-sleeved, high-collared white blouse fastened with a cameo, and a straight black skirt that reached to the middle of her calf, her silver hair drawn up in a tidy bun, the woman might have been a schoolmarm from the 1890's.

It was, Sydney thought, the elderly woman she'd noticed yesterday morning tending the rosebushes. A moment later, she wasn't so sure: the woman's twin appeared beside her. The only difference between them was the smile on the twin's face.

"Are either of you Mrs. Devlin?"

"We are both Miss Devlin," the stern one said. "Who are you?"

Sydney introduced herself. "I'm here about the deaths of Denise Reilly and Gayle Honeywell last year."

"Oh," the second Miss Devlin said, "that was so tragic. As young as they were . . . such a dreadful shame."

"It was," Sydney agreed. "I'm a private investigator and I'd like to talk to you, if I may—"

"Why? We don't know anything. We keep to ourselves, and always have."

"Oh, Faith," the second Miss Devlin said, "that makes us sound like hermits."

Faith scowled. "It does nothing of the kind."

"It does, and besides that, you're being very rude. Come in," she said to Sydney, "won't you?"

"Thank you." The house smelled of roses, and properly so; there were vases filled with roses everywhere Sydney looked. The walls were papered with an ivy and rose print, and the sofa was upholstered in a similar design.

"I'm Hope," the genial sister said, "and even though she has little, that of course is Faith."

"Charity is dead," Faith said without expression.

Hope sighed. "You are in a mood, aren't you? Have you had your medicine today?"

Faith ignored her, crossing the room to a rocking chair near the fireplace. She sat down, picked up an embroidery hoop, and soon was jabbing the needle through the taut fabric at a furious pace.

"I saw you," Faith said, "snooping around that house."

"It's part of my job."

"Imagine, a private investigator." Hope clasped her hands to her bosom. "Is it terribly dangerous?"

"Not terribly," Sydney said, and smiled. "But I do have to ask a lot of questions."

"By all means, do." Hope perched on the edge of the sofa like an eager student waiting for a chance to show off what she'd learned.

From Faith came only the popping sound of the needle as it punctured cloth.

"When I was in the neighborhood yesterday—"

"—snooping around—"

So Faith *was* listening, despite feigning disinterest. "—I noticed that you have an unobstructed view of the Reilly house."

"Oh, we have the best view of all," Hope agreed. "Our house was built many years before the others. Our brother Arthur, may he rest in peace, picked out the perfect place for us, with beautiful views. And in the summer, we get the most delicious breeze . . ."

"You're blathering," Faith said, but didn't look up from her embroidery.

"Am I?"

Sydney smiled encouragingly. "You're doing fine. You were telling me about the view."

"Yes, I was, wasn't I? You wanted to know about

the Reilly house, didn't you? As I recall, it was built in 1985, or was it 1986? I know it couldn't have been later than that—"

"Hope," Faith interrupted, "pay attention. She's here about the murders, not the house."

A blush colored Hope's cheeks. "I know that. I'm only trying to give her a proper perspective."

"Save it for the historical society." Faith tied a quick knot, brought the thick embroidery thread up to her mouth and bit through it. "And I'll save us all some time. What are you after, young lady, and what makes you think we can help you?"

"I'm after the truth about what happened last April. I need to know if either of you saw or heard anything unusual that night."

The Devlin sisters exchanged a glance.

"Maybe you passed by the window and noticed someone at the door, or an unfamiliar car parked in the driveway, or—"

"From what I read, it was very late when they were killed," Faith interrupted. "After midnight."

"That's right, it was."

"We retire early in this household. In case it escaped your notice, we're old. At midnight we would have been long since asleep."

"Except," Sydney said, "whatever transpired that evening prior to the murders could have had its origins earlier in the day."

"Oh my!" Hope said. "I never thought—"

Faith silenced her sister with a look. "I can assure you, Ms. Bryant, that if there had been anything out of the ordinary that Sunday or Monday, we would have done our civic duty and reported it to the police."

"Then you didn't see or hear anything?"

"No," Faith said, "I did not."

Sydney turned to Hope. "Did you?"

Hope squared her shoulders and looked Sydney directly in the eyes. "I did see something."

"Damn it, Hope." Faith stood abruptly, her needlework falling forgotten to the hardwood floor. "Haven't I told you it was nothing?"

"What was nothing?" Sydney asked.

"A car," Hope said quickly, before Faith could respond. "I saw a car parked in front of their house."

"What time was this?"

"A little after one in the morning. I got up to drink some seltzer . . . my digestion isn't the best."

"Tell me what you remember about the car," Sydney urged, and added after noting Hope's frown, "was it light-colored or dark? Full-sized or compact?"

"Oh yes," Faith all but sneered. "Tell her about the car."

"Well . . . it was a dark color, I think. Or at least, not white. And the size, my goodness, the size. I don't know much about cars, you understand, but it wasn't one of those tiny little cars—"

"There you have it," Faith said, with an expression of triumph. "The police will be able to track the killer down now! It's not white, and not tiny."

"You're doing fine," Sydney said to Hope. "Every little bit of information helps."

"Does it? Does it really?"

Sydney nodded. "What else do you remember? Did you see anyone?"

"No, just the car. It was dark out that night," Hope added with an apologetic smile, "and Faith kept telling me to forget it—"

"Mark my words," Faith said, her slender frame stiff with rage, "the day will come you'll wish you'd listened to me."

"Faith, please! I'm trying to think."

Sydney sat next to Hope on the sofa as a way of offering moral support. "Take your time."

"Take your time," Faith mimicked, "and think hard, because as soon as you've done this *thing,* they'll swarm down on us like locusts. The police. Reporters. And when they hear what you have to say, dear sister, there will be no question but that you are a foolish old woman who saw nothing."

"I saw that car."

"And if that isn't bad enough, what if your incessant blathering has put us in harm's way? What if someone out there *thinks* you know more than you've told?"

"That won't happen," Hope said, and hesitated. "Will it?"

Sydney recognized the uncertainty and fear in Hope's eyes, and sought to reassure her. "The District Attorney's office isn't inclined to release witness statements prior to trial, except of course to the defense."

"Trial?"

"Did you think," Faith asked, "that you wouldn't have to testify?"

Always respect your elders her mother had taught her, but right now Sydney had to fight to keep from telling Faith Devlin to shut up.

"Maybe you'll be on Court TV," Faith persisted.

"Now that's enough!" Hope stood to face her sister, her hands clenched into fists at her sides. "You saw that car, too, and if I testify, that's the first thing that I'll say."

Sydney looked from one to the other in surprise.

"Then we'll see who the foolish old woman is, and I don't think it'll be me. *I* was up to fix myself a seltzer. I wasn't walking the floors and peering out the windows at all hours—"

"It's a family matter, Hope, don't you forget."

"I haven't forgotten. But compared to murder, the boy's childish wanderings are a mere annoyance."

At a loss, Sydney asked, "The boy?"

"Our great-nephew, Corey. He lives with us."

"Honestly! Isn't there anything you won't tell anyone?" Faith asked bitterly, and stormed from the room.

Hope sank back down onto the sofa. "That was why Faith was up that night. Waiting for Corey to come home."

"How old is Corey?"

"Sixteen." Her smile was a sad one. "A very confused sixteen. His mother died a year and a half ago, and we're the only family he has left."

"His mother was your niece?"

"Yes, Arthur's only child. Arthur was the youngest, you see, but our mother wanted another girl. He hated being a disappointment, so when he grew up and married, he named his daughter Charity to complete the set."

"Faith, Hope, and Charity."

"It's old-fashioned, I know, but I was touched."

"About Corey . . . he goes out at night?"

Hope nodded. "I'm sure he does it simply to breathe. I feel sorry for the boy, having to live with his two spinster great-aunts. The way Faith and I have ordered our lives must be suffocating to him."

"When he was out that night, did he see any-thing?"

"Corey refuses to talk to either of us about where he goes at night, or what he does." She sighed. "Faith is scandalized by his behavior. It infuriates her that he disobeys, but he's nearly grown, and there's little she can do to control him."

"Where is he now?"

Hope glanced at the clock on the mantle. "Well, it's after three, so he's out of school. Often he comes home for a nap—"

"Because he wanders at night," Sydney mused. It might be a good idea to talk to Corey.

"Yes."

"What's Corey's last name?"

"Devlin, same as ours. That's another family se-cret. Faith would have apoplexy if she knew I was telling you all of this. Charity never wed. None of us knows who the boy's father is."

Sixteen, orphaned, and illegitimate. Any one of the three would produce anxiety; taken together and the kid was probably bouncing off the walls.

"I'd like to meet Corey," Sydney said.

"Well, you're about to."

Faith had returned. How long she'd been stand-ing in the doorway listening, Sydney didn't know. There wasn't time to wonder before the front door opened and Corey Devlin walked in.

He was slight for his age, about five-foot-three, and he'd inherited the family trait of being thin. His brown hair was collar-length, and somewhat greasy. Blue-eyed, his lashes were as long and dark as a girl's.

"Corey," Hope said, rising. "There's someone here who'd like to talk to you."

"Yeah? Well, too fucking bad."

Sydney caught his eyes then, and noticed for the first time an abrasion on the side of his face. The skin was raw and reddened, and there were a few drops of blood welling up. "What happened to you?"

"None of your business." His hand went to his face, covering the injury. His knuckles were also abraded, and there were smears of blood on the back of his hand.

"Were you in a fight?"

"Oh, Corey!" Hope fussed. "Are you hurt?"

"What's it to you?" He glared at Sydney, ignoring his great-aunt.

She knew better than to back down. Instead she smiled. "Let's just say I'm the curious type."

"Corey, Miss Bryant is a private investigator—"

"Big deal."

"—and she's been talking to us about the, uh . . ."

"The murders at the Reilly house." Sydney walked over to him and took his hand in both of hers, examining the wounds. "I hope you didn't open your knuckles on someone's mouth. Human bites are nasty business."

Caught off-guard initially, he recovered quickly and yanked his hand away. "Who gives a—"

"Corey." Faith took him by the arm. "Let's clean that up. Upstairs, right now."

Surprisingly, the boy went along.

"Oh my," Hope said, wringing her hands. "Maybe this isn't a good day for this, Miss Bryant."

"Don't worry. There'll be another time."

Fifteen

The cellular phone was ringing when Sydney returned to the Mustang, and in her rush to answer it, she dropped the keys while trying to unlock the door. The urgent summoning of a ringing phone was something she'd never anticipated about having one in the car.

The phone stopped ringing at the exact moment she got the door open.

Naturally.

"Have a little patience next time, will you?" Sydney tossed her notebook on the passenger seat and got in. As if in response, the line rang again. "Hello?"

"Sydney, good, I found you."

"Xavier," she said, "what's up?"

"Wade Cooper needs to talk to you. He's been calling the office every hour on the hour."

"Did he say what he wanted?"

"Nope. But he sounded amused."

"Amused? As in—"

"Tickled pink." Xavier chuckled. "You must be doing something right."

"Okay, I'll call him. Thanks."

"Wait! Don't hang up yet." Paper rustled in the background. "You have a couple of other messages."

"Is it anything that can wait?"

"I'm not a mind reader, hon, you tell me. Your mother called, and so did the love of your life—"

"Mitch?"

"No, the other one, Ethan."

If she hadn't coveted the phone for so long she would have smacked it against the dashboard. "Knock it off, Brutus, or I'll run you through with my dagger."

"Hey, I only repeat what I hear."

"Then I suggest you consider the source. What did Ethan want?"

"To talk to you. Obviously the man has a heretofore undetected death wish."

"Very funny. All right, anything else?"

"I thought you might be interested to know that I'm making significant progress in our search for the perfect secretary. I've narrowed it down to three candidates, and tomorrow—drum roll please—I'll have them all in for a final interview."

"That's great. How did Hannah do?"

"Hannah is one of the three. And before you ask, I did not include her just to humor you. Her typing test timed out at ninety words a minute, with no errors."

"Wow."

"Yeah, that's what I said."

"So," she said, "we'll actually have a secretary next week."

"Did you ever doubt it?"

"Me? No!"

"Sydney, your lack of faith astounds me. Damn, there's the other line. Gotta go."

Sydney dialed the law offices first and was put immediately through.

"Sydney," Wade Cooper said, "I'm glad you called. I don't have a lot of time, but I thought you ought to know that the District Attorney's office has been calling each and every person who was questioned or gave a statement in the Reilly case, asking for a follow-up interview."

"That's interesting."

"It is, indeed. I've also heard from a reliable source that Mr. Scott wants to sit in on every interview."

"No shit," she said, and frowned. "I talked to Jake this morning—"

"Yes, I heard."

"—but I can't recall saying anything that would warrant that kind of response." Unless he'd felt he'd tipped his hand by telling her about his tend-the-baby theory? But that didn't make sense.

"Well, you must have done something to rattle his cage." Cooper laughed quietly. "And whatever it was, it's had an effect. He's worried, make no mistake about that."

"Worried about what? I mean, I know Jake is highly competitive and hates to lose, but reinterviewing all of the witnesses? What's he afraid of?"

"I'll let you figure that out. For now, I just wanted to offer my congratulations."

"Thanks, I guess. Listen, while I have you, there are a few other developments you should know about." She outlined what she'd learned from Rebecca Aiken and Hope Devlin. "As for the boy, I'm sure I can find some way to convince him to talk."

"I'm sure you will," Wade Cooper said. "Keep up the good work."

"I'll do my best." Sydney hesitated. "Since we're legally obligated to share information with the D.A., will you advise him, or shall I?"

"If you don't mind me stealing your thunder, I would very much like to have the pleasure of breaking the news to Mr. Scott. But not yet." Cooper laughed again. "I don't think the prosecution needs to know what we're up to just yet."

"He won't like that."

"I'm sure he won't. But it's coming up on the weekend, and another day or two won't matter. I'd rather give you the time you need to develop your leads more fully, and see what comes of that."

"Whatever you say, you're the boss."

It wasn't until the connection was broken that she remembered she'd wanted his office's assistance in setting up an appointment with Miriam Reilly.

Tomorrow would do.

"Sydney," her mother said, "I'm sorry to bother you at work, but since you never seem to *stop* working—"

"Yes, Mom."

"—I never know when to call."

"Now is fine. What's up?"

"I was thinking about our shopping trip—"

Sydney stifled a groan.

"—and I wondered if there is any way you could take tomorrow off."

"Tomorrow?" In her rearview mirror, she

watched a car drive down the hill toward where she was parked. "I don't think so, Mom, I've got a lot to do."

"I understand that, dear. But you were willing to take Saturday morning off, and I wondered if you couldn't switch days. It's so hectic and crowded in the malls on weekends. Wouldn't it be nicer if we did our shopping on Friday?"

The car, a tan Ford Taurus, pulled into the driveway of the Sorvino house.

"Friday?" she said absently.

"Tomorrow."

"Hmm." A man dressed in a dark suit got out of the car and went to the door, where he rang the bell.

"Sydney, are you listening to me?"

"Yes."

"Then what do you think? Is there anything you had planned for tomorrow morning that you can't put off until Saturday?"

The man had no better luck than she had: his ring went unanswered. He stuck his business card in the door, glanced at his watch, and returned to his car. In doing so he looked straight at her. She smiled with satisfaction, recognizing him as one of the investigators from the D.A.'s office.

"Sydney?"

"What?"

"You weren't listening," her mother accused. "Have you heard a word I said?"

"Yes," she said and winced, waiting for the lightning bolt to strike her dead. Guilt over her little white lie prompted her to add, "Whatever you want to do, Mom, is fine with me."

"Good. Come by the house tomorrow at nine, and we'll get an early start."

An early finish was more like it, she thought, but said, "I'll see you at nine."

Finally, she dialed Ethan's office, after bracing herself with a few deep breaths.

"Law Offices. May I help you?"

Sydney recognized the dulcet tones of Valentine Lund, Ethan's ultra-efficient secretary. There was something in the hush of Miss Lund's voice that conveyed her reverence for the law, and her conviction that in her modest way she was facilitating its design.

"Is Ethan in?"

"Mr. Ross," Valentine said, "is in conference."

Which could mean anything. "Would you tell him Sydney is returning his call?"

"Miss Bryant?"

"Yes."

"Mr. Ross called you?"

Did she detect a hint of disapproval? "Yes, Miss Lund, Ethan called me."

"Very well. If you'll please hold."

"As if I have a choice." Classical music came over the line, something by Vivaldi, she thought, a little too energetic for her taste.

"Sydney?"

"Hello, Ethan," she said. "Xavier told me you'd called."

"Yes. I wanted to apologize."

"For what?"

"Being such a jerk yesterday."

It felt as if a hand were squeezing her heart. "You weren't that bad."

"I was out of line, Sydney, and you know it.

What's worse, we both know I have no excuse for acting that way."

"Well . . . it was an awkward situation."

"Which I made worse. You suggested that we should talk about it, and I brushed you off."

"That's true."

"But I've been thinking about it, and I changed my mind. We need to talk."

"I'd like that. The problem is," she said, "I really am incredibly busy right now."

Ethan was silent for a moment. "Okay. What I have to say will keep. I'll wait for you to call."

"As soon as I come up for air."

"Good."

"Good." Her hands were sweating and she tucked the phone between her shoulder and chin, then wiped them on her jeans. "I'll talk to you soon."

"Sydney?"

"Yes?"

"You will call?"

"I promise. Swear to God and hope to—"

"Never say that," Ethan interrupted. "In your line of work, it's inviting trouble."

"Then I won't say it, but I promise, I'll talk to you soon."

As she waited at the red light at Genesee and Governor, the phone rang one more time.

"It's me again," Xavier said.

"What a coincidence, I'm five minutes away from the office. I suppose you're ready to leave?"

"You suppose right."

"Another date?"

"Not tonight. I'm playing racquetball. Got to keep this body in shape."

Sydney smiled. The light changed and she accelerated smoothly through the intersection. "I guess you owe it to your lady friends."

"Among other things. Anyway, the reason I called is to give you a message from Mitch."

"Which is?"

"He wants you to meet him for dinner, down in Pacific Beach."

"Tonight?"

"At six. You got a pencil? He gave me directions . . ."

Sixteen

They met just off the beach at a hole-in-the-wall fast food place that had aspirations to be a sidewalk cafe. There were six bright orange tables bolted to the pavement—to deter theft by the color-blind?—and an assortment of wobbly, three-legged stools.

The ambiance was nothing to write home about, but the aroma of spicy food was divine.

Sydney looked at the chili dog as Mitch placed it on the table in front of her. "Keep this up and you'll turn my head."

Still standing, Mitch tilted her face up toward him, leaned down and kissed her. "Looks like you're on to my master plan."

He tasted of salt. "You ate one of my french fries?"

"I'm trying to save you from yourself." He sat beside her, handing her a plastic fork and knife, along with a wad of paper napkins. "French fries may be hazardous to your health."

Sydney dabbed a fry in the chili and ate it. "But they taste good."

He kissed her again. "So do you."

"This is a public place," she protested, laughing,

"and people are watching. Behave yourself, or I'll call a cop."

"You know how it goes," Mitch said, and kissed her again, this time harder. "There's never a cop around when you need one."

A little breathless, she pushed him away and smiled. "Isn't that the truth? Speaking of which, why aren't you on the street?"

"I'm supposed to meet a witness in a Filipino gang-bang down here at seven-thirty." He spooned salsa onto his fish taco. "The victim died this morning, and my source wants to turn in the gun, a double-deuce."

Translated, that meant a .22. "Sounds like fun in the big city."

"Always," he nodded. "It's what they pay me for."

The tide was out, and after dinner they walked along the wet sand, dodging the occasional wave. Sydney picked up a delicate, tiny shell, which fit like a thimble over the tip of her little finger.

"What do you think?" She showed it to Mitch. "A new way to keep from leaving fingerprints."

"I think you have a twisted, devious mind."

He reached for her, but she evaded him, walking backward a few steps ahead, the wind blowing her hair in her face. "Which reminds me . . . did you have the tech dust the nursery at the Reilly house?"

"Sydney . . . it's too nice of a sunset to waste talking shop."

"There'll be another one tomorrow," she said with a glance at the sky, then persevered: "Jake Scott told me that the nursery *had* been dusted, but

I no sooner left his office this morning before he was dispatching his investigators all over town."

"What does one have to do with the other?"

"That's what I'm trying to figure out."

"Figure it out later. This is supposed to be a romantic walk on the beach."

"It is romantic. Answer my questions and I'll prove it to you."

His expression was skeptical. "Let me warn you in advance, I'll require a lot of proof. Beyond a reasonable doubt."

"Whatever it takes, Lieutenant. Go on."

"All right. Yes, we dusted the nursery, and every other room in the house."

"I didn't see a lot of residue." The fine powders, both dark and light in color, which were commonly used to develop fingerprints tended to adhere to most surfaces even after the prints were lifted.

Mitch shook his head. "You amaze me, kid. You went through the house looking for residue?"

"Not exactly, but it's kind of hard to miss. And I didn't see any in the nursery."

"Then they must have had a cleaner in after we released the property."

Sydney was familiar with the practice: murder was a messy business, and cleaning bloodstains and splatters off the walls and furniture was the kind of thing which exacted a heavy emotional price. There was at least one company that she knew of that specialized in cleaning up the graphic leavings of violence. She didn't even want to think about what kind of aptitude testing the company used in hiring its staff.

Instead, she asked, "They being?"

"The family." He shrugged. "Hell, even Cooper

might have authorized it. That way if we missed anything, it'd be our tough luck."

"You'd need another search warrant to get back in the house at this late date?"

"Absolutely, *if* we could manage to convince a judge to sign it. But what's with the nursery?"

Sydney recounted her conversation with Jake Scott, leaving out only the suggestive remarks; she could handle Jake without anyone's help.

"But if he's right," she said, summing up, "and the killer stayed until Daniel fell asleep again, it stands to reason that he or she was in the house for quite a little while. And that would mean it was more likely there'd be prints in other areas of the house."

They had stopped walking, and were standing facing each other. The wind was brisk, and Sydney fastened the snaps on her jacket.

"Well," he said, "the problem is that from our perspective, the shooter lives in the house. Reilly's prints were all over everything anyway. But we didn't find, say, his bloody thumbprint on a door-jamb."

Chalk one up for her side. "Whose prints did you find?"

"I thought you had the reports."

"I have them—" she stepped closer to him and tugged on his belt loops "—but I haven't had a chance to read them, because I'm here on the beach with you instead of at home, okay?"

"And you think I memorized them?"

"Why not?" She looked up into his hazel eyes. "What else do you have to do?"

"Good question." He put his arms around her,

and ran his hands lightly over her back. "Very good question. What was the question?"

"Fingerprints."

"Right, fingerprints." His mouth hovered over hers, barely touching, and then he nipped at her lower lip gently with his teeth.

Sydney felt his nearness as a kind of gravitational pull. She was aware of a not unpleasant density in her body, as if there were metal shavings in the very marrow of her bones, and he was a magnet drawing her in.

It had been this way the first time she ever saw him, four years ago. It had been this way every time she'd seen him since.

The feeling was intoxicating and, she suspected, quite possibly dangerous.

"Mitch."

"What?"

"I've been thinking."

"That's a relief." His fingers kneaded the muscles in the small of her back. "I'd hate to be responsible for distracting you from your work."

She kissed the hollow of his throat. "Maybe we'd better talk about this later."

"Maybe we shouldn't talk at all."

When he was right, he was right.

Seventeen

At three A.M. Friday morning, after seven hours spent reviewing the Reilly files, Sydney closed the last of the classification folders, and tossed it on the floor with the others.

"It was Colonel Mustard in the parlor with the candlestick," she said, and yawned. "Or Miss Peacock in the conservatory with a pipe."

She closed her eyes and let her head fall back to rest on the couch. A sudden wave of exhaustion made her feel light-headed, though, and she had to straighten up to keep the room from spinning.

Add to that the stiffness in her legs and back from sitting Indian-style while reading, and she was a prime candidate for about twenty hours in bed.

She'd be lucky to get four.

But at least she'd found answers to a few more of her questions.

As far as the physical evidence went, other than the victims' fingerprints, the technicians had lifted and the crime lab had confirmed positive ID's on the prints of Keith and Miriam Reilly, Talia Sorvino, Nigel Fox . . . and two of the patrolmen who'd been the first on the scene.

Eliminate the cops, and what did they have? Nothing, since the others were presumed to have had legitimate access to the murder scene in the days and weeks prior to the crime. Given that on certain surfaces and under the right conditions, an undisturbed fingerprint might last for years, there was no direct connection between the crime and any one person's prints.

The techs had also lifted numerous partial prints which were of such poor quality that they could not be identified or classified, and two clear prints belonging to a person or persons unknown.

San Diego used an automated fingerprint identification system similar to that of the Department of Justice, but not even the most sophisticated AFIS could identify a print without having a record card from its owner. There had always been—and she hoped would always be—people who lived circumspect, quiet lives and never had cause to be printed.

A disturbing number of others, less domesticated and barely socialized, ran wild but had never gotten caught.

The fiber or trace evidence was inconsequential. A thorough vacuuming of the house had been done; and while the crime lab had identified synthetic and plant fibers—notably sisal, presumably from Gayle's purse—there had been nothing which pointed with any specificity to the identity of the killer.

Likewise the particulate matter recovered from the scene was limited to what might be expected: soil which matched that outside of the house; microscopic splinters of wood; an occasional paint chip; several types of plant pollen; and baby powder.

There was a quantity of human hair found. Analysis showed the majority of samples collected were consistent with Denise's hair. Hair matching Keith's had also been found, but for obvious reasons, no conclusion had been drawn from that.

Blood samples collected from the carpet and walls were typed and matched with Denise and Gayle. Both were type O, according to the serology results. The killer had not bled while in the house.

After his arrest, Keith had been tested using neutron activation analysis to see if he had traces of gun powder on his hands. The test was negative for barium and antimony—primer residue from the bullet cartridge—but the results were considered to be inconclusive, since at least sixteen and as many as eighteen hours had passed between the time of the shootings and his arrest.

As sensitive and specific as NAA-testing had proven to be, its downfall was the simple passage of time. No one would ever know what the outcome would have been if they'd tested Keith at 7:30 that morning, instead of twelve hours later . . .

The report from Ballistics identified the bullets recovered on autopsy from Denise and Gayle only as nine-millimeter in caliber, with six grooves and a right twist to the rifling. The make and model of the murder weapon could not be determined with any degree of certainty. No spent cartridges were found.

In other words, the evidentiary value of the physical evidence meticulously collected at the crime scene and analyzed using the latest scientific methods was essentially nil.

The taxpayers, who paid for it all, would doubtless be thrilled to hear about that.

Even so, a negative answer was better than no answer. At least she had verified that the District

Attorney's case was circumstantial, and would in all probability remain that way unless the murder weapon was found. And any conclusion based solely on circumstantial evidence could be viewed as subjective, or as a matter of interpretation, susceptible to change.

As for the statements of the neighbors, she picked up a couple of interesting details. First, that Talia Sorvino had been baby-sitting at the Merediths', the employers of the Latina maid, who were away on a four-day vacation to Catalina Island.

In her initial statement, Talia asserted that she'd put the Meredith kids, ages two and three, to bed at eight, and had fallen asleep on the couch in the living room during the eleven o'clock news. Everyone had slept soundly through the night, according to Talia, but she had been awakened shortly after five by a baby crying.

It was Daniel; she recognized his distinctive, hiccoughing cry. At nine months of age, Daniel startled too easily to be considered a good sleeper, but he usually could be coaxed back to sleep by his beloved dinosaur mobile, which played "Rockabye Baby."

She had, Talia said, tried to wait it out, hoping to get back to sleep herself. But after half an hour or so of Daniel's wailing, it occurred to her that something might actually be wrong. She tried first to reach Denise on the phone, but got no answer and decided—for unspecified reasons—to call the police rather than go over and knock on the door.

That was all Talia knew.

There was no reference to her being in possession of a key to the Reilly house, nor did she mention having had an affair with Keith. She denied having heard gunshots or screams.

The second item of interest was a transcript of the notes taken by the officer who'd arrested Nigel Fox the night of the murders. The officer had pulled Fox over at 2:08 A.M., after observing him driving erratically, which included unnecessary braking, jackrabbit acceleration off the line, and swerving into opposing traffic lanes.

Fox had also been flashing his emergency blinkers, and his wipers were zipping back and forth at high speed over a dry and dirty windshield, making what the officer described as "an annoying squeaking noise."

Fox had flunked every element of the field sobriety test. With his head tilted back and his eyes closed, he could not touch his nose—or even find it—with either hand. When he tried to walk a straight line, heel-to-toe, he nearly fell on his face.

The alphabet was beyond him. He could not or would not count backward; when the officer tried to demonstrate how it was done, he kept saying "Lift off!" and laughing uproariously at his "little joke."

The officer noted that Fox reeked of alcohol, and that his shirt was wet from spilled booze. His speech was slurred and nonsensical.

The odd thing was, the Breathalyzer test gave a .09 reading, marginally in excess of California's .08 drunk driving standard. A blood test taken shortly thereafter registered only slightly higher at .10.

Sydney thought it curious that his blood alcohol level was that low while his state of drunkenness seemed so high. She wasn't an expert, but a point ten reading probably could be achieved by ingesting two drinks. Two drinks to a man who was admittedly a habitual drinker should *not* make him falling down drunk.

As for the flashing emergency blinkers and the rest of it, she got the distinct impression that Nigel Fox had been trying to draw attention to himself. As if he'd wanted to be arrested.

As if he needed an alibi?

Then there was the field interrogation report on Corey Devlin. It was remarkable only in its brevity, taking all of ten words: "Devlin refused to answer any questions without benefit of counsel."

What to make of that, she didn't know. Except that it suggested that perhaps Corey Devlin had more than a nodding acquaintance with the law.

Or was your typical smart-ass kid.

Finally, buried in an interview with Betsy Honeywell, she'd found a new name to add to her list of people to talk to, one Eddie Monroe. Mr. Monroe had dated Gayle on and off for a number of years, but the relationship turned sour the summer before her death.

According to Mrs. Honeywell, Eddie had pursued a reconciliation in unorthodox ways. He'd started benignly enough, sending flowers and showering Gayle with gifts of perfume, lingerie, and candy. When Gayle didn't respond, the niceties stopped, the nasty phone calls began, and before long he began stalking her.

He would park outside her apartment building after following her home from work, and sit in the dark, waiting and watching.

Gayle had told her mother that she could see his silhouette in the car, and the red glow of the cigarettes he chain-smoked through the night. Unwilling at first to believe he meant her any harm, she'd tried to ignore it. Gayle hoped he'd tire of playing his one-sided game, give up and leave her alone, but seeing him there, night after night after night, finally got on her nerves, and she reported him to the police.

California had passed the country's first anti-stalking law in 1990, and the police didn't take Monroe's harassment lightly, as they might have in the past.

Eddie found himself on the receiving end of un-wanted police attention. Whatever his other faults, the man was a quick learner; after being warned that he was heading for trouble and could end up behind bars, he slunk off with his tail between his legs.

As far as Betsy Honeywell knew, that had been the end of it. Gayle never mentioned seeing or hear-ing from Monroe again.

That didn't mean that he hadn't come back.

After a hot shower, Sydney slipped beneath the covers and tried to will herself to fall asleep. But as tired as she was physically, her mind refused to wind down.

It seemed the more she learned about the Reilly case, the less it made sense.

Nigel Fox had a serious alibi problem, but what reason would he have to kill Denise? Financial? As a silent partner in The Quick Gold Fox, it could be that Denise's life had been insured to guard against business losses in the event of her death. But if profit was the motive, and the insurance money was meant to solve the company's cash flow deficit, why continue to go through the painstaking process of applying for a loan?

Unless that had been a ruse?

As for Talia Sorvino, the baby-sitter appeared to have had a motive, the means, and an opportunity to murder her rival, but why involve herself by calling the police? Every cop who'd ever worn a uniform knew to be wary of witnesses, since the bad guys—and girls—often showed a proprietary interest in their own crimes. Perpetrators of all ilks had been caught because they couldn't keep their distance, and had to be involved.

Talia reportedly wasn't very bright, but there was a world of difference between not being bright and being downright stupid.

Eddie Monroe could also be a possibility—in which case Gayle had been the primary target instead of Denise—but if she had been afraid of the man, why would she let him in the house?

Corey Devlin was the dark horse in this race, but she couldn't discount him. He hadn't been at home on the night of the murders, and he'd refused to talk to the police. The news was full of stories of youthful killers, who murdered without rhyme or reason.

And then there was Keith. Jake Scott hadn't proved him guilty, but nothing she'd uncovered so far proved him innocent.

No wonder she'd felt dizzy: her mind was going in circles.

Sydney pulled the covers over her head to block out the light. Gradually, the darkness and warmth began to soothe her, and she felt herself drifting. But even as she gave in to it, her thoughts pursued her . . .

Who am I missing?
What can't I see?

Eighteen

"Stand up straight," Kathryn Bryant ordered, "let me see how the dress hangs."

Sydney gazed heavenward. "Yes, Mother."

"Oh, it's gorgeous," the saleslady said. "What a beautiful bride she'll make."

This was the third bridal salon they'd been to, and about the fifteenth gown she'd tried on. Each and every one of the gowns had been proclaimed "gorgeous" or some variation thereof, by stylish saleswomen who couldn't quite keep their amazement in check at her transformation after changing from her Charger's sweatshirt and faded jeans into white satin and lace.

Of course, what else *would* they say? "We have some lovely burlap veils, would you care to try one on?"

"Are we done yet?" she asked. "I'm about to itch to death."

"Hush!" Her mother straightened the wrist-length lace sleeves. "You haven't fidgeted this much since I took you to shop for school clothes when you started kindergarten. The way you carried on, it was a miracle they didn't ask us to leave."

"Hmm." She surreptitiously scratched an itch on the inside of her elbow, at the same time sneaking a peak at her watch. "Obviously another childhood trauma I'd forgotten. No wonder I hate shopping."

"That's all right, dear, no one would ever guess." The saleslady laughed discreetly.

"What do you think of this one?"

Nearly surrounded by at least eight dressing-room mirrors, Sydney studied her reflections. She looked, she thought, kind of frothy, like she'd been caught at ground zero during an explosion of meringue. "Maybe we'd better elope."

"Don't say that, Sydney Térèse, even as a joke. Do you like the gown or not?"

"This—" she held the full skirt out at the sides, as if preparing to curtsey "—just isn't me. It's too . . . much. The lace itches like crazy. I'd never make it through the ceremony without grabbing Mitch's gun and putting myself out of my misery."

Her mother sighed and shook her head. "I'll take that as a 'no.' "

"Definitely no."

"My daughter," Kathryn said to the saleslady, "isn't a fan of frills. I was, or rather *we* were, thinking of an elegant satin gown, slightly flared skirt, no lace, but maybe with pearls on the bodice and just the hint of a—"

"I have exactly what you're looking for," the saleswoman announced with a triumphant smile. "It's absolutely the most stunning gown."

When Sydney turned to face the mirrors, she couldn't deny that this time the saleslady had been right. And so had her mother, whose conception of

the gown and how she would look in it, had proved
to be far more perceptive than her own.

Equally startling was seeing herself as the bride—
for the first time in her life.

"Oh my," the saleslady said. "That wedding
gown was *made* for you."

Her mother smiled, and then sniffled. "If only
your father could see you now . . ."

Sydney stepped off the platform, feeling light-
headed and a little numb, probably from a lack of
sleep. "I need to sit down."

"I imagine you do," her mother said, and turned
to the saleslady. "We'll take it."

"Sydney," Kathryn Bryant said, leaning down to
look in the car, "are you sure you don't want to
come inside? I can fix lunch—"

"I'm not hungry."

"Then you could take a nap; you said you were
tired."

"Mom, it's after two." Her knuckles were white
from gripping the steering wheel, and she made a
conscious effort to relax. "I've got to get some work
done, or the day will be wasted."

"How can you say that? We found the perfect
wedding gown, and—"

"That's not what I meant. This is an important
case; a man's life is on the line. You know?"

"Yes, and I also know every case is important to
you." Kathryn smiled. "What you forget sometimes
is that you have to live your own life, too."

"I am."

"What I'm trying to say is, there's more to life

than working eighteen-hour days. You're getting married, Sydney. That will change things."

"I know that."

"Do you?"

"Yes. When the time comes, I'll deal with it. Right now, I've got to go."

"All right, I won't keep you." Her mother reached to brush the hair back from her face. "But take care, you hear?"

Sydney patted her mother's hand. "I always do."

Nineteen

Sydney stopped at a self-service station to gas up the Mustang, which was running on fumes. As the tank filled, she dropped quarters into the vending machines, selecting an ice-cold Pepsi and a bag of corn chips.

"Lunch," she said, walking back to the car, "is served."

After paying for the gas, she pulled off to the side of the station lot and parked. She ate a couple of chips, then opened her notebook on the seat beside her, ran a finger down her list of phone numbers, and began making calls.

Or trying to. All of the lines at Cooper & Associates were repeatedly busy, as were the two at her own office. When she tried Miriam Reilly's number, she got the machine—and Cullen Reilly speaking from the dead?—once again. There was still no answer at the Honeywells'. She called the Sorvino residence, with the same result.

"Where is everybody?" she muttered, hanging up the cellular phone.

In her review of the records, she had discovered the name of the sixth and final home owner in the cul-de-sac. According to the field interview report, ninety-one-year-old Jefferson Davis Brown lived alone in the house next door and to the right of the Reilly's.

The interviewing officer reported that Mr. Brown was blind but otherwise claimed to be in good health. He managed for himself with the assistance of various social-service agencies, which provided him with meals, home health-care visits, and a part-time companion.

It was the companion Sydney hoped to reach, to arrange to call on Jefferson Brown. Mr. Brown had in fact been at home on the night of the murders, but obviously hadn't seen anything, nor had he admitted to hearing the gunshots, or an argument preceding them.

The report ended with a notation that Mr. Brown had refused to cooperate further after becoming irritated with the officer for "shouting" and asking too many "damn fool questions."

Sydney dialed the phone number she'd copied from the report. She got a recording instead which informed her that the number was no longer in service. Directory assistance was of no help.

"I'm sorry," the operator said, "I have no listing for a Jefferson Brown at that address."

The man had been ninety-one at the time of the murders; maybe he'd fallen and broken a hip, had a heart attack, or suffered a stroke in the past year, and had been forced to enter a convalescent hospital. Then again, it was entirely possible he had died.

"Thank you anyway." As she was about to hang up a thought occurred to her. "Oh, wait!"

"Yes?"

"Do you have an address and phone number for

a bar called Harvey's out in Borrego Springs?" She had the number already, but figured that asking for both would at least prevent her from being relegated to the dreaded automated voice.

"One moment." After a pause, the operator reeled off the number and address, on Fire Canyon Road.

Sydney scribbled the address in her notebook, thanked the operator again, and hung up. She reached under the seat where she kept her Thomas Guide, and within seconds found the correct map.

Fire Canyon appeared to be one of many dead-end roads out in the desert, branching off of Borrego Springs Road, which was also known as Country Route S3. It wasn't exactly in the middle of nowhere—there was a golf course in the general vicinity—but it came close.

"To go or not to go," she said aloud, studying the map. It'd take a couple of hours to get there—if she were lucky—and she didn't really have a clue what or who she was looking for at Harvey's, but she'd have to go sooner or later, and today was shot anyway . . .

At the very least, she could show the bartender photographs of Denise and Gayle, and run some other names by him—like Fox and Sorvino and Monroe—on the off chance it had been one of them who'd called the bar. Even if Harvey's proved to be a false lead, it would leave her with one less detail to check out.

"Hell," she said, and turned the key in the ignition, "nothing ventured, nothing gained."

*   *   *

During her senior year at college, Sydney had taken an extension class that required the students to spend a weekend in the Anza-Borrego Desert. Nature study was a distinct change of pace from her classes in Criminal Justice, a change that she sorely needed at that point in her life.

All of the focus on criminal psychology, forensic pathology, and aberrant behavior had left her feeling as if there was nothing good left in the world.

Nature study seemed . . . natural. What was odd was how much she remembered, even now, of the days spent identifying the cacti and trees; of climbing on the rocks to find a good place from which to bird-watch; of unexpectedly encountering the desert creatures—a Blacktail jackrabbit, or kit fox, or chuckwalla.

Driving along an empty stretch of road, she searched out the desert willow, tamarisk, cottonwood, and smoke trees. She knew that in the blur of landscape passing by were the cholla, hedgehog, beaver-tail, and barrel cacti. There among the honey mesquite, fan palm, brittle bush, and creosote were also ocotillo, yucca, palo verde, and the great agaves, or century plants, which bloomed only once—hypothetically after a hundred years—and then died.

Adding color to the stark beauty of the desert were the annuals: the evening primrose, desert sunflower, sand verbena, and wild heliotrope.

Beside the coyote's wail, the eerie silence might be broken by the call of a mourning dove, a mockingbird, or loggerhead shrike. Sometimes a roadrunner would dart across the blacktop.

Vultures circled lazily in the sky, waiting with endless patience for death.

Borrego, she remembered, apropos of nothing, was the Spanish word for yearling sheep.

As grand as the name sounded, Fire Canyon Road turned out to be little more than a glorified dirt path, with deep ruts connecting the even deeper potholes. She had to drive slowly, but even so, plumes of dust rose into the dry air in her wake.

The road did indeed dead end, at Harvey's. The bar was the typical desert dive, a wood shack with a metal roof. The unstained lumber had grayed, the metal had rusted, and it looked as though a brisk wind might bring the whole thing crashing down.

A hand-painted sign proclaiming the bar's name was situated precariously on the roof directly above the screen door. There were no neon signs advertising brands of beer in any of the grimy windows, or for that matter, any liquor advertisements at all.

The parking lot was dirt and gravel, with an occasional cracked patch of blacktop. There was a shed off to the left of the bar from which came the distinctive sound—and smell—of a gas-powered generator.

Business at Harvey's wasn't exactly booming; there were only three vehicles in the lot. One was an old Ford pickup that looked as if someone had taken a hammer and methodically dented every square inch. In the truck bed were a couple of bales of hay and a five-gallon water jug with a tin cup tied to the handle.

The second truck was a Toyota with over-sized wheels and a custom paint job. Its windows were tinted nearly black—a violation of the California Motor Vehicle Code—and its bed was littered with

crumpled beer cans. If the Ford was for work, this
Toyota was for play.

The last vehicle was a motorcycle, a big hulking
Harley that somehow seemed more substantial than
either truck. The way it was tricked out, the Harley
had probably cost more, too.

Sydney parked off to the side of the others, got
out of the Mustang, and went to the trunk, where
she retrieved her .38 from the strongbox and tucked
it in the waistband of her jeans at the small of her
back. She pulled her sweatshirt down over her hips
to better hide the gun's distinctive shape.

She would have to remember not to sit back too
abruptly or hard; the last time she'd carried, she
forgot the gun was there. And while the bruises
along her spine were more colorful than painful, it
was a lesson she preferred not to forget *or* repeat.

The inside of the bar was covered wall-to-wall
and floor-to-ceiling with hub caps. It was a wonder
that the combined weight didn't pull the walls in.

There was an old-fashioned jukebox in one corner, and a pool table in another. A wall rack held
five cues; a sixth lay across the rail. One of the two
middle-aged men at the table was twirling the eight
ball on the felt surface, while the other collected the
rest from the ball return box to set them up.

Overhead, ceiling fans stirred the warm, boozy
air. On the jukebox, Clint Black sang sorrowfully
of—what else?—his lost love.

The bartender, young and good-looking, stopped
what he was doing to watch Sydney cross the room.

"Well, hello," he said, and grinned.

"Hi." She sat on a bar stool. "Can I get a Pepsi?"

"Honey, from me you can get whatever the hell you want." He opened a cooler and brought out a can with crushed ice still adhering to it. "Want a glass?"

"The can's fine."

Without taking his eyes from her, he popped the top and then licked his thumb which had been sprayed with foam. He grinned again and handed the Pepsi to her, making certain their fingers touched. "Something else?"

"How about a few minutes of your time?"

"Anytime, anywhere."

"Here and now will do," she said. She debated showing him her investigator's license to cool him off, but decided he was more likely to talk if he felt he was doing himself some good. "What's your name?"

"Joey." He came around the bar and sat on the stool next to hers. About five-foot-seven, lean and wiry, he moved with the insolent grace of a young Marlon Brando.

Watching him, she noted that the employee dress code at Harvey's was casual at best; Joey wore a white T-shirt, and there were fashionable holes in the knees of his jeans. His paratrooper boots were polished, though.

"I'm Sydney."

"Sydney, well." He sucked his breath through his teeth. "I hope you won't take this the wrong way, but you are really hot."

"In the desert, I'd think everyone is."

"Not in your life. Most of the women who come around here are pug-ugly bitches. On Ladies' Night we serve Milk Bones."

Across the room, the pool players laughed.

"Tell me," she said to change the subject, "is it always this quiet?"

"Hardly. The thing is, it's early . . . hang in for a couple of hours, till the Friday-night crowd arrives. The place'll be packed."

"I suppose most of them are locals?"

"I'd guess ninety-five percent live hereabouts." He leaned toward her, smiling his cocky smile. "I know you'll find this hard to believe, but Harvey's isn't what you'd call a trendy kind of place."

"You never know," she said. "Have you worked here long?"

"Ever since I turned twenty-one." He shifted on the bar stool so that his knee brushed against hers.

Sydney pretended not to notice. "Then maybe you know some friends of mine."

"Could be."

"Denise Reilly? Gayle Honeywell?"

"I've never met a Denise." Joey rested his hand on her knee. "Of course, until today I'd never met a Sydney, either, and that's a fact."

This definitely was not working. In a minute, if left to boil, Joey would be all over her. If she had to, she was pretty sure she could handle him, but she'd rather it not come to that. She reached into her shoulder bag and brought out her wallet, which she opened to reveal her license. "The reason I ask is because I'm a private investigator, and I'm working on a case."

"Are you shitting me?" Furrows formed on his brow as he peered at the license.

"Not at all."

"Damn," Joey swore, but moved his hand back to the safety of his own knee. "And here I thought we were getting along."

"Unfortunately," she said, smiling to take the sting out of it, "I'm on the clock. But it would really help me out if you'd take a look at these." She placed photographs of Denise and Gayle in front of him.

Joey picked up the picture of Denise, frowned, and tossed it back on the bar. "Never saw her."

"How about the other one?"

He leaned forward for a look, scratching his nose. "I don't know. Maybe."

"Her name is Gayle Honeywell," Sydney added, hoping that would help.

"Gayle? Doesn't sound familiar. She go by any other name?"

"I'm not sure." Anything was possible; when and if she ever reached Gayle's parents, she'd have to ask. "Have you seen her in here?"

He didn't answer immediately, but picked up the photograph for a closer look. "I can't say for absolute sure. But I think so."

"Did she come in alone?"

"No, if this is the gal I'm thinking of, she always came in with a guy." The grin was back. "I remember, because I'd have liked to ask her out. Never got a chance, though. Crazy Eddie never let her out of his sight."

"Eddie Monroe?"

Joey shrugged. "I only knew him as Crazy Eddie."

It had to be the same guy. "What's so crazy about Eddie?"

"The dude was a weirdo, plain and simple. He liked to pretend he was a biker. You know, decked out in leather and kind of scruffy-looking, but I know it was nothing but an act, all for show."

"How do you know it was an act?"

"Because I called his bluff. Eddie was bitching that his bike had been repossessed because he missed a couple of payments, and talking up how much he missed riding the line. I offered him a chance to take my hog out, catch some bugs in his teeth, and he turned fucking *green*. I thought he was gonna puke."

So Joey owned the Harley. She'd have thought the Toyota was more his style. "A minute ago you said Eddie never let his girlfriend out of his sight. I take it he was the jealous type?"

"In spades. He didn't want anyone to even look at her, and as for anything more . . . man, if he caught anyone talking to her, he came unglued."

"What would he do?"

"Invite them outside," Joey said, and laughed. "Crazy Eddie is fearless, let me tell you. I saw him jump on some big motherfuckers. He didn't always win, but he did enough damage to make his point."

"Does he live in Borrego?"

Joey nodded. "He's got a trailer off a little dirt road maybe fifteen miles from here. You want, I can draw you a map. Or I'll take you there myself."

"I wouldn't want to trouble you—"

"It's no trouble," he was quick to add.

"—not while you're working."

"Hey, no problem. The second bartender gets here at seven, and things don't start hopping till eight. I can take a break, show you the way to Crazy Eddie's, and be back before the karioke starts."

"Karioke?" She knew of a few places in San Diego where the patrons got up on tiny, makeshift stages and sang to prerecorded songs, but she'd never have guessed that kind of faddish silliness would be tolerated out here.

"Yeah, karioke. Of course, the way we do it, it's a hell of a lot dirtier."

"By that you mean . . ."

"The singers change the lyrics to suit the mood of the crowd. By closing time, the songs are so raunchy, they'd make a Marine blush."

"Sounds charming," she said.

"That's Harvey's all right. Charming. So, what do you say? Wanna take a ride?"

"I appreciate the offer, but . . . it's getting late. I think the best thing to do is to pay a call on Eddie another day." Preferably not alone, and definitely not with Joey, who still had that I-know-you-want-me look in his eye.

"That's cool." Joey grabbed a paper coaster and turned it over. "Got a pen? I'll draw you a map."

Twenty

By the time she'd reached the end of Fire Canyon Road, Sydney had changed her mind.

It would be foolish to take a pass on talking to Eddie Monroe, since she was already in Borrego. According to the map Joey had drawn for her, Monroe's trailer was at the most twenty minutes away.

As frustrated as she was at not being able to connect with virtually anyone and everyone she wanted to interview, it made absolutely no sense to forgo an opportunity to talk to the man who'd allegedly stalked Gayle Honeywell. And given how fast news traveled in small towns, Monroe would soon know that someone had been asking questions about him and Gayle.

If he had anything to hide, he might be gone by the time she came back.

Sydney simply couldn't take that chance.

Safety was always a concern, but even though it had been ten years, she'd never forgotten what she'd learned in Defensive Tactics back in the Academy. If that didn't work, she could cut and run.

And if all else failed, she had the Smith and Wesson.

It was a left turn to go home, a right turn to get to Crazy Eddie Monroe's.

She turned right.

It was getting near dusk, but there was still enough light to see the marker—an inverted pie pan nailed to a post—that Joey had described. Sydney slowed the Mustang and eased off the pavement onto a narrow dirt road that made Fire Canyon look like Interstate 5.

The Mustang's suspension was stiff, the shocks unforgiving, and it rode low to the ground. Only by careful maneuvering around the deepest potholes did she keep the undercarriage from bottoming out.

The road meandered along what she suspected was the path of least resistance, curving around an occasional boulder, and threading between a cluster of yucca plants, which had grown as tall as trees. There was a gradual incline to the road, and when she crested the rise, she saw the trailer on the other side.

It was an old Silver Stream, and it sat among the hulks of half a dozen abandoned cars. An ancient refrigerator, minus the door, stood like a sentry where the road entered the compound, if you could call it that.

"Home sweet home," she said, taking in the view.

There were no lights on inside the trailer as far as she could tell. Floodlights had been mounted on wooden poles extending up from the four corners of the trailer, but they were off.

The place looked uninhabited.

Looks, she reminded herself, could be deceiving. For all she knew, Monroe might have black-out shades on the windows. Out here in the desert, darkness was valued as a way to ease the heat.

She'd come this far; she might as well knock on the damned door.

Sydney parked the Mustang only after making a three-point turn in the narrow road so that the car was facing back the way she'd came.

Getting out, she put on her Levi's jacket even though it wasn't cold, and moved the .38 around to the front, tucking it up to the grip under the waistband of her jeans. If she had to, she could reach the gun in seconds. If she kept her distance from Monroe—and she certainly intended to—a few seconds would be enough.

The huge air conditioner on the Silver Stream's roof was silent, which would seem to indicate that no one was home. April temperatures weren't as blazing hot as they would be midsummer, but it had been warm today. Under the desert sun, the metal-skinned trailer would hold the heat in like an oven.

She took her time approaching the trailer, keeping a watchful eye on the derelict vehicles, which provided the perfect cover if someone wanted to hide. She'd even heard of desert rats who'd dug subterranean caves beneath a junked car in their quest to avoid the heat . . . and any unwelcome visitors.

Off in the distance, a dog barked.

Reaching the trailer, Sydney knocked on the door, the heat stinging her knuckles. She waited and listened, but heard no sound coming from inside. She knocked again, harder.

A minute or two passed. She tried the door, and

found it locked. The windows on this side of the trailer appeared to be shut tight, so she slowly walked the perimeter looking for signs of recent habitation.

As she came back around to the front of the Silver Stream, she heard a scuffing sound, like a boot kicking dirt.

A paratrooper boot to be exact.

"Hey there, Sydney," Joey said.

He was about eight feet away from her, between her and the Mustang. His Harley was parked up the dirt road, near the bend.

"Joey. I didn't hear you ride up."

"Yeah," he said, "I walked that big son of a bitch all the way from the main road."

"Why'd you do that?"

He grinned, and tucked his thumbs in the front belt loops of his jeans. "Guess."

"So I wouldn't hear you."

"There ya go."

She regarded him thoughtfully. "You knew Eddie Monroe wasn't here, didn't you?"

"Why the hell would he be? This is my place."

His place; no wonder the super-detailed directions. "And you wanted me to come out here," she said, cursing herself for not catching on to his game.

"You wouldn't have if I'd asked."

"What about the bar? Friday's a busy night . . . won't you be missed?"

"The guys will cover for me," he said. "They understand you gotta strike while the iron's hot. Besides, this won't take long. Unless, of course, you want it to."

Sydney felt her pulse quicken. In the gathering

darkness, she couldn't read his eyes. "What is it exactly that you have in mind?"

"Well, I thought we'd get better acquainted, for starters."

"You know," she said, with an edge to her voice, "the problem is, you're not really my type."

Joey snorted. "Don't give me that shit. I saw you checking me out."

"Not a chance."

"That's bullshit." He pointed a finger at her. "You women think you can flirt and tease, and do whatever the hell you want. Then some guy takes you up on it, and you're *offended,* like you weren't sending signals."

"I wasn't sending signals," Sydney said flatly. "You're imagining things."

"Hell, you don't know the half of it. I've got myself a great imagination. I close my eyes, I can see us together, naked and sweating . . ."

He took a step forward, and she took one back. "It's not gonna happen, Joey."

"I wouldn't be so sure."

"I am." She'd shoot him if she had to, if she couldn't find another way out. In a few more minutes, twilight would give way to the night. Her best chance to get away without a physical confrontation was under the cover of darkness, which meant she'd have to stall.

"So what's it gonna be?" He gestured toward the trailer. "You wanna come inside?"

"Willingly, you mean?"

"Yeah, willingly. I'll be nice to you if you're nice to me." He took another step in her direction.

Sydney moved backward and then sideways. "I

don't get this, Joey. What you're talking about is rape."

"Come off it," he scoffed. "You'll never be able to prove it. The guys at the bar saw us sitting together, having a good ole time. I think everybody knows a woman who comes in to a place like that by her lonesome is looking for something other than a beer."

"What I was looking for was information."

"Tell it to the judge. The guys saw me drawing you a map out to my place—"

"To Eddie Monroe's."

"That's *your* story. It'll be your word against the three of us. Nowadays, you want to cry rape, you'd better be a nun, and an ugly one at that. Otherwise, people are gonna figure you got what you were asking for."

She side-stepped again. "So might you."

"I'm counting on it. But don't make out like it's so bad. I'm not gonna hurt you—"

"You're right about that."

"—I just want to love you a bit." He laughed suggestively. "And honey, the iron is *hot.*"

That exceeded the limit of her tolerance. Knowing it would be the last thing he expected, Sydney moved quickly toward Joey, acutely conscious of the ground she was walking on. When she was five feet away from him, she bent down, grabbed a handful of soft dirt, took another two steps and flung it in his face. "You bastard."

"Shit, my eyes!"

Another step and she pivoted, kicking out sideways, aiming at and hitting him directly in the knee.

His leg buckled, and Joey stumbled to the ground. "What the—"

She didn't give him a chance to finish. Yanking the .38 from her waistband, she whacked him on the back of the head with the wood grip.

Joey started to stagger to his feet, and she hit him again on the back-swing, this time striking him in the face. She heard a pop and a crackling sound—cartilage tearing?—and he collapsed in the dirt like a puppet whose strings had been cut.

Even in the dark, she could see blood staining the ground.

She didn't wait around to see if he was conscious or not, instead turning to run to the car. The adrenaline had kicked in and her hands were shaking badly, but she managed to yank the door open, got in, and reached for the key, which she'd left in the ignition—

The key wasn't there.

Joey must have taken it.

As she saw it, she had no choice: she would have to go search him. Locking herself in the car and waiting for help wasn't a viable option; out here passersby were few and far between. Neither could she use the cellular phone to call for help without the key.

Cussing under her breath, she got out of the Mustang and, gun in hand, hurried back to where Joey lay in the dirt. He was groaning and scrabbling around as if he were trying to get to his knees.

She hated to touch him, hated to get close enough for him to grab her, but there wasn't an alternative. She stood over him and put the barrel of the Smith and Wesson next to his right ear. "Do you feel that, Joey? Do you know what it is?"

By his sudden stillness, she knew that he had and did.

"Lay flat and don't move," she ordered, and began to pat him down. His back pockets held a wallet, which she tossed off to the side, and a jackknife, which she kept. "I need my keys, where are they?"

"Shirt pocket," he mumbled, his voice sounding strangely congested.

Maybe she'd broken his nose.

"Let me turn over, I'll give it—"

"I wasn't born yesterday, Joey. Your shirt doesn't have a pocket." She pressed the gun harder against his neck, then knelt so one knee was in the middle of his back. "Don't move, don't even breathe hard."

"Whatever you say."

With her left hand she reached under him, searching his left front pocket. All she found was some change. She switched hands with the gun, and tried the right front pocket. There she encountered a tangle of keys which she removed.

There were two sets, and one was hers. Then again, with possession being nine-tenths of the law, maybe both sets were.

With the gun still near his ear, she cocked the hammer. "I'm going to go, now. You are going to stay where you are until I'm gone. Is that clear?"

"Yes, ma'am."

"Good. Put your hands on the back of your head, fingers entwined." She didn't want him reaching for an ankle to pull her down.

He complied. "I wasn't gonna hurt you," he said.

"Tell it to the judge." She straightened up and backed away. "And have a nice day."

When she'd put a good number of miles between

herself and Borrego, she pulled off the road into a well-lit service station and, engine idling, made a couple of calls.

True to form, the lines were busy.

Twenty-one

At midnight, back at her apartment and alone, the reality of her close call finally hit her. Sydney sat on the floor of her shower and let the water beat down on her until it ran cold. Even after turning the taps off, she sat there, wet and shivering, replaying the scene with Joey over and over again in her mind, while blocking out what might have been . . .

"Stupid, stupid, stupid," she said, hugging her knees to her chest. She was too civilized to scream, and far too angry to cry.

The worst of it was that she'd walked straight into that punk Joey's transparent scheme. Thinking him harmless—distracted and preoccupied with finding Eddie Monroe—she'd let her guard down. It was a mistake she should not have made.

About the only thing she'd done right was taking the offensive, instead of waiting for him to make his move. The element of surprise had been on her side; evidently it never entered his mind that she would not submit docilely to his demands.

As she saw it, at that point it was either him or her. Defensive tactics aside, there were few women who could hold their own, one-on-one, against a

man. If she'd let it come to that, she had little doubt
what the outcome would have been.

Still, she was sickened by what she'd had to do,
by the sound of her gun striking flesh and bone.
There was blood on the grip; she'd brought the .38
in so she could clean it before locking it away.

*What if I hadn't had the gun with me? He was
down, but he wasn't out.*

"Damn." She stood up, reached for a towel and
wrapped it around herself, then grabbed another for
her hair. "Son of a . . ."

She let the words trail off. The way she felt,
swearing a blue streak wouldn't help.

Wide awake and restless, Sydney put on her robe
and went into the kitchen to make a cup of hot
chocolate, hoping that it might help her get to sleep.
It had been awhile since she'd done any grocery
shopping, and she sniffed the milk to determine if it
had soured.

It hadn't. She poured the milk in a pan, added
two heaping spoonfuls of Nestlé's Quik, and a taste
of vanilla. She turned the burner on low—few
things tasted worse than scalded cocoa—and waited
for it to heat.

The doorbell rang.

She looked at the kitchen clock; it was one A.M.
straight up, an unusual hour for visitors, even by
her night owl standards.

Maybe it was a neighbor coming to complain
about her forty-five minute shower.

With a sigh, she turned off the burner and went
into the living room. After switching on the lights,

she looked through the peephole, one hand on the top dead bolt.

"Mitch," she said, unlocking the door. "What are you doing here?"

"That should be obvious." He came in, locked the door behind him, and took her into his arms. "I heard you had a rough night."

"You heard?" She'd talked briefly to a deputy, but since Joey hadn't actually touched her, whatever his intentions, she'd decided not to file a complaint against him. "I've underestimated your sources."

"No kidding. Are you okay?"

"More or less." She pulled back and looked up at him. "Why? What exactly did you hear?"

Mitch gave her his most engaging smile. "Basically, that you kicked some punk's ass."

"Great." She adjusted her robe, tightening the belt, belatedly recalling that she wore only a thigh-length T-shirt beneath it. "I know the way this works. I've spent my entire career trying to earn a reputation for working clean and keeping my cool, and from now on all anyone will remember is this one incident."

Mitch cupped her face in his hands and kissed her. "It's not as bad as that."

"Convince me."

"It won't go any further than this room . . . unless Joey decides to press assault charges against you for breaking his nose."

"Right, I feel *much* better now." She ducked away from him and started for the kitchen. "Do you want some hot chocolate?"

"Sure. Anyway," he said, following her, "I have some information you might be interested in."

"Such as?"

"Such as the whereabouts of one Edward no-middle-initial Monroe."

Sydney stopped halfway through the swinging door and turned to face Mitch. "How did you know I was looking for Eddie Monroe?"

"I have my—"

"—sources, right." She'd only mentioned Monroe's name once, in passing, and would have bet the deputy hadn't bothered to write it down. "I never realized the San Diego P.D. and the Sheriff's Department were joined at the hip. Whatever happened to interdepartmental rivalry, for crying out loud?"

Mitch took her by the shoulders, turned her around, and escorted her through the doorway. "We can cooperate when necessary. Make your hot chocolate."

"What's going on, Mitch? How come everyone knows what I'm going to do before I do it?"

"Kid, you have Jake Scott and the District Attorney's office jumping through hoops trying to figure out what you're up to. He can't stand the thought of being upstaged by a private investigator."

She took that to mean a *female* private investigator. "I heard he's interviewing the witnesses again."

"And again and again. One of the people he wants to talk to happens to be Eddie Monroe."

"Fancy that." As far as she knew, the D.A. hadn't talked to Monroe prior to the trial. At least, she hadn't come across any paperwork that would indicate otherwise. "So who found him?"

"An old friend of yours, Lieutenant Grant."

Dwight Grant was anything but a friend. He'd been the primary investigator for the Sheriff's Department in the Blood Bride case, and had made it clear from the start he had no use for "wannabe" P.I.'s.

"That figures," she said.

"Small world, isn't it?"

Sometimes the world was too damned small.

"Anyway, with Eddie Monroe on every Attempt to Locate sheet in the state, naturally the deputy's ears perked up when you mentioned the name."

"Naturally."

"They picked him up at noon, by the way. They're holding him on a probation violation."

At noon she'd been trying on wedding gowns. All at once tired, she sagged against the counter. "That's just . . . that's . . . I don't believe this. Here I am out looking for him, and he's in custody?"

"Yep."

"I should never have gotten out of bed this morning," she said, and ran her fingers through her still-wet hair. "Shit. Hand me that dishtowel, would you?"

Mitch complied. "You're taking this well."

"I'm trying. Are you going to tell me what the deal is with Monroe?"

"The deal is he's not talking to anyone about anything. Not Gayle Honeywell, not Denise Reilly, not the price of tea in China."

"Oh." She took some satisfaction in that, knowing that Jake Scott must be livid. "What are my chances of getting in to see him?"

"That depends. His attorney is trying to broker a deal to get him released, but I don't think the D.A. will consider letting him go until after his arraignment on Tuesday."

"Hmm." Sydney picked up a wooden spoon and

skimmed the skin that had formed off the milk. She turned on the heat. "That gives me a few days, anyway."

"That gives all of us a few days."

"Speaking of which, how did you guys miss talking to him on the first go-around? I mean, it's right there in black and white; Betsy Honeywell stated unequivocally that Monroe had been harassing Gayle."

"We didn't miss it. The harassment was old news by the time she was killed. They hadn't seen each other in seven or eight months."

"Maybe." She made figure eights in the chocolate milk with the spoon. "That you know of."

"What do you mean by that?"

Sydney told him about the last-number-dialed feature on the guest room telephone. "That's how I ended up at Harvey's in the first place, trying to track down who was on the receiving end of that call."

"You think Gayle Honeywell called Eddie Monroe?"

"Stranger things have happened," she said, echoing one of her father's favorite sayings.

"Well, if they had any contact, Ms. Honeywell didn't bother to notify the police. There was a valid restraining order on Monroe; we would have picked him up."

"On the other hand," Sydney went on, pursuing her train of thought, "maybe Eddie Monroe is the killer. And after he got in—"

"Was let in," Mitch corrected. "No one broke in."

"—and shot them, he made a call to Harvey's."

"Why?"

Sydney considered that for a moment. "You're right, why would he? It works better if someone else was the shooter, and that person called to report the deed was done. Do you have the phone records, by the way? Borrego Springs would be a toll call."

"I honestly don't know. We don't always get phone records, especially not when it appears to be an open-and-shut case."

"Do you still believe that?"

"That it's open-and-shut? Let's just say, I'm willing to reconsider the alternatives."

"I'm glad to hear it."

"Jake Scott won't be."

"That's his problem. *My* problem is getting in to talk to Eddie Monroe." She'd call Wade Cooper in the morning to request that he arrange it. That, and schedule an interview with Miriam Reilly . . .

Mitch came up behind her and put his arms around her waist, easing her back so she was leaning against him. "The hot chocolate is boiling," he murmured in her ear, reaching to turn off the burner.

She hadn't noticed. "Forget the hot chocolate, I think it's time for me to go to bed."

"Want company?"

"Mitch . . ." Although they'd been lovers four years ago, they had not taken up where they'd left off. As badly as she wanted him—and sometimes she ached from the wanting—her guilt over having an affair while he was still married stood between them.

"No?"

"Not tonight."

"Then I'd better go." He kissed her on the neck. "The last thing I need is a broken nose."

Sydney started to laugh, helplessly, and found she

couldn't stop, until her sides ached and there were tears running down her face. She began to shake, then, as if with fever.

A moment later, regaining control, she caught her breath and shook her head. "I guess that qualifies as a classic illustration of a delayed reaction."

"The Department psychologist would call it 'borderline post-traumatic stress disorder.' " Mitch kissed her wet face. "Either way, you're tougher than you think."

Except, she thought, I don't *feel* tough . . .

Twenty-two

Miriam Reilly lived in one of the older sections of San Diego, not far from Old Town. The houses here were small, mostly stucco, and sat back from the street in the middle of generous lots.

The Reilly property was the only one in the neighborhood enclosed by a white picket fence. There was a child's wading pool in the front yard, and a swing set was visible in the back.

Sydney let herself in through the gate, and shut it behind her. A toddler's bright red plastic rake and shovel were propped against an exterior wall. A slightly deflated neon yellow beach ball blocked the walk, and she stepped around it.

These were Daniel's toys, she realized. He'd be twenty-one months old now; in the year since the murders, he would have learned to walk, to feed himself, started to talk, and been potty-trained. It was sad to think his mother had missed all of that, and that if his father was convicted, the little boy— the most innocent victim—would grow up without either parent.

This was, she knew, the house Keith Reilly had

grown up in. That his son lived here now, under
these circumstances, was a sad kind of continuity.

Sydney rang the bell.

"I was surprised when Wade mentioned you
wanted to talk to me," Miriam Reilly said, leading
the way into the living room. "I really don't know
what I could do that would be of any help . . ."

"I have a few questions," Sydney said, "about
Denise and Keith. It shouldn't take long."

"Not that I'm complaining," Miriam was quick
to add. "It's just that Danny's at his play group and
I usually use the free time to pick up the house, run
to the store, or—" she laughed ruefully "—take an
aspirin and put my feet up for a while. Having a
little one around can be tiring for a woman of my
age."

"I can imagine." Sydney sat on the floral-print
couch and removed the microcassette recorder from
her shoulder bag. "Do you mind if I tape our conversation?"

"No, not at all."

Despite her ready agreement, there was a look of
apprehension in Mrs. Reilly's eyes. Sydney pressed
the record button. "Why don't you tell me about
your son's marriage to Denise?"

Miriam blinked several times. "Their marriage?
That's um . . . what is it you want to know?"

"Did Keith ever talk to you about the trouble
they were having?"

"Not in so many words." Her smile was tremu-
lous, and there was a hint of a quiver playing at her
chin. "Keith is very much like my late husband, you
understand, and a Reilly simply doesn't talk about

his private life unless matters have progressed beyond his control."

"Not even to you?"

"Oh, especially not to me. I'm sure Keith is horribly embarrassed at having his—how shall I put this?—his indiscretions made public."

Sydney thought that embarrassment was the least of Keith's worries. "But you must have drawn some conclusions on your own?"

"I had my suspicions," Miriam agreed. "I could tell that Denise wasn't happy—"

"She didn't confide in you?"

"Never. To be honest, Denise and I were never very close."

"Keith mentioned when I spoke to him that you disapproved of the marriage."

A crease appeared between the older woman's eyebrows when she frowned, and she said crossly, "I wish he wouldn't tell people that."

"It isn't true?"

"I thought Denise was too young to be married, and too flighty. She had to be the center of attention. If she wasn't . . . watch out. But if he'd listened to me when I told him it was a mistake to marry her, none of this would have happened."

If it walks like a duck and talks like a duck, Sydney thought, it's a duck. She looked down at her notes so Mrs. Reilly would not see her smile.

"They had absolutely nothing in common; Keith had *ambition,* you understand. He was an entrepreneur all the way back in grammar school. The boy had a paper route and mowed lawns, the usual ways that kids earn money, but he also had his coin collection, even then. He wanted to make something of himself."

"And Denise?"

"Denise." Miriam sniffed. "All that girl ever wanted was to have a good time."

"She was young," Sydney pointed out.

"I was young when I married, and I never wasted a moment concerning myself over what I might be missing, or what my friends were doing that I wasn't. Selfish and self-absorbed, that's what she was."

Sydney wondered in whose book any or all of that added up to equal a death sentence.

"I know what you're going to say, that times have changed since I was a bride, but *not* for the better," Miriam went on. "Keith needed a more traditional wife, a helpmate. Denise's proper place was at her husband's side. Call me old-fashioned if you will, but a good wife puts her husband's needs before her own."

"Did you tell her how you felt?"

"I may have mentioned it once or twice."

For some reason, Sydney found that hard to believe. "When Denise found out about Keith's affair and he moved into the spare room, did you know?"

"Of course, by then I did. There was no way he could hide it, given his predicament. Keith told me that Denise had asked him for a divorce."

"What was his reaction?"

"He was upset, of course," Miriam Reilly snapped. "He couldn't stand the thought of losing little Danny."

Not one word yet of regret for the loss of Denise. "I assume he told you of Denise's threats to take the baby and leave?"

"Yes!" Her eyes flashed with indignation. "She wanted to hurt him as badly as she could—"

As badly as Keith's infidelity had hurt her? Sydney wondered but didn't ask.

"—and that was the punishment she came up with. She said she'd take Danny out of the country, and that we'd never see him ever again."

"Did you believe her?"

"I'm sorry, what?"

"Did you believe she'd actually do something that drastic?"

"She was *very* angry," Miriam said, blinking rapidly, obviously angry herself.

"Yes, but isn't it possible she could have been bluffing? People often make threats they never intend to carry out."

"Oh, she meant it all right; if you'd seen the hateful way she looked at me, and heard the spite in her voice . . . you'd understand why we couldn't take that chance. Not and risk losing that precious child."

"Then you talked to Denise?"

"I . . . I may have spoken to her."

Sydney regarded her for a moment, wondering at the cause of the woman's evasiveness. "Did you or didn't you?" she asked.

Miriam covered her face with her hands briefly, then folded them in her lap. "This is difficult for me to admit . . . I'm afraid I did."

"This took place at their house?"

"Yes. I went over one afternoon, when I knew Daniel would be taking his nap."

"What happened?"

"I was thoroughly unpleasant to her. You don't know how much it pains me to remember that, considering how it all ended. If it *has* ended."

"Go on."

She took a shuddering breath. "I did my best to talk some sense into her. Whatever Keith had done, however badly he'd behaved, he didn't deserve to lose his son."

In another room, a clock chimed eleven A.M. Neither of them spoke until it fell silent.

"Did she repeat her threats to you?" Sydney asked.

"Yes. I begged her not to do anything foolish. 'Daniel needs a father,' I said, 'he needs a home. The children always suffer the most,' I told her."

"What did she say?"

"She informed me it was none of my business. It was between *them*. And she would do whatever she wanted. She said there was nothing that Keith or I could do if she decided to run off."

"You knew that wasn't true, didn't you? You had legal recourse. Parents can be charged with stealing their own children—"

Miriam shook her head vigorously. "None of that legal nonsense matters. What good would it do for a court to rule in Keith's favor? Would that give him back the years he'd lost with his son?"

"No," Sydney conceded, "it wouldn't."

"No. And I would have lost the most precious days of that sweet baby's life." Tears glistened in her eyes. "Any grandmother would do what I did. Perhaps I shouldn't have said some of the things I said, or raised my voice, but I did it out of love."

Sydney resisted the urge to point out that appallingly horrible acts were committed in the name of love every single day. Instead, she asked, "Did anything change, after you talked to her?"

Miriam squared her shoulders and lifted her chin. "Oh yes, it got worse. Denise wouldn't speak to me after that, or let me in the house. If she heard my voice on the phone, she'd hang up. If she was home when I went over to see Keith, we had to stand in the yard and talk, like common trash."

"Were you able to see Daniel?"

"For fifteen minutes at a time. Keith would bring the playpen out and set it up under the willow tree, there in the shade. Then Denise would hand the baby out to Keith, and we'd have those few minutes together."

"That must have been awkward for all of you."

"Not all of us." Her smile was bitter. "Denise enjoyed having her way."

"And now she's dead."

Miriam's expression did not change. "Yes, and now she's dead. Don't expect me to mourn her, Ms. Bryant, because I cannot."

"Keith is in jail," Sydney continued matter-of-factly, "facing a second trial—and the death penalty—in the murder of his wife. Did he do it, Mrs. Reilly? Did your son kill Denise and Gayle?"

Miriam came straight off the couch, and then, as if shocked by her own reaction, sat down just as quickly. "No! My son is not a murderer."

"You're certain of that?"

"I am."

"You have no doubts at all? I mean, you know better than almost anyone what he'd been going through. Living in that tiny room, using a curtain rod for a closet, eating TV dinners off a tray . . ."

Miriam Reilly glowered, narrowing her eyes. "Keith may have wished her dead in a weak moment—and I'll not deny that the Reilly men can be as weak as any other man—but he did not kill her.

He took her abuse and turned the other cheek, as his father and I taught him."

"Who do you think killed your daughter-in-law?"

"I don't think about it. Until Keith is set free, I can't spare the time."

Keith's response had been much the same. Sydney thought them both short-sighted; finding the real killer was the most expedient way to prove Keith Reilly innocent. If innocent he was.

"When was the last time you saw or spoke to Denise?" she asked, looking at her notes.

"I spoke to her on the phone last, since I hadn't seen her in weeks. That was on Wednesday."

"Five days before the murders?"

Miriam inclined her head in agreement. "She called me that morning in a fury because Keith had cancelled her credit card."

"Why call you instead of him?"

Miriam frowned. "I can't say for certain, but she blamed me for a lot of things. I did encourage my son to have all his mail sent here, so she couldn't fool with it, or destroy any important papers. The way she'd been carrying on, I thought it for the best."

For a mother whose son kept his problems private, she took an active interest in the consequences. "Were you aware that he'd cancelled her card before she called?"

"I knew he was considering it. He was worried she'd use it to buy airline tickets. And she had been charging a lot of clothes—"

"Did they have a joint checking account?"

"Keith closed it, the day after. He paid all the

bills and even did the grocery shopping so she couldn't hoard cash and run off."

"Couldn't she get money from her father?"

"I'm sure she would have, eventually. Or maybe from that friend, the girl who got killed with her. But Keith wasn't going to make it easy for her," Miriam Reilly said, and nodded as though satisfied.

"Obviously not." The entire situation reminded her of a chain-reaction collision, with one crash leading to another until it no longer mattered what or who had started it, the damage was done.

In this case, the damage was irreparable.

"Is there anything else you remember about your conversation?"

"It was, as I said, a very unpleasant call. I tried to put it out of my mind as soon as I hung up."

"She didn't mention any plans she had?"

"No. I knew she had company—I could hear the other one talking in the background—but by then, Denise had said all she had to say to me. She slammed the phone down, and that was that."

The recorder clicked, signalling that the tape had run out. Suffering from information overload, Sydney welcomed the diversion. Rather than turning the cassette over, she dug a fresh tape from her bag.

Unfortunately, installing the new tape took only a few seconds, and she looked up to find Miriam Reilly watching, her expression closed and guarded.

"You must think I'm a horrible person," Miriam said. "This sordid mess makes us all look like monsters. It depresses me to remember the petty cruelties . . . and some not so petty."

"It must have been a devastating experience to live through."

A tear ran down her cheek. "No one can imagine

how bad it was, how helpless a mother feels when she can't do anything to make it better. Mothers are supposed to make it better, you know?"

"It'll be over soon," Sydney said, although she was far from convinced of that.

But Miriam was no longer listening. She stared vacantly out the bay window at the backyard. When she spoke, her tone was almost dreamy: "There was nothing, really, that I could do."

Twenty-three

After leaving Miriam Reilly, Sydney drove once again to the Sorvino house. Rebecca Aiken had said that Tony Sorvino would be back in town by today, and with any luck, she'd get to talk to both father and daughter.

The neighborhood seemed abnormally quiet for a Saturday—there were no kids playing outside—but that might be the lingering aftereffect of double homicide. In a community of six households, murder in one of them came disturbingly close to home.

She'd heard of cases where, following a tragedy such as this, the neighbors sold their homes and moved away, one by one, unable to cope with having to face their memories every time they walked out the front door.

There were wounds that time alone was too slow to effectively heal.

As she approached the Sorvino residence, she saw the curtain flutter at one of the windows, and knew she was being watched. At least someone was at home.

The door opened before she reached the porch,

and a short, stocky man dressed in army fatigues stood framed in the doorway.

"Who the hell are you?" he asked, crossing his thickly-muscled arms over his chest.

"My name is Sydney Bryant." She held up her wallet, displaying her license. "I'm a private investigator—"

"I can read, chickee."

"Are you Tony Sorvino?"

"Cut the crap; you know I am."

"Mr. Sorvino, I'd like to talk to you about the murders last April—"

"I was out of town."

It was what she'd expected him to say. He'd refused to give a statement—which was his legal right—but according to Mitch, his whereabouts the night of the murders had been verified by the police. They'd confirmed that Sorvino had booked a flight to Atlanta, where he'd spent the night in a Holiday Inn.

His signature appeared on the American Express receipts for both the flight and accommodations; handwriting analysis had eliminated any possibility that the signatures had been faked or forged.

"I'm aware of that," Sydney said, "but your daughter was here."

"What of it?"

"It's common knowledge that Talia was involved with Keith Reilly."

Tony Sorvino did not appear to be pleased. "Common bullshit is more like it. She wasn't *involved,* Reilly was taking advantage of her."

"May I come in and talk to you about it?"

He looked her up and down. "Eh, I guess I can live with that. You don't look too intimidating."

She couldn't say the same for him; she noticed he was wearing a hunting knife strapped to his thigh. Still, she entered the house when he stepped aside and waved her in with a sweep of his arm.

"Go on back to the kitchen," he instructed. "To the left, there."

Sydney felt uneasy with him following her, out of eyesight, but that, she told herself, was a delayed reaction to yesterday's confrontation.

The kitchen was all-white and spotless. Sorvino went to the stove in the cooking island at the center of the room, where simmering pots and pans occupied every burner. There were several hardwood cutting boards lined up on the tile counter, with parsley, onions, garlic, and tomatoes in various stages of preparation.

"Have a seat," he said, picking up a slotted spoon.

Sydney brought a director's chair from the breakfast bar to sit at the island. "What are you cooking?"

"Spaghetti sauce, marinara with a pinch of sweet basil, hollandaise, and béarnaise," he said, pointing to each in turn with his little finger. "I cook on weekends when I'm home, and freeze the stuff, so Talia won't have to eat out of cans. My little girl isn't what you'd call domestic."

"Is she home, by the way?"

"Talia? No."

"Will she be? I need to talk to her, too."

Sorvino began mincing parsley. "She'll show up sooner or later."

"How much later is later?"

He considered it for a moment, apparently oblivious to how close the blade came to his fingertips.

"Probably before three. Or if not, definitely by five; she's got a baby-sitting job tonight."

Sydney glanced at her watch. "Two hours?"

"Or four." He dumped parsley into the spaghetti sauce. "On the other hand, she could walk through the door any second now. You never know with Talia; she's never been a slave to the clock."

"If I came back at three—"

"Hey, you're here now. Stick around. Maybe she'll show. Ask me some questions." Sorvino laughed. "I can't promise I have any answers or that I'd tell you if I did, but it'll pass the time."

"There are a couple of other calls I need to make today," she said. Corey Devlin was on the list, and so was Nigel Fox, whose blood alcohol level had been weighing on her mind. Plus she really ought to try to reach the Honeywells again.

"On a Saturday? Nobody's at home on a beautiful day like this. Listen, have you had lunch? I can cook up some spaghetti—you'll excuse, I'm not high-toned enough to call it pasta—throw in some meatballs, and we'll have ourselves a feast."

Sydney hadn't expected to like Tony Sorvino, and was surprised to find she did. "That's the best offer I've had in days."

"Now you're talking."

Sorvino gently swirled the red wine around in his glass. "The thing is, a girl needs a mother to teach her how a lady is supposed to act. What they show in movies, you'd think women were the same as men, always on the make, which we all know isn't gonna work, cause of the double standard, which isn't supposed to exist anymore, but it does."

"You're probably right," she said when he took a breath.

"Hell yes, I'm right. You seem like a nice girl, your momma taught you better. Talia's momma died when she was eight. I shoulda done right by my little girl and married again, so there'd be a woman in the house, but I couldn't. I just . . . couldn't."

Sydney looked at his face, his features rigid with pain, and saw a man deep in mourning twelve years after the death of his wife. "What about family?"

"Like an aunt or grandma or something?" He shook his head. "There was no one like that. Talia was on her own, and I guess with me on the road so much, she got the wrong ideas about love and stuff."

"What do you do?"

"For a living? I buy and sell guns. I can get you anything you want, for a price. Automatic, semi-automatic, assault rifles, submachine, whatever." He finished his wine, and gave her a sly smile. "Maybe the odd Stinger for the serious collector. You know, your basic home protection weapons."

Startled, Sydney laughed, and reminded herself Sorvino was a survivalist; selling guns fit right in with that. "Do you keep them here in the house?"

"Yeah, I try to keep a decent inventory on hand, but it's locked up most of the time. I got a walk-in safe with six-inch steel walls. I had to reinforce the floors to bring that big mother in here."

"I assume it's kept locked while you're away?"

"Has to be. I can't have someone breaking in and making off with my profits."

"Do you have nine-millimeter automatics?"

The look he gave her was shrewd. "That's what was used to blow those gals away, eh? Yeah, I got nine-millimeters, sure. And before you ask, the answer is no, Talia does not have the combination."

"Does she shoot?"

"Growing up with me for a father, she'd have to, wouldn't she?" Sorvino leaned forward, his elbows bunching up the white tablecloth. "On her worst day, she could qualify as an expert marksman."

"I appreciate your candor—"

"I'm only telling you what you could find out anyway. It's no secret. She's also damned good with a bow and arrow, but she didn't kill Cock Robin."

"I wasn't—"

"What was done to those two women could've been done by someone who'd never touched a gun before. As a matter of fact, what I know of it, it was a sloppy kill. If Talia had done it, it would have been over like that." He snapped his fingers.

Which, Sydney thought, would have been a kindness, considering.

"Talia doesn't have it in her to let someone suffer," her father said. "Okay, she's a little mixed-up about sex, and she's been known to confuse lust with love, but she's not cold-hearted."

"Has she said anything to you about that night?"

"Not a lot." Sorvino poured himself more wine, then held the bottle out to her. "Are you sure you don't want some?"

"Thanks, I have to keep a clear head."

"Eh, that's no way to stay sane."

"Mr. Sorvino—"

He stopped with the glass an inch from his mouth. "We ate together, you like my cooking, I give you permission, you can call me Tony."

"All right, Tony. What *has* your daughter told you about that night?"

"Give me a minute, and I'll tell you."

"Take as long as you need." She watched him, intrigued by the incongruities of the man. A survivalist gun dealer and gourmet, who taught his daughter to shoot but not cook. He struck her as being honest and forthcoming, in marked contrast to others she'd talked to in this case, many of whom seemed to have something to hide.

Unless . . . could it all be camouflage?

"Well," Tony Sorvino said finally, "you know she was sitting with the Meredith kids. That's the house next door to the Reilly's—" he gestured with a nod of his head "—on the other side."

"Right."

"She'd spent the weekend with 'em, from Friday night on. The parents were due back sometime Monday. She did say that she'd seen Denise that afternoon."

"On Sunday?"

"Yeah, Sunday. Denise and the other one were in the backyard, and Talia was right across the fence, squirting the kiddies with a garden hose. Kids love to play in the water, you know? It can be three degrees out, but if the sun is shining, they think it's warm."

Sydney smiled at that.

"Where was I? Oh . . . Talia said Denise looked right at her, but didn't say a word."

"Did Talia speak to her?"

"Nah. Talia had tried a couple of times before to make up, to apologize, and Denise cut her off cold. My girl might not be a rocket scientist, but she knows better than to rub salt in an open wound."

"Was there anything else? Did she overhear them talking?"

"She didn't mention it if she did. What with the canyon down there, words tend to drift and get swallowed up by the trees. Anyway, she told me they were out there for at least an hour."

"Did she notice if they seemed upset?" Sydney wondered if Gayle had heard from Eddie Monroe, or perhaps Denise had argued with Keith.

"You'll have to ask Talia."

Sydney nodded. "What has she told you about the next morning, when she called the police?"

"Only that she heard the baby crying, and it wouldn't stop. Denise wasn't one of these mothers who leave their kids to bawl it out, so after a while, Talia began to think something was wrong. So—"

"She tried to call Denise?"

"I guess so. When no one answered the phone, she called the police."

His account matched his daughter's official statement, but Sydney was still bothered that Talia hadn't gone over and knocked on the door first. Even if she and Denise weren't speaking, calling the cops on a wailing kid had always seemed to border on the extreme.

"Tony," she said, and hesitated, mindful that this was a sensitive issue. "At one time, didn't Talia have a key to their house?"

"Who told you that?"

"I heard it from a couple of sources, including Keith Reilly."

"Oh sure, I'd believe a cradle-robbing, adulterer like *him*."

"Actually, Keith said that Talia gave the key back. But there has been speculation that she might have had a copy made."

Tony Sorvino sighed and scratched the back of

his head. "Speculation, huh? It's funny how a fancy word can dress up talking behind somebody's back."

"But she did have a key?" Sydney persisted.

"Yeah, but it's no big deal. At the time she was practically living over there. And if she made a copy—which I'm not saying she did—it was probably because she misplaces things sometimes. It had nothing to do with wanting to kill anyone."

Sensing that it would do more harm than good to press him further, she said nothing, content for the moment to let the silence grow. Instead she met and held his eyes.

Sorvino drummed his fingers on the table but did not look away. A minute or two passed and then his mouth quirked with a crooked smile. "You're good," he said. "Know when to ease up a little, how far to push, not asking the obvious question . . . you are good."

"What's the obvious question?"

"Turn it around," he said, nodding, "so you don't have to be the one to say it. Let me wrestle with the nagging doubt that every parent has, deep inside; how well do I know my own child? Is it *possible?*"

"Is it?"

"Damn, but you're a pro. Have you ever thought of working for the feds?"

"Never. All I want, Tony, is the truth."

The smile disappeared. "The truth is, I wasn't here, and I don't know. I wish to God I did."

"I'm sorry," Sydney said.

"For what? You're only doing your job."

He was right about it being her job, but that

didn't make it any easier. "One last question: who do you think killed them?"

"Honestly? I don't know, but I hope it was Reilly. The son of a bitch deserves to rot in jail."

"Did I mention I was working for the defense?"

"No kidding?" Sorvino said, and started to laugh. "In that case, as poor a shot as the killer was, a blind man would be my second guess. Why don't you try next door? There's an idea, ask old man Brown."

"Jefferson Brown? I thought he was dead." It was out before she realized what she was saying, and she shook her head at how callous it sounded. "I mean, his phone's been disconnected."

"Yeah, he gets mad at Ma Bell a couple of times a year, and cancels his service." Tony Sorvino favored her again with his crooked smile. "But he's alive. The man's too ornery to die."

Twenty-four

The man who was too ornery to die looked as if a brisk wind would blow him away. Jefferson Brown sat in a rocker in a sunny corner of the deck behind his house, bundled up in an afghan, with knitted booties on his feet.

Brown wore every one of his ninety-two years on his wrinkled, leathery face. His eyes were a pale, milky blue, occluded by cataracts which were, she supposed, a redundancy, considering his blindness.

He clutched the afghan to his chest with his left hand—knuckles deformed with arthritis—and held a cane across his lap with his right. Dark blue veins showed beneath thin, age-spotted skin.

"Mr. Brown," the male attendant said, "you've got a visitor."

"What is it?"

"Not what, who. You've got a lady caller, Mr. Brown. Aren't you glad we had a bath today?"

"Piss," Jefferson Brown said.

The attendant gave Sydney a what-can-I-do? look. "I'll leave you alone to talk. Call me if he gets rowdy, I'll be right inside. And good luck."

She thought she might need it, but merely nodded

and waited for the sliding door to close behind him. Then she pulled up a foot stool and sat down in what she judged to be beyond cane-swinging range.

"Hello, Mr. Brown. My name is Sydney Bryant and I'm a private investigator. I'd like to ask you a few questions, if that's all right."

His mouth moved for a minute as if he were chewing furiously, before he licked his lips and spoke. "You from the government?"

"No."

"Good. I hate the government."

"The reason I'm here is in regards to what happened next door about a year ago."

"The murders."

"Yes, the murders. I know the police were here to talk to you—"

"Gestapo is what they are. Not worth a cup of warm spit."

Apparently, Jefferson Brown had a problem with authority figures. "The thing is, Mr. Brown, after reading the field interview report, I wasn't sure the policeman had gotten the whole story."

What might have been a smile flitted across the old man's lips. "You don't say?"

"The officer noted that you became upset, that you felt he was shouting—"

"He *was* shouting. Damned pup couldn't get it through his thick skull, I don't hear with my eyes. I'm lucky I didn't go deaf after the way he hollered at me."

"Yes sir. Anyway, the officer indicated in his report that you'd cut the interview short because he was asking foolish questions."

Brown tilted his head, as if remembering. "That sounds about right. 'Cept 'foolish' seems to be putting it mildly; I never heard so many ignorant questions, that is, outside a Social Security office. Those people are the worst; I think they got some kinda device sucks their brains outta their heads every morning when they report to work. And they say we're senile."

In view of the fact Jefferson Brown did not seem like a man who would tolerate being humored, she decided against agreeing with him. Instead, to get back on track, she said, "I came to find out if there's anything you'd like to tell me about that night."

"Why should I tell you anything?"

"It's the right thing to do."

His hand tightened around the cane. "Right thing to do, my foot. Nosing into other folk's business isn't neighborly. Who're you working for?"

She told him, adding: "But anything I find out working for the defense can't be concealed from the District Attorney's office, or we'd be in violation of Section 135—"

"Piss on that regulation tripe, like I give a fig. Is he innocent?"

"That's what I'm trying to find out."

Brown turned his head, his sightless eyes staring right at her. "Which means you don't know."

"Exactly. I don't know."

"Aren't you afraid you'll find out the wrong things if you ask too many questions?"

"No. I worry I won't ask the right questions."

His laugh rumbled around in his chest, sounding more like a bronchial spasm than mirth. "Good for you. All right, young lady, ask your questions."

"You were home last year on April fifth?"

"Yes."

"Were you alone?"

"Yes. My helper only stays until after dinner. He cleans up the dishes, helps me into my pajamas, locks up the house and leaves."

"What time is that, usually?"

"Seven o'clock."

"But you don't go to bed that early . . ."

"No. One of the joys of aging is you don't seem to need as much sleep."

"What do you do, after he's gone?"

"That depends. I might have the television on. That was a Sunday, so I would have listened to Sixty Minutes, to the end, unless they were doing one of those sappy celebrity interviews. Those I turn off. Can't stomach a serious journalist fawning over some *actor* who needs someone else to put words in his mouth."

"Anything else?"

"Not on Sunday. Afterward, I go to my room and listen to Books on Tape."

"What then?"

"I'm usually in bed by midnight, or half past. Some nights I can get to sleep easy, other nights I can't."

"That night?"

"I couldn't sleep."

Sydney felt a prickling of excitement. "Where's your bedroom in relation to the Reilly house?"

"My bedroom is the left front room."

Which made it opposite the nursery. "Do you sleep with a window open?"

"Except when it's raining, yes."

"Did you hear anything unusual that night? A baby crying, or—"

"That baby crying was not unusual. He cried a couple of times a night."

"Did you hear him on April fifth?"

"I heard him."

"More than once?"

"More than once," Brown confirmed. "You want to ask what time it was, don't you? Only you know I can't see the clock."

"I'm not an expert on blindness, Mr. Brown. How do you tell time?"

"Well, there are watches if you press a button, a little voice tells you the time." He let go of the afghan and extended his left arm; his wrist was bare. "I haven't worn a watch since I retired. But the clock by my bed has Braille markings on the hour and minute hands, as well as the face."

"So you know what time it was when you heard the baby cry."

"I do. It was one-thirty, give or take a minute."

Which kept Keith Reilly in contention as the killer. "How about before that? Did you hear gunshots?"

"No, but I figure that's because I was in the bathroom; the exhaust fan is out of balance, and it makes a sound like a plane taking off."

"The baby was already crying when you came out of the bathroom?"

"Yes."

"Can you estimate how long you were in the bathroom?"

"Ten minutes." He chuckled again, the rattle in his chest unsettlingly like a death wheeze. "The old plumbing doesn't work as well as it used to. I get the urge, can't always purge."

Sydney considered those ten minutes; almost certainly, Jefferson Brown had been in his bathroom as the murders were committed. She asked, "Had you been asleep prior to getting up to—"

"To piss? No."

"Had you heard anything before that?"

"You mean voices, don't you? That damned fool cop kept yelling in my face, 'Did you hear people arguing? Did you hear a scream?' "

"Did you?"

"I only heard one voice, and it wasn't human."

"Not human?"

The old man leaned forward, using the cane to brace himself. "I haven't told a living soul this, and I probably shouldn't tell you, but I'm gonna, yes sir, since you're not from the blasted government, and haven't yelled at me even once."

Sydney sent a thankful glance heavenward. "Go on."

"It was one of those mechanical voices, a machine talking. It said, 'The key is in the ignition.' "

"A car." Sydney suddenly remembered the dark-colored car Hope Devlin had seen parked in front of the Reilly's near one A.M. Keith Reilly would have been driving his Lexus that night; did the Lexus talk?

She'd have to find out.

"The other thing," Brown said, "is that I heard it twice."

"The car said the same thing twice in a row?"

"No, just twice. First time was earlier, I can't tell you exactly when, I'd guess twenty minutes or so. But later, it said it again."

"How much later?"

"Must have been near dawn."

Her heartbeat quickened. "Are you sure?"

"Pretty sure. It woke me that time, and I heard a

car engine start. I tried to get back to sleep, only it wasn't long before I smelled coffee brewing. It's on a timer, you see, and switches on automatically at quarter to six. I get up at six."

"The cops were here at 5:57," Sydney said, more to herself than to him.

"Yeah, I heard them, too. And the baby."

"Wait a minute." Keeping the time sequence straight in her mind wasn't easy. "When did you hear Daniel crying for the second time?"

"Just before the cops arrived."

Talia Sorvino had said in her statement that she'd been woken by the baby's crying at five A.M., and claimed that he was still crying some thirty minutes later when she called the cops.

Somebody's timing was seriously off, and she had a hunch it wasn't Jefferson Davis Brown's.

Twenty-five

Sydney went to the Mustang to make a few calls before returning to the Sorvinos. Now more than ever, she was looking forward to her interview with Talia, who presumably had returned home.

First, though, she wanted to advise Wade Cooper of what appeared to be a major discrepancy in time: if Jefferson Brown was right, the killer would appeared to have stayed in the house until approximately five A.M.

The prosecution's own witness placed Keith back at The Quick Gold Fox at two-thirty.

For the present, however, all she had was a monumental "if." It could be the break they were looking for, or it could turn out to be nothing. Perhaps Talia had invited a male friend to spend the night and keep her company at the Merediths; the talking car might have been his.

She reached Cooper's answering service, and was immediately put on hold. "What a surprise," she said to the silent line.

While she waited, she looked around the neighborhood, and tried to imagine it as it had been on that morning. The police cars parked at all angles, lights flashing initially, until someone thought to turn them off. Yellow crime-scene tape creating a flimsy barricade against the nosiness of the neighbors.

The neighbors, some still in their nightclothes and robes with their coffee mugs in their hands, would have gathered in ever-changing groups of two or three or four, eyes riveted on the front door, speculating in hushed tones about what terrible thing had happened inside. At some point, the demands of the real world—where murder occurred in *other* neighborhoods—would siphon off those who had to go to work, curiosity unquenched.

Eventually, the others would go back inside, although they'd find themselves drawn to the window time and again. The arrival of the forensic van might tempt them back onto the doorstep; the arrival of the coroner's wagon definitely would.

No one wanted to miss the bodies being removed on a stretcher, zipped in heavy black polyurethane bags, or under a velvet drape. The television crews always showed up in time for that . . .

None of it would have seemed real.

Sydney wondered if the killer had watched the news coverage. Or if he or she had been standing on a doorstep nearby, and had seen it all first hand.

"Thank you for holding," the operator said. "May I help you?"

After unsuccessfully trying to reach Wade Cooper, Sydney was patched through to Ayanna Parke.

Ayanna listened without comment as she described her interview with Jefferson Brown. "I don't know that any of this is definitive proof of anything, but at the very least, it warrants a closer look."

"Wade will be thrilled. If nothing else, it ought to qualify as reasonable doubt. And just think; we might have to put a *car* on the stand." Ayanna laughed. "That'll be a first."

"Where's the Lexus, by the way?"

"Still in impound."

"Well, if it can talk, I hope it's smart enough to take the Fifth."

"God yes. Listen, I'll keep trying to locate Wade, and if I do, I'll have him call you."

"While you're at it," Sydney said, "would you do me a favor?"

"Name it, girl, and you've got it."

"I need to make an appointment to see Gayle Honeywell's parents . . ."

Next, she tried Mitch's private line, with no answer. She called Homicide directly, and was informed he was "in the field." Judging by the level of noise in the background, something big was going down.

Invited to leave a message, she declined, reasoning that as defense counsel, Wade Cooper was the logical messenger to relay to the police *and* District Attorney new developments in the Reilly case.

As Cooper had said earlier, another day or two wouldn't matter.

A woman answered the phone at Xavier's with a giggly, "Hello?"

"Is Xavier there?"

"Is he ever! Snooky, you've got a call. Now stop that, you bad boy!"

Bemused, Sydney listened to more giggling and her partner's hearty guffaws before Xavier finally came on the line.

"Yeah?"

"Snooky, it's Sydney," she said. "I'm sorry to bother you at home, but something's come up."

"Don't tell me you're working today?"

"All right, I won't tell you. I need you to do a little research—"

"You don't mean now?"

"Actually, yes."

"Sydney, don't do this to me. It's Saturday, I've got plans."

She frowned at her reflection in the side-view mirror. One of these days she'd probably need intensive psychotherapy to deal with the guilt, but she said, "I know it's inconvenient—"

"Hell, yes, it's inconvenient. Linda's going to whip up a quick dinner, and then we've got tickets to a Padres' game. *Reserved* seats."

"I know, and I'm sorry, but this is important. Don't forget you wanted us to take this case."

There was silence at his end, and then Xavier sighed as if the weight of the world had settled on his shoulders. *"Mea culpa.* Okay, what is it?"

She told him about what Jefferson Brown had heard the night of the murders. "I need to know what makes and models of cars are equipped with voice warnings."

"What?"

"Verbal idiot lights. You know, those little voices that tell you you're getting low on gas, or that you've left the key in the ignition."

"Uh-huh."

"I thought you could call the auto dealerships and ask. Or maybe go by a couple of lots."

"Talk about hazardous duty pay; you want me to *talk* to car sales people?"

"How bad could it be?"

"Trust me, we're not talking about a walk in the park. More like a swim in the shark tank."

"Xavier—"

"Sydney . . . can't you wait till the weekend's over to find out which cars are nags?"

She hesitated. If the D.A. had to wait until Monday, she supposed she could live with it; one more day shouldn't make much difference. "Well . . ."

"They're great seats," he said wistfully, "opposite first base."

"All right, you win."

He must have made some gesture of victory, because she heard Linda squeal with delight.

"But I'm counting on you, Monday morning, to make those calls."

"Bless you, child. And if I snag a foul ball, it's yours."

"Be still my heart."

"Ciao."

He hung up before she remembered to ask him who he'd hired as their secretary.

She supposed that could wait till Monday, too.

Twenty-six

"I have a baby-sitting job at five," Talia Sorvino said, leading the way to her bedroom. "And I can't be late or Mrs. Kritch will have a cow."

"You won't be late."

"That's good, because this lady is, like, a super bitch." Talia glanced over her shoulder at Sydney. "It rhymes, you know."

"Excuse me?"

"Kritch, bitch. No one can tell me that's a . . . what do you call it? A coincidence."

"Why do you work for her, then?"

Talia opened the door to her room and went directly to flop on the canopied bed. "Money," she said, "she pays twice the going rate. Close the door, would you? I don't want my dad to hear."

Sydney closed the door and looked around the room for a place to sit. Decorated in pastel pink and lilac, with ruffled curtains, canopy, pillow shams, and bedspread, it struck her as being appropriate for a girl of twelve or thirteen.

There were posters on the wall, of country singers, including the chunky one with the naughty-boy sneer whose name she never could remember.

Photographs of Talia with male friends lined the dresser mirror; some of the men appeared to be in their forties.

Keith Reilly was not among them.

A cardboard cut-out of Batman stood in one corner with a pair of sexy black mesh pantyhose draped around his neck. The caped crusader—if Sydney hadn't gotten her superheroes mixed up—did not look amused.

There was a cherrywood chest at the end of the bed, miraculously clear of the clothes tossed every which way throughout the room and, not seeing anything better, Sydney sat on that.

Looking at Talia, she understood what Rebecca had meant by "all body." If she were limited to a single word to describe the young woman, that word would be ripe. More curvy and voluptuous than perhaps was in style, Talia was of a type more favored by B-movie directors than fashion designers.

Dark-haired and pretty, she had tawny skin and almond-shaped eyes. Her mouth was sensuous, although the little-girl pout was a bit much for a young woman of twenty.

Talia snapped her gum. "So what do you want to talk about?"

"The murder of Denise Reilly and Gayle Honeywell."

"Bummer." Reaching in with two fingers, she pulled the gum like taffy until it seemed ready to break, whereupon she gathered it into a ball and stuffed it back in her mouth. "Me and Denise were good friends until, well—" she rolled her eyes "—you know."

"Let me make it clear, I'm only interested in your

affair with Keith Reilly as it relates to what happened on April fifth."

Talia frowned and momentarily stopped chewing. "Was that the night?"

"Yes. Or rather morning."

"Okay. I was at the Merediths, and—"

"I read your statement," Sydney interrupted, hoping to forestall a well-rehearsed recitation of that account. "We can get to that later. For now, I want to talk about some of what you haven't testified to."

Talia's expression went blank. "I don't know what you mean."

"I think you do, Talia," she said, deciding to cut to the chase. "The key."

"The key?"

"Rebecca Aiken said that she saw you coming out of the Reilly house one day last March, and when she confronted you, you showed her a key. Mrs. Aiken went to Keith, and he admitted that he'd given you a key."

Talia looked doubtful. "That was a long time ago."

"Not that long, and the point is, I know you had a key," Sydney said. "You had a key to the Reilly house three weeks or so before the murders."

"I must of given it back."

"To Keith?"

"Yeah, to Keith."

"When?"

Talia shrugged. "I don't remember."

"Did you have a copy made?"

She stopped in midchew. "What?"

"Did you make a copy of the key before you returned it to Keith?"

"Who told you that?" Talia had been sitting cross-legged, but she shifted around so that she was kneeling on the bed, her arms wrapped tightly around a body-length pillow, as if that would protect her. "It was Mrs. Aiken, wasn't it? I'll bet she told you."

Sydney didn't answer.

"Okay, I made a copy, but it wasn't so I could break in or anything. That deal with the sweater was different; it was *my* sweater, and I tried to ask for it back, but Denise kept hanging up on me."

That sounded familiar.

"Anyway, I just like to have . . . extras. I lose a lot of keys."

"How many extras did you have of that particular key?"

"Maybe . . . five?"

Sydney had to trust that her amazement didn't show. One copy, she'd expected, or even two, but five? "Where are they now?"

"In my jewelry box. Do you want them? I'll give 'em to you." She hopped off the bed and crossed to the dresser. "It kinda gives me the creeps knowing they're there, if you know what I mean."

"Maybe you'd better." Sydney would pass them on to Wade Cooper, and let him take it from there.

Talia opened the third of six drawers and dug around, coming up with a ballerina jewelry box very similar to the one Sydney had had when she was eight. Sure enough, when Talia opened it, the small figurine of a ballerina in pink tutu began to twirl.

Sydney watched as Talia dug key after key out of the jewelry box. There were, in the end, at least two dozen, of assorted shapes and sizes. Talia picked through them, and handed five silver keys to her, which appeared on first glance to be identical.

"Good riddance," Talia said, returning the jewelry box to the drawer. "I feel better already."

"So do I." Sydney stood up and slipped them into the front pocket of her jeans, and sat down again. "Tell me about the Sunday before the murders."

"Like I said, I was baby-sitting next door at the Merediths." Talia returned to the bed and the safety of her pillow. "From Friday at noon on."

"Your father said you told him you'd seen Denise and Gayle in the backyard on Sunday?"

"I saw them a couple of other times, too, coming and going, but that time, I knew they saw me."

"Denise didn't speak to you."

"Ha! She looked right through me like I wasn't even there."

"What about Gayle? I assume you two had met prior to the estrangement—"

"The what?"

"When things got bad between you and Denise."

"Oh, yeah, gotcha. Gayle was all right, I guess. The three of us went out once—"

"Just once?"

Talia nodded, blowing a small pink bubble which popped, sticking to her lips. Peeling it off, she said, "Gayle wasn't keen on going places with me. She was jealous, I think. I get a lot of attention from guys."

Remembering the photograph on the beach, Sydney figured Gayle could hold her own. "When did the three of you go out together?"

"Gee, it had to be the summer before. Or maybe September. That's it, it was September. Classes were in the second or third week—"

"You go to school?" Sydney asked, surprised. What with everyone's dismissal of Talia as a dim bulb, she'd assumed otherwise.

"Yeah, at State."

San Diego State, her own alma mater. "Go on, I'm sorry to keep interrupting."

Talia shrugged. "No biggie. People are always interrupting me. Anyway, it must have been September. We went to a club Denise knew."

"In Solana Beach?"

"Yeah—" Talia's eyes widened like a child's at a magic show "—how'd you know that?"

"A lucky guess." Sometimes it was too easy.

"Huh. Anyhow, we got along fine, although like I said, Gayle was maybe a little upset with me because of all the guys asking me to dance. See, she'd just broken up with her boyfriend—"

Eddie Monroe?

"—and she wanted to have some fun. She said she felt like she'd just busted out of prison; her boyfriend kept her on a short leash."

"She wasn't having fun at the club?"

"Well, yeah, only not as much fun as I was having, and that ticked her off. I got all the cutest guys," Talia added with unmistakable pride.

Sydney bit her tongue to keep from asking Talia where she kept all the guys she "got." Maybe she had a stud box to go with the ballerina. If so, she didn't even want to know what popped up when the lid was opened.

"But," Talia sighed, "after that, when Gayle came around, the two of them would go off together. I wasn't invited."

"Back to that Sunday . . . how did Denise and Gayle seem to you? Did either of them seem upset?"

Talia shook her head. "Not that I could tell. They were sitting and talking, normal like, there on the deck."

"Could you hear anything they said?"

"Not much. The water was on, you know, and the kids were making a lot of noise."

In court, "Not much" would not qualify as a responsive answer. "Let me rephrase that: what did you hear?"

"Oh, Denise was going on about signing some papers. My first thought was she'd filed for divorce, you know, the way things were so bad, but then she said 'weasel' and I knew she was talking about *him.*"

"Keith?"

"No, Nigel Fox. That's what she called him, at least behind his back. Not that I blame her or anything; he was a major creep." Evidently tired of chewing, she tore the corner off a page of a *People* magazine and wrapped her gum in it. She tossed the gum into a wastebasket with scarcely a glance.

Her aim was dead on. In the phraseology of basketball, the shot was all net. Some people were blessed with perfect pitch; at least one of the Sorvinos was blessed with perfect aim.

Even so, it was difficult to make her as the shooter; Tony Sorvino's little girl seemed to lack the grit necessary to kill in cold blood. As much as Sydney hated to admit it, she rather thought Jake Scott was right when he'd said Talia wasn't bright enough to lay a smoke screen.

There were others, though, who well might. "Talia . . . did Nigel Fox hang around much?"

"Not really. Except on the first of the month.

Then he'd come over to the house, and he and Keith would do the books."

Accounting for his fingerprints.

Talia giggled suddenly. "Keith told me that doing the books made Nigel so upset and nervous, he'd drink an entire bottle of Maalox."

"That's interesting." What exactly, she wondered, did Nigel Fox have to be nervous about? "Did they do the books on April first?"

"I don't know. I went to an April Fools party, and, like, spaced it out."

"Back to Denise and Gayle . . . was there anything else you overheard?"

"No, not really. Except on the way back in Gayle asked if she could make a long distance call. Denise said sure, she wasn't paying the bills. Denise was cool about things like that."

Sydney had decided at the outset not to tape or make notes of their conversation, hoping that Talia would feel less pressure, but now, purely on instinct, she reached into her jacket pocket and ever-so-gently pushed the Record button. "Okay, about that night . . ."

"Sunday."

"Sunday night. You put the kids to bed at eight—"

"That's right. And they went straight to sleep." She looked pleased with herself. "I wore 'em out, playing outside in the water and—don't tell their mother—jumping on the beds."

"That's . . . nice. What did you do after that?"

"I made myself a sandwich, and went in the living room to watch TV. Don't tell Mrs. Meredith about the sandwich, either. It's a family rule, no eating except in the kitchen or dining room."

Sydney counted to ten in her head. "Don't worry, that particular secret is safe with me. Now, were you alone all evening, or did someone come by?"

"Oh no! That's a—"

"Family rule, right." She refrained from pointing out that Talia's compliance with the Meredith family rules seemed to be a hit-or-miss proposition. "At any time did you happen to notice anyone visiting next door?"

Talia shook her head. "It was just Denise and Gayle, I'm positive. The way the road curves, the headlights shine right in the living room. And company usually parks on the street, so I'd have seen the car."

That didn't mean no one had walked down. "Did Gayle have a car?"

"Not that I know of. She always came down by train. Denise would pick her up at the Del Mar station; I remember because she always complained that there wasn't enough parking."

"All right, the kids are asleep, you're alone and you're pretty sure they're alone next door."

"Gee, it sounds spooky, talking about that night like it's happening right now."

"I'm trying to help you remember."

"Oh boy." Talia rubbed her arms, as if she were cold. "Okay. Where was I?"

"You're in the living room, watching television and having a sandwich. You said nobody comes over . . . does anyone call?"

"No, the phone never rang all evening, which is kinda strange because I was expecting Mrs. Meredith to check on the kids. But she didn't."

"According to your statement, you fell asleep sometime during the eleven o'clock news."

"Right. I remember being crashed out on the couch, watching the weatherman with one eye open, and that's the last thing I remember, until I woke up."

"What woke you up?"

She chewed on her lower lip. "Daniel was crying."

"What time was it?"

"Five A.M.?"

"That sounds like a question, Talia."

"No, it was five."

It occurred to Sydney that she hadn't read an explanation as to how the baby's cries could be heard from the Merediths' living room. "Was the television still on when you woke up?"

"Yes."

"The sound was on?"

"It must have been."

"And you heard the baby over the TV?"

"Yes." Talia frowned, her brow furrowing in concentration. "I turned it off after a minute, you know, to try and figure out what the noise was."

"Were the windows open?"

"I don't know."

"But you heard Daniel cry."

"I did," Talia said, a hint of desperation in her voice. "I really did."

"What did you do?"

"Nothing, right that minute. I waited for the crying to stop."

"And when it didn't?"

It took a moment and came out a whisper, but she said, "I got scared."

"Why?"

"Denise would *never* let Danny cry like that. And

I started thinking all these crazy things, like what if she fell in the shower, and broke her leg or hit her head or something."

"Gayle was there . . ."

"I forgot all about Gayle."

Sydney thought that part might be true, but continued to press for the rest: "If you thought Denise was hurt, why call her on the phone? Why not go over there?"

"I . . . I . . ."

"You did go over, didn't you?"

"No, I called the police."

"You called the police after. Wasn't it after, Talia, when you came back?"

"Oh God." Talia buried her face in the pillow.

"You had the key to the house. If you honestly were worried about Denise being hurt, and Danny left to cry, why not go over? Anyone would, under the circumstances. And a crying baby isn't necessarily an emergency; the police might not have shown up for hours."

"No, no," she said into the pillow, "they came right away."

"Talia, did you know there's someone else who heard the baby cry?"

Her body visibly tensed, and she looked up. "What?"

"The neighbor on the other side, Mr. Brown. He sleeps with a window open, and—"

"He's blind! He couldn't have seen anything!"

"Not seen, heard. He told me that Daniel wasn't crying until shortly before the police cars drove up."

"Well, he's wrong." Her lower lip trembled slightly. "Who'd believe him, anyway? He's an old man, he can't see, maybe he's deaf, too."

Sydney shook her head. "I know he's not deaf. And I believe him."

Talia stared at her with stricken eyes. "Why are you doing this?"

"I need to find out the truth."

"Oh God." She got off the bed and began foraging through one of many piles of clothing. "I've got to go, Mrs. Kritch will never use me again if I'm late."

Sydney went to stand in front of the door, just in case. "Why don't you tell me what's bothering you?"

"Nothing's bothering me. Everyone is gonna believe an old man instead of me, but—" she broke into tears "—that's nothing new."

"Talia, sit down."

Surprisingly, she obeyed.

"I want you to tell me about that morning." Sydney sat on the bed beside her. "What really happened? The truth, now."

Tears ran down her face, and she made no attempt to brush them away. "I went in," Talia said, her voice husky. "I saw them."

On some level, she'd known it had to be something like that. "They were dead?"

It took her four attempts to get the word out: "V . . . v . . . v . . . very."

"What were you doing there?"

"It's so stupid, no one will believe me. That sweater, my cashmere sweater. I wanted it back."

"Five A.M. is an unusual time to go calling."

"I guess," Talia sniffed. "But something woke me up, and I thought, gee, it's so early, nobody'll be awake. I thought I'd sneak in while they were asleep, no one would see me, and I'd get my sweater. Which I paid seventy-five bucks for, you know?"

"What woke you up?"

"Something, a noise." She grabbed a blouse off the floor and used it to wipe her eyes. "Maybe it was the little pervert sneaking around in the bushes outside."

Sydney ventured a guess: "You mean Corey Devlin."

"Yeah, how'd you—never mind. For a Peeping Tom, he's awful loud and clumsy. I've caught him looking in my window before."

Which explained the night wandering. "You didn't tell your father?"

"Are you kidding? My dad would kill him."

"He didn't kill Keith Reilly," Sydney pointed out, "and what Keith did was worse."

Talia blinked and frowned. "I never thought about that."

"Back up for a minute. You went over to the Reilly house to find your sweater. Was the door locked when you got there?"

"Yes."

"You went into the living room and saw Denise and Gayle on the floor . . ."

Talia closed her eyes. "It was the worst, most horrible thing I ever saw in my life. God, the blood!"

"Why didn't you call the police then?"

"I didn't want anyone to know I still had the key, that I'd been inside. My reputation ain't that great to start with, and something like that, no one would hire me to watch their kids ever again. All I could think was . . . get out of there."

"And yet you called the police later."

"I couldn't let them lie there. And I didn't want Keith to come home and find them like that. I mean, he can be a real shit sometimes, but she was his wife."

Sydney nodded and squeezed her hand. "You did the right thing."

The tears returned, with a vengeance. "So I made up a story, and called the police, and when the baby *wasn't* crying, I called the house and let the phone ring, so it woke Danny up."

For the first time since she'd signed on, Sydney had the impression that the pieces of the puzzle were beginning to fit into place.

Twenty-seven

"She didn't do it, did she?" Tony Sorvino asked, following Sydney out to her car.

"No, I don't think so." She opened the door, but instead of getting in, turned to face him. "You said she didn't have it in her, and you were right."

"For once, thank God."

"But Talia didn't tell the whole truth, either," she said, and gave him a condensed version of what she'd learned. "The District Attorney will be wanting to talk to her again. I don't know how much trouble she's in, if they'll charge her with perjury or what."

"We'll get through it," Sorvino said, and thrust his hand at her. "And thank you. Living with a lie like that could really mess with someone's head. Maybe she'll grow up a little, you know?"

Her hand disappeared in his grip. "I hope so, for Talia's sake."

Sydney slowed as she drove past the Devlin house, and briefly considered stopping, but she wanted to talk to Master Corey alone, and she had an idea as to when and how best to accomplish that.

In the meantime, she had a few questions for Nigel Fox.

She'd gotten proficient at using the phone while driving, so she flipped open her notebook, located Fox's home number and dialed.

"Fox resident," a woman's voice answered, her accent all but indecipherable.

"Is Mr. Fox in?"

"No."

"Do you know when he'll be home?"

"No."

Sydney paused, wondering if the woman understood what she'd asked, or if "no" was simply her standard reply. "Do you know where he is?"

"No."

She vaguely recalled seeing Saturday hours listed in gold lettering on the door to The Quick Gold Fox. "Is he at work?"

"Work?"

"Work, his place of business."

"Si, work."

Now they were getting somewhere. "Okay, thank you. *Gracias."*

Evidently, having established communication opened a floodgate of sorts; the woman said, in tortured syllables, *"Si,* at business work fliming."

"Fliming?"

"Si."

A believer in quitting while she was ahead, Sydney thanked her again and hung up. "Fliming," she said, "huh. Must be some kind of numismatic term." She made a U-turn, back toward the freeway.

* * *

When she turned into the parking lot at The Quick Gold Fox fifteen minutes later, she realized she was wrong on both counts: she was not ahead by any criterion, and "fliming" had nothing whatsoever to do with collecting coins.

A van from one of the local indy stations was parked in front of the coin shop, and Victor Griffith was standing beside it, deep in conversation with the cameraman, at the same time waving and flapping his bony arms around like a land-bound pterodactyl.

"Filming," she said, and winced.

Victor saw her at that moment, and started in her direction, a big smile on his face. "Sydney, what great timing!"

Resigned to her fate, she put the car in Park, engaged the brake, and turned off the motor. "Victor, this is a pleasant surprise."

"Anyone who didn't know might think you actually meant that." Ever the gentleman, he opened the door for her. "But I'll forgive your insincerity, for you know not what you do. Plus I could use a second opinion . . . we're just about to reenact that Sunday night—"

"Excuse me, but why? Nothing happened here."

Victor raised his eyebrows at her. "It's background. I'm setting the scene."

"Is something going on that I don't know about? Doesn't your show try to enlist the public's aid in catching the bad guys?"

"Well, yeah," Victor said modestly, buffing his fingernails on his Hawaiian print shirt. "That's the franchise."

"Then I don't get it. The last I heard, Keith Reilly was still the prime suspect—"

"Oh, he is. But see, the buzz I'm hearing is the State's case is all of a sudden starting to look like it was built outta balsa wood."

"That's encouraging."

"And I didn't get to where I am today by sitting around waiting for opportunity to knock me upside the head. So we're doing some preliminary exteriors, taping a recreation here and there. That way, we'll be one up on everybody else. Brilliant, isn't it?"

"Oh, definitely. Is Nigel Fox around?"

"Inside, in make-up." He leaned closer and lowered his voice marginally. "Between the two of us, I think he wears the stuff everyday."

"Is that so? Would it disrupt your schedule if I talked to him for a minute?"

"I can spare him till it gets dark, and he has to do his bit," Victor said, and grinned. "Then it's time for his fifteen minutes of fame."

Nigel Fox was indeed in make-up, sitting on a corner of one of the desks in the back office. He had a towel wrapped backward around his neck with a smock over it to protect his clothes. The make-up lady was using a series of small, thin sponges to blot the perspiration that had beaded up on his forehead.

"Are you nervous?" she asked. "You're sweating like a pig."

"I'm fine," Fox said. "The lights are hot. I had no idea they'd be that hot."

Sydney knocked on the open door. "Hi."

Fox nearly jumped out of his skin. "What are you doing here?"

"Can we have a moment?" she asked the make-up lady, who shrugged, handed Fox some sponges and left. "I have a few more questions for you."

"There's nothing I can tell you."

"Maybe there is." She closed the office door, evaluated his state of nervousness to be nearing low earth orbit, and decided to bluff. "You didn't mention when we spoke last that you were at the Reilly's on the first of April, doing the books with Keith."

"Didn't I?"

"No. You said Denise came in that Friday to sign papers, but—" she shook her head "—why didn't she sign them the night before?"

The color drained from Fox's face. "Oh, sweet Jesus, you think that I—"

"I don't think anything yet."

"Let me explain—"

"Please do."

He yanked off the smock and used the towel to dry his face, unmindful of the effect it had on his make-up. "I should have known I'd never get away with it. I told her, 'This is a bad idea, we'll get caught.' But she wouldn't listen."

"By 'she' you mean Denise?"

"Yeesss, Denise," he hissed. "Who else?"

"I'm asking you," Sydney reminded him.

"God, what's going to happen to me?"

"I honestly don't know. Why don't you tell me about this idea of yours."

"Hers! It was her idea! She wanted money, and Keith had cut her off."

"Money to run away?"

"Of course."

She noted with some amazement that behind his blue contacts, his pupils were contracting. His fear was having more than one physiological response. "Why come to you? Other than your 'pleasant social relationship' I mean. Isn't that how you described it?"

"Because she knew that I'd been skimming."

"Ah. The Maalox moment. Did she threaten you? Was she being as unreasonable with you as she was with Keith? What was that you called her? Mary, Mary, quite contrary?"

"No, no, it wasn't like that."

Sydney shook her head. "It doesn't sound good, my friend."

"Actually, I was on her side."

"Convince me, only start at the beginning."

"The beginning." He took a breath as if to steady himself. "Well, it got bad about a year and a half ago. I'd been having financial problems—"

"Due to what? Gambling? Drugs?"

"Hardly. I have always tended to live beyond my means. A nice car, a beachfront apartment, exotic vacations, that sort of thing."

"If you say so."

"I certainly do. At first, it was a simple matter of floating myself little loans from the business. I'd fudge a receipt; or at the shows out of town, I'd sell a couple of coins off the books and pocket the cash. It wasn't like stealing—"

No, just embezzlement.

"—because a third of any profit was mine. Anyway, I tried to pay it back as soon as I could, only after a while, I couldn't seem to get even."

"And Denise found out?"

Fox nodded, and gave his head a sideways jerk.

"She did the books one month when we were at an estate sale in Kansas. You'd be surprised how many of those old farmers like to hoard gold."

"But she didn't tell Keith?"

"No. They'd been having their own problems for some time. As a matter of fact, I don't remember them ever *not* having problems."

"But it got worse."

"Worse is putting it mildly." He ran a hand through his bristly hair. "Keith messed up royally, doing it there in the house. Women will take a lot of shit off a man, but not many will tolerate another woman in their bed. And who can blame them?"

"Not me."

"So things got ugly and Denise was really leaving. Keith listened to his Mommy, who said Denise didn't deserve a dime, and he cut her off. He closed their checking account, got her name removed from our business account, cancelled her credit cards, you name it. It's a wonder he didn't go after the fillings in her teeth."

"Which brought her to you."

"Yes. The idea was, I'd lift about twenty thousand dollars worth of gold out of the safe. It's liquid, and hard to trace."

"No kidding." Twenty thousand in one-ounce gold Eagles would amount to perhaps sixty coins. "Did you do it?"

"Yes."

"When."

"That night, April fourth."

Sydney shook her head. "I don't understand. There wasn't any gold in the house."

"No, because I never gave it to her. The plan was to wait until Keith had finished doing inventory in the vault—otherwise he'd know right then it was missing—sign it off, and take the gold."

"Go on."

"I did just that. I waited until he went to take a leak. I had the gold with me when I left at midnight. I dropped it off at my apartment, had a couple of quick drinks, sloshed some booze on my clothes, and went out, looking to get arrested."

So she was right about that much. "Why get arrested?"

"Because I wanted to be somewhere else. On Monday we were having an independent auditor come in to double-check the books and whatnot for the bank."

"Who would have discovered the loss."

"Exactly."

"And since Keith had been the one who was alone here all night, while you were in the drunk tank, he'd be the one with explaining to do, at least initially."

"That's it in a nutshell. After I got out of jail, I was supposed to go home, get the gold, drive over to meet Denise in the parking lot at Horton Plaza, and hand it over. It was her share of the business, the way she figured, and who was I to argue?"

"Only she was murdered," Sydney said, and frowned. "What happened to the gold?"

Fox glared at her. "I put it back."

She ran the scenario through once or twice more in her mind, and everything seemed to fit. "When you found out Denise was dead and had been murdered, what did you think had happened?"

"What else could I think? I figured Keith had found us out somehow, and knew if he didn't do something, she and the baby were as good as gone. So he did what he had to, to stop her."

It was distressingly plausible.

"Damn." Potential suspects were dropping like flies. To be thorough, she asked, "What kind of car were you driving last April?"

His expression showed his confusion at the abrupt change of subject. "A Corvette. It's parked in the lot."

Sydney looked out and spotted a late model, silver Corvette convertible. Quite distinctive, she thought, even to someone who knew nothing about cars. "What happens if you leave the keys in the ignition when you get out?"

Fox looked at her as if she were crazy. "It goes to Tijuana without me."

Sydney laughed. "Right. I meant, does it talk?"

His eyebrows arched. "Not in your life; it's too well-bred and discreet for that."

The door opened behind her, and Victor Griffith stuck his head in. "Night is upon us," he said to Nigel Fox. "And you're on."

"Are we done?" Fox asked her.

"You are," she said with a nod, "but I'm not."

Twenty-eight

After a quick stop at her apartment to change into a black sweatshirt and pants, and an equally brief stop at the office to pick up a pair of night-vision binoculars, Sydney returned to the Reilly neighborhood. She parked up the hill from the cul-de-sac, in the shadow of a pepper tree.

She took a moment to snap an opaque plastic shield over the Mustang's interior light, so that when she had to get out of the car, it wouldn't give her away. She also pocketed the keys.

From her vantage point she could see the Devlin house clearly. There were lights on in the living room, as well as upstairs, in what she suspected was Corey's bedroom. With any luck, he was in there.

Then again, it was eight o'clock on a Saturday night. She hadn't gotten the impression that the boy had a lot of friends, but if he had even one, he might already be gone for the evening, hanging out or cruising or doing whatever this generation of kids did—and thought they'd invented.

Sydney was betting that Corey was a loner, and that he was biding his time until his great-aunts went to bed. Then he would leave the house, and wander, looking for whatever it was that drew him into the night.

In the meantime, she settled in, waited, and watched.

Time passed slowly.

It took some effort to keep her mind off other aspects of the case, but she couldn't afford to be distracted; as it was surveillance could be incredibly dull. If she didn't focus on Corey Devlin—and Corey Devlin only—she very well might find herself zoning out and missing him entirely when he left the house.

An amateur mistake, but easy to make, isolated by the darkness and the need not to attract attention, to stay out of sight.

Sydney brought the binoculars up and scanned the Devlin house. A second light had appeared upstairs. One of the sisters, turning in?

The thought made her yawn. By her tally, she was about eight hours behind in her sleep, and nearing the point at which exhaustion began to take its toll, both physically and mentally.

The living room lights turned off. A quick look at her watch showed it was nine-thirty. "Early to bed, thank you very much."

Several minutes passed, and the upstairs light—the one she assumed belonged to the sisters—switched off. Give them half an hour or so to fall asleep, and if Corey ran true to his billing, it ought to be show time.

Sydney lowered the binoculars and rubbed her eyes, which were tired from gazing through the dim, greenish night-vision light. Her throat was dry and itchy, but she didn't dare drink anything.

She drummed her fingers on the console, and waited. After an indeterminate period, she saw the second upstairs light go out, she sat forward with the binoculars and studied the house.

"If you're going," she said, "go."

As if in answer to her summons, the front door opened and Corey Devlin came out onto the screened porch. He, too, was dressed in dark clothing.

Fifteen seconds later he was walking along the sidewalk, uphill, toward her. She got out of the car and closed the door quickly, the sound covered by a passing truck with a faulty muffler.

She circled around behind the Mustang and moved closer to the pepper tree, which would provide cover until she could determine in which direction Corey was headed. He passed under a street light, and she caught a glimpse of his face, but at this distance, not his expression.

When he reached the top of the hill, he turned right, into the heart of the residential area.

She followed, staying about fifty feet behind him on the opposite side of the street. The roads up here were winding; the developer must have had a fondness for circles, cut-backs and cul-de-sacs. It would be easy to get lost, she thought, in the maze, but Corey never hesitated, seeming to know where he wanted to go, and how to get there.

Oddly, he never looked back, never glanced over his shoulder to see if anyone had noticed him. A few years ago she'd read an interview with a man who the police termed a career voyeur, and he'd said that early on, he'd begun to feel like he was invisible.

That he could go anywhere and do anything, and no one was ever the wiser.

The watcher, unseen.

Eventually, Corey turned back down the hill toward the canyon, into a cul-de-sac very much like the one he lived on. Sydney allowed the distance between them to increase. If he were to turn, he'd probably see her, but he might not realize she was following him.

Then, so quickly that she would have missed it if she'd blinked, Corey Devlin disappeared into the shrubs that lined the property of the house at the furthest point of the road. Sydney heard a gentle rustling, and nothing more.

She raised the binoculars and searched the bushes. It took three slow passes before she located him, squatting motionless between two bushy junipers, facing the house. The living-room drapes were wide open.

The woman standing inside wore a sheer white negligee that left little to the imagination. She was prancing back and forth in front of the window like it was the runway on a burlesque stage, pretending to be unaware of the show she was putting on.

Sydney walked a few yards closer to the house, and could see in the blazing light that the woman had to be in her late forties or early fifties, with fleshy thighs and a sagging derriere. Still, bare skin was bare skin, and the woman was displaying a lot of it, from her deep decolletage to the peek-a-boo hemline.

The woman's mane of hair was an incendiary shade of red, although it paled in comparison to the lipstick she wore, which made her mouth look like an angry wound, a violent slash across her face.

Even so, it was possible to imagine that once she had been beautiful. Once the men flocked eagerly to her side, and would have gladly paid to see what she now had to pretend to accidentally reveal.

A glance at the other houses in this neighborhood did not reveal any other watchers. To the contrary, all of the curtains, blinds, and shades appeared to be drawn. Quite possibly the redhead's neighbors had seen enough. Maybe one or two had even complained, and been met with feigned innocence.

Who me? An exhibitionist?

It was, Sydney thought, very sad.

And sadder still that this was how a sixteen-year-old boy had chosen to spend his night, crouched in the bushes, hot young eyes taking it in.

Unwilling to confront him while he was so engaged, Sydney found another tree to lean against, and prepared to wait.

It was nearly midnight before the lights went out in the redhead's house. A short time later, Sydney saw Corey hurrying up her side of the street.

She had no way of determining whether or not he was done for the evening or if this had been merely the first stop on his route. She did know she had no stomach for witnessing any more of it. What bothered her most was the knowledge that Peeping Toms often evolved into flashers who sometimes mutated into rapists. A significant percentage of rapists learned to kill.

Ten years from now, who knew what he'd be?

When he was five feet from her, she stepped out

of the shadows. She saw the recognition on his face—the street light was behind her—and she said, "Hello Corey."

His body tensed like he was going to run, but he didn't, perhaps because he seemed to be out of breath. Instead he fixed her with a cold stare. "Are you following me? Have you been following me?"

"No, I'm thinking of setting up a concession stand. What about it, did you enjoy the show?"

The temptation to lie battled in his eyes with teenage bravado, and bravado won out. "Yeah, I did. Not the best I've seen, but not bad for an old broad."

"Oh?"

"Yeah." He wiped under his nose with the back of his hand. "What's it to you?"

"How's your hand?" she asked, ignoring his bluster. "Did it get infected?"

He made a sound of disgust. "No, not that it's any of your business."

"I think it is. It occurred to me that maybe you got popped by some guy who found you in the bushes spying on his wife."

"Bullshit!"

"Or did it happen while you were running away?" she asked, knowing he'd have to be mad or scared before he'd tell her anything. "You want to run now, don't you?"

His teenage bravado wasn't up for it, though, and Corey averted his eyes. "I don't have to talk to you."

"Maybe not, but I think you'd better listen."

He snorted derisively, but made no move to leave. Which was good, because she didn't want to chase him. "I know from your great-aunts that you

were out—shall we call it wandering?—in the early
morning hours of April fifth last year."

"So?"

"So possibly you saw or heard something pertaining to the murder of Denise Reilly and Gayle
Honeywell."

"I didn't, okay? I was nowhere around."

"Where were you then?"

"I don't know, out."

"You'll have to do better than that."

"I don't have to do anything. I don't have to
stand here and listen to this shit."

He took a step and Sydney straight-armed him,
pushing him a step back. Mad wasn't working, so
she decided to try scared. "Let me repeat, I think
you should. Because one of the other things that
occurred to me, while I was watching you tonight,
was that maybe you were looking in on them."

"On who?" he asked before realization dawned.
He raised his hands as if in surrender and took a
couple of shuffling steps back. "Wait a minute,
there's no way."

"Come off it. Talia Sorvino said you've tried your
act on her, which suggests you don't mind messing
in your own neighborhood. Denise was an attractive young woman, and so was Gayle."

Corey was shaking his head emphatically. "No
way, no fucking way."

"Maybe they caught you peeping in at them.
You're what? Five-foot-three? A hundred and
twenty pounds? The two of them together could
have dragged you inside easily. Maybe they threatened to tell your aunts."

"No, no, no, no, no."

"Would you kill to keep your dirty little secret, Corey? Would you?"

"The . . . they were shot." He swallowed hard and licked his lips. "I don't have a gun. Where would I get a gun? I'm only sixteen."

"The sad thing is," Sydney said, "you could probably get one in any schoolyard."

"But I didn't. I didn't kill anyone."

"No? Then why did you refuse to answer any questions after the murders? If you had nothing to hide . . ."

"I had *this* to hide," he said, and waved an arm in the direction of the redhead's house. "The cops start asking questions, hook you up to that machine, and you can kiss your ass good-bye."

"Do you mean the lie detector?" Sydney asked with a frown. His nod of affirmation made her shake her head. Kids these days watched too many movies, too much TV, and came away thinking they knew it all.

"But I swear, I was nowhere around that night. When I got home that morning, the cops were already there." His eyes welled with tears, and his nose began to run. "I don't know anything else."

"That's a little hard to believe; the cops didn't arrive until almost six. Are you telling me you were out all night? Doing what?"

"There's a lady a few blocks over," he said, looking thoroughly miserable. "She doesn't sleep at night, I guess she's got amnesia—"

"Insomnia," Sydney corrected.

"Whatever. Anyway, she walks around the house totally naked. She even vacuums and stuff."

"You watched her all night?"

"Pretty much. Then I walked home. The cops were there. I swear, that's all I know."

"What time did you go out that night?"

"Ten, ten-thirty."

That was well before the killer had arrived, she thought, but asked anyway, "Did you notice a car parked in front of the Reilly house?"

"No."

Sydney hesitated. Maybe she was being snowed, maybe not. About the only thing she was sure of, Corey Devlin was going home early tonight.

Twenty-nine

Sunday morning, she slept late, undisturbed by dreams. Or at least none that she remembered.

She got up at eleven and took a shower, ignoring for the moment the blinking light on her answering machine. Instead she luxuriated in the force of the hot water, stinging her skin and easing her aching muscles. She must have walked ten miles, tracking that kid last night.

Afterward, she dressed in an oversized navy-blue T-shirt and a favorite pair of jeans that had faded to near-white. Barefoot, she went into the living room, hit the rewind button on the answering machine, and manhandled the box of Reilly files into the center of the room.

Leaving a space for herself in the middle of the floor, she laid the case materials out in a big circle, then tossed the empty box aside.

Push was about to come to shove.

On the way into the kitchen to grab a Pepsi, she hit the play button.

"Sydney," Ayanna Parke's voice said, "I reached the Honeywells for you. They can see you on Sunday at four, but you'd better call to confirm—"

"Yes!" Sydney said, pushing through the swinging door. She grabbed a can out of the refrigerator and was back in the living room before Ayanna finished.

"—to call in a couple of favors, but he got you in to talk to Eddie Monroe—"

When it rained, Sydney thought.

"—still, you'd better arrange it for today if you can, because come Monday, his attorney will either have him out or in deep cover. When you call, ask for Deputy Rick Morgan," Ayanna said, and gave a phone number.

The next message was from her mother, reminding her to bring "the magazine with your veil" when she came for dinner on Wednesday. And Mitch had left a message, telling her he would have to work on Sunday and possibly Monday, because of a triple homicide in an industrial park in Kearny Mesa.

Sydney sat on the arm of the couch, letting the tape run for another thirty seconds to make sure that was all of it before picking up the phone. She confirmed her four o'clock appointment in Mission Viejo with "a friend of the family" who answered the phone at the Honeywells. Allowing time for heavy traffic on the drive back from Orange County, she reached Deputy Morgan and scheduled an eight o'clock visit with "Crazy Eddie" at the County Jail.

"So much for a lazy Sunday afternoon," she said, hanging up the phone.

Still, the morning wasn't technically over—it was a quarter till twelve—and she didn't have to leave for the Honeywell interview until about two.

Sydney stepped into the center of the circle, and

sat down, Indian-style, ready to review the files, once again.

The sound of the doorbell made her jump, and she had to grab for the Pepsi can to keep it from tipping over. She considered not answering the door—she doubted anyone she wanted to see would come over unannounced—but curiosity was her weakness, and she got to her feet.

When she opened the door on the chain, Trouble squeezed through, followed in short order by his new friend, Galaxie. Startled, she laughed and looked up to see Ethan standing in the hall.

"Ethan, what . . ." She quickly shut the door, undid the chain, and let him in.

"Sorry I didn't call," he said, and held up a white paper bag. "I brought lunch, if you're hungry."

She hadn't been until then, but the smell of Chinese take-out remedied that, making her stomach growl. "Tell me you bought egg rolls."

Ethan smiled.

"There is a God," she said, shutting the door behind him and throwing both dead bolts.

The cats were in the kitchen, Trouble on the counter poking the cookie jar with his nose, while Galaxie sat, very much the lady, in front of the stove.

"I didn't know you were running a home for wayward cats," Ethan said.

Sydney reached down to pet Galaxie and rub a silky white ear. The cat looked at her with one blue eye and one green, and started to purr. "Wait till they find out I'm fresh out of cookies."

"Will they eat Chinese?"

"Stranger things have happened," she said, and went to the cupboard to get paper plates.

Trouble sniffed everything before deciding on the meat and scrambled egg in the Mu Shu Pork, while Galaxie would settle for nothing less than the tiny shrimp from the house's specialty fried rice.

Sydney felt Ethan watching her as she picked morsels from her plate to feed to the cats, but each time she looked up, he averted his eyes.

Whatever had brought him here, he obviously wasn't ready to reveal . . . yet.

"So," she said twenty minutes later, after she'd tossed the empty cartons and paper plates away, and let the cats out, "exactly when did you get into the home food delivery service?"

"Just today," Ethan said, and laughed.

It had been awhile since she'd heard him laugh.

"I know you're busy—" he nodded, indicating the files on the living-room floor "—and that we agreed this could wait until you had the time, but I'm not sure waiting isn't going to make things worse."

She sat on the couch and tucked her bare feet beneath her. "Can it get worse? I mean, it's been months since you, since *we* had our . . . falling out. A few more days, what harm will it do?"

"Well," he ran a hand through his short-cropped hair, "it'd be nice to get it over with." He cleared a space on the coffee table, and sat down directly across from her, their knees almost touching.

He'd changed his after-shave, she noticed. "That's an interesting choice of words, *over with.*"

"You know what I mean."

"What you usually mean is that it's up to you to set Sydney straight. A dirty job, but somebody's got to do it, right?"

"That isn't it at all."

She frowned, but said nothing.

"I was wrong," Ethan said, "to try and tell you how to run your life."

"I agree, you were wrong."

"And I'm sorry."

"So am I. The question is, will anything change?"

He looked away for a moment, his eyes seemingly restless, unwilling to meet hers. "I have a problem, Sydney, with you and Mitch . . ."

"Yes?"

"It bothers me."

"What bothers you?"

"I don't think he's the right one. For you."

"Don't you think that's for me to decide?"

"Yes," he said, "but . . ."

Sydney felt an odd mix of emotion; irritation at his presuming to know what or who was right for her, and a tingle of anticipation that maybe, just maybe, Ethan would admit for the first time that his feelings for her were more than brotherly.

There was also, unquestionably, a feeling of loss. Because if he did say what she thought he might, she'd have to tell him that, for her, their time had passed.

"Do you remember," Ethan said, "when you broke it off with Mitch, and I took you away . . ."

As if she could forget. They had stayed at his family's beach home in Baja, just the two of them.

On the first day, she'd done little more than cry. Ethan sat on the bed with her and held her for hours, never once saying I-told-you-so.

On the second day, he'd coaxed her into walking on the beach, and by the third, she wore herself out swimming in the ocean, the waves smoothing the sharp edges of her pain.

On the fourth day, they went into the village, to a small cantina where she drank tequila shooters until she was numb. That night, they'd stayed up till dawn, sitting in front of a roaring fire, and playing Monopoly with Baja rules they made up as they went along.

The fifth day, she slept. She still didn't know whether she'd dreamt it, or whether he'd been there in her room. She did hear his footsteps, pacing, somewhere in the house.

On the last day, she had taken his wrist as he moved past her in the kitchen, and reached up to kiss him on the corner of his mouth. If right then, he'd put his arms around her, she would have not said no.

But although she felt his sudden intake of breath, he stepped back from her, and she from him, and the moment was gone.

Of course she remembered. There were nights when she would have sworn she heard the sound of the waves whispering up onto the sand . . .

Now she merely nodded.

"There are days," he said, touching her knee with two fingers, "that I wish we'd never come back."

She took his hand and pulled, so that he had to sit next to her, then turned to face him directly. "Ethan, when I was thirteen and my friends were having matinee dates, I wanted desperately for you to be the one sitting next to me in the theater, holding my hand. But you were twenty-one, getting ready to graduate from college."

He gave her a quizzical look.

"When I was sixteen, I used to dream about you taking me to the Junior prom. I used to pretend, in my room, late at night, that we were slow-dancing. But you were twenty-four, and a cop."

"Sydney, I didn't know—"

"What I'm trying to say is that I've been trying to catch up to you for as long as I can remember, but it seems like it's always the wrong time or place. Or—" it hurt her to smile "—you didn't see me."

"I did, I always did."

"Then you were awfully good at hiding it."

"Sydney, you were a kid. It would have been wrong."

"I know, damn it. But the thing is, I loved you. I loved you, and I waited, until I couldn't wait anymore. Only now, there's Mitch, and . . . I love him, too."

Ethan blinked, and looked away.

Sydney felt the muscles in her throat tighten, and raised her hand to her neck. "I'm sorry, Ethan."

He shook his head. "It's not your fault."

"It isn't anybody's fault."

"I don't know." Ethan stood up, took a couple of steps toward the door, and stopped. With his back to her, he said, "I wanted to tell you in Baja that I was in love with you, that I realized it the first time I saw you with Mitch. He'd been my partner, I considered him a friend . . . hell, the man had saved my life, and yet when I saw him touch you, I wanted him dead."

"I had no idea."

He made a sound that might have been a laugh. "I'm very good at concealing my worst impulses."

"Ethan . . ." Sydney got up and stood behind him and slightly to one side so that she could see his face. "I want you to know, I never wanted to hurt you. What you said about me getting even . . . that wasn't true."

"I know."

"You are now and always will be important to me. I do love you." She touched his forearm gently. "I hope we can be—"

"Don't say friends," Ethan turned toward her. "We'll always be more than that."

She knew before he did it that he was going to kiss her, it was in one sense, inevitable, and that somewhere inside of her, she wanted him to.

What she didn't know was how it would make her feel.

Thirty

The drive up the coast to Mission Viejo in southern Orange County was more pleasant than she'd expected. Often on weekends it seemed as if the populations of San Diego and Orange County— and L.A. to a lesser degree—were playing an exaggerated game of musical chairs. For reasons unknown, everyone in San Diego headed north; everyone in Orange County headed south.

When the music stopped, so did the traffic. The normal sixty minutes it took to drive from La Jolla Village Drive to Oso Parkway doubled. An accident in either direction might triple it, given the inclination of those inching by to slow even further for a really good look.

Today, however, the traffic was light and moving briskly. The sky was a clear if milky blue, although a gray fog bank lurked out at sea, held at bay by an off-shore breeze that in warmer months might aspire to grow up to be a Santa Ana wind.

Frank and Betsy Honeywell lived in a ranch-style home in the gently rolling hills near the Mission

Viejo Golf Course. Turning left from Oso onto Montanosa, she'd noted that the players were out in full force, even late on a Sunday afternoon.

She parked the Mustang on the street, angling the wheels into the curb. The neighborhood was quiet; the only sound she heard was the far-off whine of a hedge trimmer.

The door opened before she reached the trellised porch. The resemblance between Gayle and the woman standing there was nothing less than astonishing. Gayle not only had her mother's eyes, but her face. If not for the sprinkling of gray in her hair and a subtle softening of her features that came with age, Betsy Honeywell could have easily been mistaken for her late daughter.

"Miss Bryant?" Her voice had just a hint of huskiness to it. "Elizabeth Honeywell, but everyone calls me Betsy. Come in, won't you?"

Frank Honeywell was seated on the couch, a martini in his hand, complete with olive. He nodded when they came into the family room, but didn't rise.

Judging by the gin flush on his cheeks and his watery gaze, he'd chosen—or perhaps needed—to fortify himself for their meeting.

People dealt with grief in different ways. Sydney had often heard—and believed—that the worst fate for a parent was to outlive his or her child. A year now since they'd laid Gayle to rest, but it was evident that the loss still cut to the bone.

"We were surprised," Betsy Honeywell said when they were seated, "to hear from Mr. Cooper's assistant that you wanted to talk to us."

Frank Honeywell nodded again. "Considering."

Sydney understood they were referring to her working for the defense, presumably to benefit the killer of their child. "I won't insult you by telling you I know how you feel—quite obviously I don't—but I hope that you're as interested as I am in seeing that the right person is convicted for murdering Gayle."

"You don't think Keith Reilly did it?"

The sixty-four thousand dollar question. "To be honest, Mrs. Honeywell, I'm not sure. But the case against him is circumstantial—"

"Good enough for me," Gayle's father said, and downed his martini. He got up, a little shakily, and went to the breakfast bar where a glass pitcher, beaded with condensation awaited.

"I do know," Sydney went on, "that the worst outcome would be if the killer, whoever it is, never had to answer for his crime."

"Yes," Betsy Honeywell said absently. Her attention was on her husband, who had filled his glass to the brim and now was puzzling out how to add the olive without spilling a drop of his drink.

He settled it by eating the olive, taking a gulp, and then skewering another olive with a plastic spear. Crisis averted.

Sydney waited until Mrs. Honeywell looked at her before resuming. "I was hired to fill in some of the blanks. When I read over the statement you gave to the police, I wondered why no one ever talked to Eddie Monroe."

"Monroe!" The flush on Frank Honeywell's face darkened. "That bum."

"We questioned that, too, Miss Bryant. Our attorney informed us that since the last documented contact between Gayle and Eddie had occurred the summer before, I guess that would be seven or eight months, the police concluded that he was no longer a threat."

"Was he?"

Betsy Honeywell shook her head. "I don't know. He never made any verbal threats. Eddie was more subtle than that; the calls were nasty but—Frank, how did our attorney put it?"

"Non-specific," Frank Honeywell muttered.

"You said 'documented contact.' What do you mean by that?"

"When Eddie began harassing Gayle, our attorney instructed us to make written notes of everything he said and did. We also recorded him every time he called her, took pictures of him in his car when he would park outside. And the gifts and . . . *things* he sent her, we would hand over to the police."

"What kind of things?"

"In the beginning it was flowers and candy, that kind of thing. A teddy bear. Heart-shaped Mylar balloons. Red lace underwear. Perfume."

"And later on?"

Her expression showed her distaste. "Later on, it was condoms that glowed in the dark. Sex toys. The last box we opened ourselves contained a dead rattlesnake. Thank God it *was* dead. After that we delivered the packages intact to the police."

"I assume they were not amused."

"No, not much. When they finally managed to catch up with Eddie, it stopped, of course, in a New York minute. But not before he'd put an ad with Gayle's photograph in one of those singles newspapers, including *our* phone number, since Gayle had changed hers by then."

Sydney wondered if stalkers had a grapevine; she'd heard of similar tactics before.

"The ad was disgusting." Betsy Honeywell glanced toward her husband, who'd gone to stand near the sliding glass door, overlooking the pool. "We had calls you wouldn't believe, some from women."

"But you say the harassment stopped after the police talked to him?"

"That's correct. An officer from the Threat Management Division called us afterward and said if Eddie as much as breathed in my daughter's direction, they'd send him to jail. The police department's policy after one warning was zero tolerance, the officer told me."

"Good for them."

"It seemed to do the trick," Mrs. Honeywell said. "But when Gayle was murdered . . ." Her voice trailed off and she shook her head.

"Did Gayle ever mention seeing Monroe again?"

At the window, Frank Honeywell grunted, and said, "That son-of-a-bitching bum." He opened the sliding door and stepped outside.

"No, not to us."

"Is it possible she might have seen him and didn't tell you?"

"Anything is possible, Miss Bryant."

Sydney acknowledged that with a nod. "And you? Did he contact you in any way after her death?"

"No. Or I should say, maybe. There was one arrangement of white roses at her funeral that arrived without a card. If the roses were from him, well . . . there was nothing anyone could do to hurt our little girl ever again."

"Did Gayle tell you what happened between them? Why they broke up?"

"That," she said, and sighed. "Gayle found out Eddie had been seeing other women. Which was why she was so determined to help Denise out, having been through it herself. As a matter of fact, when things got too intense, Gayle always knew she could count on Denise."

"I gather Gayle had visited the Reillys before?"

"Many times. Denise and Gayle had been friends for a long time, but sharing going through what they did, crying on each other's shoulder, brought them even closer."

And they had died together, Sydney thought. "About Eddie . . ."

"Understand, Gayle and Eddie had been dating on and off since high school, although not exclusively. Then he got it in his head that she was the only girl he wanted. Gayle resisted getting serious—Eddie was still too wild, she said—but he pursued her until she finally agreed to stop going out with other guys."

"Did they discuss marriage?"

"God forbid, no. But Eddie had a five-year plan; he intended to prove to her he'd changed, no more fights, no more drinking, no more hanging out with the boys. He wanted to go to college. After he got his degree, he said, he'd ask her to marry him."

"How long did that last?"

"Actually, he did very well—or seemed to—for close to six months. Then Gayle decided to surprise him by taking him a cake she'd baked for his birthday. When she got to his place, she found him in bed with some little tramp he'd picked up at a bar."

"Speaking of bars, did Gayle ever mention a place in Borrego Springs called Harvey's?"

Another glance at her husband, who was still wandering outside, and Betsy Honeywell shook her head. "He's not usually like this. I'm sorry, did you say Harvey's? No, that isn't familiar."

Remembering what Joey had said about "Crazy Eddie," Sydney said, "I've heard from another source that Monroe was the jealous type. Was he ever violent toward Gayle?"

"Oh no, she'd never have stood for it. As for being jealous, I'm a marriage counselor by profession, and I can tell you that men who cheat usually *are* jealous, because they figure if they're getting away with running around, maybe she is, too."

It made sense, in a twisted way. "Did Gayle have a nickname?"

"A nickname? No."

"Or was there an endearment Eddie used, like Precious or Honey-pie, that kind of—"

"Oh! I'd almost forgotten. He called her Nique or Martinique, because he said that's where they were going on their honeymoon . . . oh God." Her face contorted, and she turned away, then abruptly stood. "Excuse me, would you please?"

Sydney winced, watching as Betsy Honeywell fled the room. She was doing great, here. Gayle's father was knee-deep in gin, and now her mother had dissolved into tears. And yet as bad as she felt for them both, at some level she was also relieved that finally, *finally,* in this case, she'd encountered someone who gave a damn.

Talia had cried, and Corey had sniffled, and even

Nigel Fox had quivered, but their emotions, whatever they truly were beyond the typical "poor-little-
me" had nothing to do with the loss of a human life.

Gayle, at least, was being mourned.

"I'm sorry I ran off that way," Mrs. Honeywell
said, a scant three minutes later, retaking her place
on the couch. Her eyes were slightly red and puffy,
but she held her chin up and attempted a smile. "It's
just that it's often not until a mother watches her
daughter leave on her honeymoon, that she realizes
she's lost her little girl. And I would give anything
and everything on this earth to have it be just that."

At a loss, Sydney merely nodded.

"I do want to help, though. That's why we agreed
to talk to you."

"I've taken enough of your time," she said,
standing. "For which I thank you. I know you
haven't granted any interviews to the press."

"We never will. Our loss is a private matter, *not*
a human interest tidbit on the six-o'clock news."

"That's understandable."

"The press was so horridly intrusive when the
trial ended the way it did, calling every few minutes,
knocking on our door, trampling the bushes, that
Frank and I flew off to visit our son in Seattle—"

"I didn't know Gayle had a brother."

"Yes. His wife's expecting our first grandchild."
Her smile, this time, seemed genuine. "We're all
hoping for a little girl. Of course, no one could ever
take Gayle's place in our hearts, but . . . a baby
granddaughter might help fill the void."

Outside, Mr. Honeywell's wandering had taken
him to a hammock slung between two flowering

cherry-blossom trees. His empty martini glass, forgotten, had tipped over in the grass.

"Anyway," Betsy Honeywell said, bracing herself. "We do need to find out who murdered Gayle. If it wasn't Keith, am I right that Eddie is the next most logical suspect?"

"Yes," Sydney said, "it would seem he is."

Thirty-one

"The best I can do for you," Deputy Rick Morgan said, with a glance over his shoulder, "is twenty minutes with Monroe in a holding cell."

"I can live with that," Sydney said, following him down the hall. The walls, painted in two shades of institutional tan, light above and dark below, were scuffed with shoeprints including one matching set at eye level.

About a size thirteen, she estimated, and wondered how they had gotten there.

"Good thing it's been quiet," Morgan said, inserting the distinctive flat turnkey into the lock, "or I wouldn't have even that."

"I'll be as quick as I can," she promised, and stepped inside.

Eddie Monroe was standing in a corner of the room, leaning against the wall, arms folded across his chest. His streaked brown hair was collar-length, framing a rather delicately-featured face. Monroe was almost pretty, which probably accounted for his predilection for macho pursuits. About five-foot-nine or ten, he was slender except for the suggestion of a nascent beer-belly.

His brown eyes regarded her benignly.

"Mr. Monroe," she said as the lock was engaged behind her, "I'm a private investigator working for—"

"I know. Word gets around."

"I have a few questions I'd like to ask you."

"Fire away."

There was no place to sit, so she went to stand at the wall opposite him, leaning her left shoulder against one of the cleaner spots. "I assume you know that the D.A. wants to talk to you about Gayle Honeywell?"

"Oh yeah. What they tell me, I'm moving up the charts with a bullet. Pardon the expression."

Sydney wondered at his lack of concern. "Where were you last April fifth?"

Monroe offered a minimalist's smile. "I'm not sure where I was the day before yesterday."

"Is that your answer? You don't remember?"

"Well, I remember that I didn't kill anyone last year, if that's any help."

"What about when you heard she was dead?"

"Sorry." He tugged on his right ear, fingering what appeared to be a diamond stud. "I must have blanked that out, too. Mental trauma or whatever they call it these days. I loved her, you know."

"You had an odd way of showing it."

"All a guy can do is try," he said. "Never know what might work."

Quite the philosopher, she thought, and decided to see if she could rattle him. "I talked to Gayle's parents this afternoon."

"Really."

"Her mother thinks maybe you sent flowers for the funeral. White roses."

"Sounds nice."

"Did you?"

He didn't answer immediately, instead scratching his head as though puzzled. He shifted his position, bracing one foot against the wall as if he were anticipating the need to push off in a hurry.

"Florists keep records. It might take me a day or two, but I can probably find out," she said, although if he'd paid cash, that was doubtful.

"What the hell," he said. "Okay, I sent the roses. Is that a crime?"

"No, but you obviously knew Gayle was dead shortly after the murders. The question is, how did you find out, and where were you when you heard?"

"It was on the news." He squinted in concentration. "I must've been out when old Frank and Betsy called to break it to me gently. I saw the story on the late news that Monday night."

"That's half of it."

"What, you don't want to know which station?" Monroe asked and laughed.

"Just where you were." If she could eliminate him as a suspect, if he'd been six hundred miles away at a crap table in Vegas, she wanted to know, and *now*. "At home, in Borrego Springs—"

"Haven't had a TV in years. Got mad and put my boot through the screen."

"A friend's house, maybe, or at a bar?"

"You don't know my friends. Sure, they've got lots of TVs, but nobody plugs 'em in."

She took that to mean his friends were thieves, only interested in moving the merchandise along. "I don't have time for twenty questions, Eddie."

"Oh, I'm sorry. Am I pissing you off?"

"No, and I'll tell you why; I think you enjoy

pissing people off. If it's all the same to you, I'd prefer not to give you the satisfaction."

"It *is* all the same to me, honey. Jail, the street, my bed or yours. You just have to learn to adapt to your circumstances."

She shook her head in mock wonder. "Why aren't you out on the lecture circuit, spreading the word? I haven't heard a line that lame since freshman Psych class."

His infinitesimal smile was back. "Glad you liked it."

"Come on, Eddie. Talk to me."

"What's it gonna get me? You're working for the other side. It's in my best interest to let old Keith swing in the breeze."

"Only if you're the shooter."

"There's where we disagree. As long as the wheels of justice are grinding him into dust, instead of me, I'm happy. Better him than me."

"The thing is, as evasive as you're being, it makes me think you know something about the murders, that you've got something to hide."

Monroe inclined his head. "I know a few things. But not anything that'll help the grieving widower."

"Why don't you let me be the judge of that?" She heard footsteps in the corridor and glanced at her watch, worried that her time was running out.

"I don't think so. My attorney wouldn't want me to devaluate my potential testimony."

So there might be a plea bargain in the works. "Are you saying Keith did it?"

Monroe simply stared at her.

"How could you possibly know?" She moved away from the wall, toward the door, deliberately turning her back to him, dismissing him. "I'll tell you what I think, Eddie. I think you must be crazy. That's what they call you, isn't it? Crazy Eddie?"

"I'm not crazy."

"No?" At the door, she turned again to face him. "Whatever you're telling your attorney, it's gotta be a lie. You were at Harvey's that night, in Borrego."

Monroe did not respond in any way, not even the blink of an eye.

"That's right, isn't it? Gayle called you there, didn't she? She called from Denise's."

"What makes you say that?"

She told him about the last-number-dialed feature on the guest-room phone. "No one's gotten the records yet, but they will, and when they do—"

"When they do, nothing. The fact that Gayle might have called Harvey's doesn't necessarily have anything to do with me."

"Now you *are* pissing me off. The records will show what time the call was made and—"

"So? No frigging record I've ever heard of can prove who was on the other end."

"I get it," Sydney said. "You think your friends will cover for you."

"Not saying I need them to, but why wouldn't they?"

"From what I'm told, there's a fair amount of illegal activity that goes on out there."

"What's that have to do with me?"

She didn't answer, asking instead, "Have you ever noticed that if someone's *own* ass is on the line, they get less concerned about covering somebody else's?"

"You're saying they'll give me up?"

"Bingo."

He pushed off from the wall, but then just stood

there, with what might have been a frown on his pretty face. He hung his thumbs in the pockets of his jail-issue jumpsuit. "Could happen," he said after a minute had passed.

Sydney tried not to show her relief; the sale wasn't made yet, and almost didn't count. "Tell me what you know, Eddie."

He held up one finger. "I still gotta ask, what's in it for me?"

"Not for you. Do it," she urged, playing her trump card, "for Nique."

Monroe's eyes narrowed, then he blinked and looked away. "You fight dirty," he said, sounding hoarse.

"You say you loved her—"

"I did, damn it."

"—and yet you don't want to help find out who killed her? That doesn't sound like love to me. Or does protecting yourself come first?"

"No matter what I do, it won't bring Nique back."

"You're right, it won't."

"So what's the point?" He took a step back and slumped against the wall. "And don't tell me it's justice, because there ain't none."

"Isn't there?"

"No. If there was, I'd have got her back. I really miss her, you know?"

Sydney watched him for a moment, and understood. "You and Nique were getting back together?"

"You could say that."

After all the things Monroe had done, Gayle had been considering a reconciliation. Then again, it was hardly unheard of; a year or so ago, she'd worked a case involving battered wives. Strange as it seemed, then and now, there were always women, ever hopeful or maybe just scared of life alone, who'd failed the first time but were willing to try, try again.

"Her parents didn't know," she said as a statement of fact.

"No. She said she hadn't figured out how to break it to them. They were, you know, still pretty ticked off about . . . stuff."

"You talked to her that night?"

"Yes."

"More than once?"

He inclined his head. "I can't give you an exact number, but there were at least four or five calls."

"What kind of time interval?"

"You expect me to remember that? I was drinking, you know."

"The last call, then," she persisted.

"Last call, huh? I guess it was about twelve-thirty."

If that was true—and the phone records should verify it—there was no way that he could have made it to San Diego by ten after one, when Jefferson Brown had heard an automobile's voice warning . . .

"What kind of car do you drive?"

He jerked his head back in surprise, but answered. "It's a candy-apple-red Mustang, a sixty-five."

"Is that what you were driving last April?" He nodded.

"When Gayle called, what did you talk about?"

"She told me she missed me. That she and Denise were going to stay up all night watching old movies. They were too excited to sleep, she said."

"Did she say why?"

"Denise was getting the money to make her getaway. The next day, I mean. Gayle and I made plans to have dinner the day after that. Tuesday, would have been." He grimaced. "They buried her on Wednesday."

"Did she mention any trouble of any kind? Had she heard Denise and Keith fighting, or—"

"No, no trouble. She did say they'd had company earlier but wouldn't tell me who."

"What did you make of that?"

"Not a lot. She and Denise had some notion that the phone lines were bugged. Talk about paranoia. I kidded her about it, but she was convinced. Wouldn't tell me the details, but somebody knew something that was supposed to be a big secret."

"She never said who it was?"

"Nope. But they were prepared."

"What do you mean, prepared?"

"They had a gun."

Sydney's heart thudded. "What?"

"Gayle had a gun. Denise had given it to her back when, well . . . you know. A nine-millimeter automatic."

"Keith's missing Beretta."

"Could be." Eddie Monroe gave her a knowing look. "The D.A. finds out about that, that it was Keith's gun, it's all over."

Sydney thought he might be right.

Thirty-two

Keith's Beretta.

It appeared Jake "I'll-win-next-time" Scott was right about that much; the murder weapon had been the missing Beretta all along.

Granted, the gun may have been in Gayle's possession, but assuming the shooter had acted on impulse, taking the gun away from Gayle and shooting both women, who stood to gain the most by *not* leaving the gun behind?

Keith.

If he knew it was his Beretta—and presumably he would have suspected it was—he certainly would have known that his ownership of the murder weapon was the kind of detail that seriously eroded reasonable doubt.

His gun, his house, his wife, dead on the floor.

"Damn." Sydney tightened her grip on the steering wheel, coming to stop at a traffic light. She glanced up at the street sign hanging from the standard, swinging just slightly in the wind. Where the hell was she?

Distracted by her thoughts, she'd somehow wound up on Pacific Coast Highway, heading north. Since it was the direction she wanted to go, if not the most direct route, she stayed the course. She'd catch Interstate 5 by taking the PCH to Fiesta Island Drive, then take a right on Sea World Drive to the freeway on-ramp, near Mission Bay.

Out to sea, the fog bank was an ominous presence, illuminated by an unknown source.

What are you missing?

"I'll be damned if I know," she answered the voice in her head. She was tired and frustrated, and the beginning of a headache was forming behind her eyes, aggravated by the bright flashing lights of the driver tailgating her Mustang as she merged onto I-5.

Maybe she just was too close to it. Couldn't see the forest for the trees. Maybe everything pointed to Keith Reilly, as Jake Scott had said.

Was she being stubborn? Refusing to see the truth because she wanted to show Jake she could play with the big boys? Or had she been influenced by Wade Cooper's faith in his client?

Her client, too.

Only it couldn't have been Keith, if Jefferson Brown was right. Keith was at The Quick Gold Fox at two-thirty A.M.; the killer had stayed until five.

What are you missing? Or who?

She didn't know.

It had been her intention to go home, sit on the floor in the middle of the files, and try to puzzle it out. She could listen to the interviews she'd recorded, then slip the videotape of the Reilly walk-through into the VCR, and hope like hell that something she read or heard or saw would jar the answers from her brain.

But as she neared her exit, it occurred to her: why watch a videotape when she could go that one better? She had the keys to the house Talia had given her.

It might not be, strictly speaking, an authorized entry, but what the hell. What harm could it do? All she wanted to do was get a deeper feel for the place, spend a little time, listening for the echoes of that night.

No one would ever have to know.

She'd spent so much time in the Reilly neighborhood, it was almost starting to feel like home. To keep from drawing attention to herself, she parked up the hill from the cul-de-sac, and walked down after retrieving her heavy-duty Lumilite flashlight from the trunk, since the electricity to the house had long ago been turned off.

And just in case, she took her .38.

Inside, she checked that the drapes and mini-blinds were closed in all of the rooms that faced the street. Only after that did she turn on the Lumilite; she sat it on its base on the floor in the living room, so that the beam was directed at the ceiling.

The effect was eerie. There was a circular shape to the light, beyond which it became more diffuse. The quality of the light, she realized, was very much like that reflected by the moon.

Somehow it fit her mood.

Sydney sat on the harem couch, and put the .38 on the cushion beside her. Seeing it there made her a trifle uneasy—she wasn't quite over Friday's inci-

dent—so she edged it under the corner of an over-
sized pillow. Still in reach, but out of sight.

"Well," she said, "I'm here."

If houses could be said to be unimpressed, this
one was. Other than an occasional creak as it settled, the silence was complete.

"All the better," she said, leaning back and drawing her right leg up, clasping her hands around her
knee. Staring at nothing in particular, she surren-
dered to her thoughts.

Imagining . . .

*Denise and Gayle, alone in the house, baby Daniel
asleep in the nursery. Denise is excited, exhilarated,
because her plans to leave Keith are coming together.
She's been clever, she thinks, letting Keith stay in the
house, lulling him into a sense of complacency. The
loan papers she signed Friday at The Quick Gold Fox
are nothing but a ruse, one affording her a last opportunity to remind Nigel Fox that he'd better do his
part, or else.*

*Best of all, the inventory required for the bank loan
will keep Keith out of her hair that last night before
she leaves. She deliberately has avoided packing her
or the baby's things—she can buy whatever they need
later—so that Keith won't suspect anything.*

*She has outsmarted them. Keith and Miriam have
pulled every nasty trick to keep her in line, closing her
checking account, cancelling her credit cards, making
her have to ask for—and justify—every dollar she
spends. But she's had the last laugh: tomorrow she'll
collect twenty-thousand dollars in gold.*

*Maybe she's already given some thought to where
she'll go to convert the gold to cash. She knows she*

shouldn't change the entire amount with one dealer, but there are lots of coin shops, and she'll have a few hours, anyway, before Keith starts to look for her.

When the time is right, she'll wire some of the money to herself in Germany, where her father is stationed, and buy traveler's checks with the rest. She and Daniel will fly out of Los Angeles, to Germany, to points beyond. By the weekend, the humiliation she's suffered because of her husband's infidelity— and her interfering mother-in-law's disapproval—will be nothing but a memory.

She can walk out the door without being afraid to run into Talia, who she thought was her friend. Keith is welcome to his bimbo, if that's what he really wants. There have been, she thinks, other women at other times, but they were faceless suspicions, and none of them had shown up, naked, in her own bed.

On Valentine's Day, no less.

I love you, too.

After tomorrow, she'll be among friends, wherever she is. She's only twenty-three, and she knows she's pretty. There has to be a guy somewhere who'll treat her well. She and Daniel will make a new life for themselves.

Gayle is a good friend, coming to stay with her in her time of need, but maybe a little more apprehensive than she should be. Gayle is worried that Keith is onto Denise's plan, perhaps because of an overheard conversation, or could it be he's wired the phone?

But Gayle, Denise thinks, is a little paranoid, because of her experience with Eddie Monroe. Denise had snuck a nine-millimeter automatic out of Keith's collection to give to Gayle when that craziness had been going on. The police might not have approved of Gayle arming herself, and the Honeywells definitely would not, but Denise felt better knowing she'd given her best friend a means of self-defense.

Wasn't it weird that after all of that, Eddie was back in Gayle's life? And kind of touching, the way she kept sneaking off to the guest room to call him, just to hear the sound of his voice?

Denise doesn't envy Gayle having to tell her parents that she's falling in love again with the guy who had them pacing the floor with worry. Tough job, that.

All Denise has to do, by comparison, is get through the night.

Except, she doesn't.

Someone comes to the house at about ten minutes after one. Someone she lets in or who has a key. They start to talk, and then argue, but Denise feels invulnerable. She's leaving tomorrow, and this is her chance to say some things she's only thought about till now.

It isn't until the killer grabs the gun that the first tingle of fear runs through her. Afraid, she turns to run, and is struck in the back. The force of the bullet knocks her to the floor.

In a closed space, a gunshot is incredibly loud, and she is almost deafened by that, and a ringing in her ears. But there's another shot—Gayle, she thinks, oh no—and after that, she can only faintly hear Danny crying.

Bleeding and frightened, she struggles to reach him, pulling herself across the carpet with her hands. Someone is behind her, though, coming near.

Another shot, and an explosion of pain.

Gravely wounded, she's unaware of the killer walking past her into the nursery. Doesn't hear the dinosaur mobile begin to play "Rockabye Baby."

At five A.M., when the killer leaves, Denise has been dead for more than three hours.

"Four hours total." Sydney closed her eyes. "The killer stayed in this house for four hours, with two dead bodies and a baby."

Why so long?

Unless . . .

Outside, she heard the sound of a car engine. Listening as it came closer, she got up and turned out the flashlight, brought it back with her to the couch. She had to feel her way in the dark. She located her .38 and pulled a pillow into her lap to cover it.

And waited.

A moment later, the engine was shut off. Then, faintly, as if in a dream, a mechanical voice said, "The key is in the ignition."

A kind of shuffling at the door, followed by the sound of a key turning in a lock.

The door opened, a woman's form in silhouette against the ambient light.

"Hello, Mrs. Reilly," Sydney said.

Thirty-three

"Who's there?" Miriam Reilly asked.

Sydney switched on the Lumilite, directing it at a far wall, the better not to blind either of them. "It's the strangest thing . . . I was just thinking about you."

"Miss Bryant?" She took a hesitant step into the house. "What are you doing here?"

"Thinking, actually." Sydney noticed that the older woman had a flashlight of her own, a big heavy job that must have taken six D batteries. The late Cullen Reilly's? "I do a lot of that."

"Oh, well, I won't disturb you then. There was something I wanted to get for Daniel, but it can wait until tomorrow," Miriam said, but made no move to leave.

"It's odd, Wade Cooper never mentioned to me that you had a key."

"Yes, I . . . I have a key." Miriam laughed, sounding uneasy. "Talk about odd, I found it today, this afternoon, in fact. I was going through my junk drawer, looking for a thumbtack to put up Daniel's latest fingerpainting, and came across it."

"Really."

Miriam nodded. "It gave me a jolt, I can tell you, finding it. I'd forgotten I ever had one."

"What was it," Sydney asked, "that you came over to get for Daniel?"

"Oh, a toy. One of his stuffed animals." In the indirect light, her expression looked mildly agitated, her eyes restlessly scanning the room.

Had she been back, Sydney wondered, since that night? "Where is he, by the way? Daniel, I mean."

"At a neighbor's." Miriam cleared her throat. "Since I'm here, do you think it would be all right if I . . . no never mind, I'll—"

"Stay." Realizing it sounded like a command to a dog, she added, "It would be foolish not to do what you came for." Whatever that was.

"Well . . ." Indecision was apparent in her body language; she shifted her weight from foot to foot, and glanced over her shoulder at the still-open door.

"If nothing else, I'd like to talk to you about Keith."

Miriam came forward slowly. "I heard on the news they have another suspect."

Sydney chose to play dumb, shaking her head as if to say, that's news to me.

"You haven't heard?"

"I just got back from Orange County," she lied. "What's going on? Who is it?"

"The other one's boyfriend." Miriam entered the living room finally, and sat on a wingback chair. "Monroe, I think his name is."

"Monroe. The name's vaguely familiar."

Miriam nodded, as if it were to her, too. "I met him once. Keith and Denise had a Fourth of July barbecue and he came with, um, what was her name? Gayle."

Also known as the other one, Sydney thought, but said nothing, lest her irritation show.

"He was quite peculiar. Long hair, scruffy clothes. And—" Miriam frowned "—he wore an earring. If I remember correctly, he had a wild look in his eyes, which made me think he was on drugs."

"Drugs, really."

Mrs. Reilly leaned forward, her clasped hands on her knees, that heavy flashlight across her lap. "Do you think this will help Keith?"

"I guess that depends on what the police can find out about where he was that night." Sydney had a curious sense that she could hear the gears turning in Miriam Reilly's head.

"Wouldn't it be wonderful if they found some kind of proof that he'd done it?"

"Proof?"

"Then Keith could come home—our home, not here—and the three of us could get on with our lives."

"And live happily ever after," Sydney mused. She had an inkling of what was going on.

"He'd have to sell this house, of course." Miriam got up, flashlight in hand and turned around in a tight circle, surveying the rooms. "Not that he'll see a dime of it; every cent will have to go to paying Wade."

"You know, Mrs. Reilly, I was wrong."

"Hmm?"

"Right before you got here, I was brainstorming, trying to figure out why the killer spent so much time in the house after the murders."

"Oh, my . . ."

"The Deputy D.A. said in court the killer stayed to make sure Denise and Gayle were dead, maybe half an hour. Off the record he told me they were also fairly certain that this person made an effort to quiet the baby, so his cries wouldn't attract unwanted attention."

"Oh? I hadn't heard that," the older woman said with a frown.

"Even so, the D.A. was thinking along the lines of, as I said, thirty minutes. But I'm pretty sure it was closer to four hours—"

"Four hours?" Miriam placed one hand on the back of the chair. "That couldn't be. Really?"

"Really. You see, I've found a witness who heard the killer arrive at a little after one, and leave around five A.M."

"Witness, did you say?"

Sydney nodded. "Anyway, it bothered me enough that someone could or *would* stay while two people were dying here, thirty minutes or so. But four hours."

"That is terrible," Miriam said, one hand pressed against the side of her face.

To control the twitch at her eye?

"I am by nature a curious person," Sydney continued. "So naturally I wondered why anyone would hang around like that. It didn't make any sense to me."

"No, of course not."

"But when I visualized it, sat here and thought it through, it came to me that the killer—you, Mrs. Reilly—stayed because you couldn't stand to leave the baby alone."

"No, no . . ."

"You hadn't seen little Danny for more than fifteen minutes at a time in six or seven weeks. The gunshots woke him, and he was crying. You had to comfort him."

"I could never—" a strangled cry came from her throat, and she covered her mouth.

"You changed his diaper, gave him a bottle of sugar water, and cuddled him back to sleep." Sydney saw both that Miriam Reilly was shaking and her grip had tightened on the flashlight. "But I was wrong thinking you'd stayed only for Danny's sake."

"You don't understand," Miriam said, a little breathlessly. "He did it. That Monroe person. Don't you see? Everything works out for the best."

"I know that's how you'd like it to be."

"It *has* to be."

"I'm sorry, Mrs. Reilly, but it can't. An innocent man is in jail now, but you can't go out and implicate another innocent man to take your son's place."

"I'm not—"

"That's really why you stayed that night, isn't it? Long after Daniel was back asleep. Not that seeing him wasn't part of it, but you had another reason to keep you here."

Confusion in her eyes, Miriam Reilly shook her head. "I don't know what you're talking about."

"The gun, Mrs. Reilly. It's here, isn't it? It's been here all along, hidden so well that the police couldn't find it."

"How can you do this to me?" Her voice was a whisper, barely audible over the sighing of the weeping willow beyond the open door.

"You did it to yourself." And because she did not want Miriam Reilly swinging that flashlight and forcing the issue, Sydney moved the pillow off her lap, revealing the Smith and Wesson.

"That won't be necessary," the older woman said, moving back to sit in the chair, the picture of resignation. She put the flashlight on the floor, gave it a little kick so it was out of reach. "How did you know?"

"It's the only logical answer." Sydney frowned. "You were always so certain of Keith's innocence . . . yesterday, a father asked me how a parent could ever really *know,* and I didn't have an answer for him. But you knew Keith hadn't done it, because you had."

"Something that simple . . ."

"Sometimes simple, sometimes not. Tell me, you came here to get the Beretta, didn't you? You were going to try to use it to implicate Monroe?"

"Yes."

The woman's expression was dreamy again, the way she'd looked yesterday morning, talking about how a mother had to make it all better.

"I know where he lives, you see. Keith had me write down his name and address the summer before last. In case anything happened to them while Gayle was visiting, I could notify the police who to look for. Keith told me he was violent, this Monroe person."

"And on the news tonight . . ."

"They said the police were requesting a search warrant for his home. I thought I could get there first, and hide the gun."

"It might have worked," Sydney said. A piece of evidence that incriminating would be nearly impossible for the police or D.A. to ignore. Monroe's drinking buddies—probably not the most savory lot—and the phone calls would be hard-pressed to outweigh the evidentiary value of the murder weapon.

"Yes," Miriam said, "it might."

"What I don't understand is why. Why kill them?"

"It was an accident."

Sydney kept silent.

"I didn't come here that night to shoot anyone. I didn't even have a gun." Her eyes got a faraway look. "It was just sitting there, on top of Gayle's purse."

"Denise let you in?"

"Yes, and that surprised me. I'd come over to plead with her not to leave the country. If she wanted to divorce Keith, that was fine with me. I was no fan of hers or the marriage. But take an apartment or let Keith move out. Be civilized, for heaven's sake."

"How did you know she was planning to leave?"

"Oh that." An odd smile flitted across her face. "You can guess, surely."

"No."

"Well, I bought one of those little tape recorders, like the one you have. It's voice-activated. Quite clever, really."

"And you had Keith hide it in the house?"

"Not Keith. I bought the baby a stuffed animal. It was supposed to talk—"

Talking cars and talking toys. Sydney shook her head at that.

"Anyway, I took out its inner workings, and put the recorder in. Denise never noticed. Most of what was on the tape was Daniel, crying. But I heard enough of Denise and Gayle to put two and two together." Her smile turned sly. "Sort of the way you did."

"Did you confront Denise?"

"I had to. Only she laughed at me, called me a meddling mother-in-law, and said to get the hell out. You'll excuse the profanity."

Ever the lady.

"I was afraid of them." Her mouth was trembling, and her cheeks colored. "Denise was saying the most awful things and her hands were clenched into fists. I thought she was going to hit me."

"So you grabbed the gun."

"It was right there."

The words were out before she could stop them: "Wasn't that enough? You could protect yourself if you had to. Did you have to shoot?"

"Denise said she was going to call the police. I was between her and the phone in the kitchen, so she turned to go to the bedroom, and . . ."

"And?"

"She said to me, 'We'll see who's high and mighty when they throw your ass in jail.'" Miriam frowned. "And I shot her. An accident."

"What about Gayle?"

"Gayle?" She blinked rapidly, as if trying to remember. "I couldn't let her interfere."

Sydney felt queasy, her stomach aching. "And the third shot?"

Miriam Reilly sighed. "Denise was crawling toward the nursery. I couldn't let the baby see her . . . like that. The blood. All that blood."

The Beretta was in a small wall safe behind the key cabinet in the service area. Keith had never told the police about its existence—had he suspected?—and no one other than Denise and Miriam Reilly ever knew it was there.

The combination had been hidden by Keith, who wrote it, lightly in pencil, a single number at a time, in the pages of the family Bible. It had taken his mother most of those four hours to find all of the numbers.

Sitting on the window seat in the nursery, with Daniel asleep, with Denise and Gayle dead, turning ever so patiently through the thin, gold-edged pages.

Sydney left the gun where it was.

Waiting for the police, Sydney asked her, "Would you have let Keith go to prison?"

Miriam Reilly tilted her head, as if wondering herself, but then nodded. "He's my son, and I love him, but the way his life has turned out, I feel that Cullen and I failed to bring him up properly."

"What do you mean, the way his life turned out?"

"Well, marrying *her* was a terrible mistake. He wouldn't listen to me, you know. I warned him, and he wouldn't listen. With Daniel, I had another chance to raise a child. Another chance to do it right, this time."

"Do it right," Sydney echoed.

"Besides, it's not as if I ever thought Keith would be convicted. My son is innocent, you know."

There was no adequate response to that. Standing in the open doorway, Sydney saw two police cars turn onto the street. Lights, no sirens.

Epilogue

By Friday, the furor had died down to the point that when the phone rang at Bryant and Walker Investigations, it wasn't necessarily the press.

Sharks in chummed waters had nothing on the media, the members of which had engaged in a virtual feeding frenzy since the story broke. The results still could be seen in photo captions, including one showing a serene Miriam Reilly being taken to Las Colinas Women Detention Facility out in Santee, which read with typical newspaper hyperbole: "Mother Love?"

Victor Griffith had, as usual, tap-danced his way to the front of the pack, managing to snag two exclusive interviews: the first with ninety-two-year-old Jefferson Davis Brown; and another with Miriam Reilly's Nissan Maxima. The Maxima, on cue, had given a flawless reading of its only line.

Victor had also found a stuffed toucan identical to the one Mrs. Reilly had used to hide the voice-activated tape recorder. The toucan, probably on advice of counsel, had remained mute.

* * *

Keith Reilly had been released on Tuesday. At his request, Sydney went with him and Wade Cooper to pick up Daniel, who'd remained in the care of the neighbor Miriam had left the child with Sunday evening.

Daniel, at twenty-one months, had Denise's blond hair and Keith's brown eyes. He had a sweet, shy grin and an infectious laugh.

On his knees hugging his son, Keith had looked up at Sydney with tears in his eyes.

"Daddy," Daniel said, his sturdy little body bouncing up and down within the circle of his father's arms. "Daddy, where you been?"

Sydney lost it, then, and had to walk away.

Later, with Daniel finally exhausted and asleep on his father's lap, Keith grabbed her hand and pressed it to his face, his skin hot with emotion. "I don't know how to thank you," he said.

"Danny already did."

On the way back to town to pick up the Mustang, Wade Cooper had looked over at her, driving his big Lincoln with two fingers. He winked and smiled. "I told you he didn't do it."

"You told me," she agreed, "but you forgot to mention his mother was a trifle unbalanced."

"Wasn't that a shocker? She seemed so damned normal. Better than normal, the way she supported Keith. And she was absolutely devoted to Danny."

"Well," Sydney said, watching an ambulance roar by east-bound on the freeway, "she was fully prepared to support him all the way to Death Row."

"Don't remind me."

"As for her devotion to her grandson, I think

taking his parents away—one way or the other—qualifies as something else entirely."

"It's a tough world," Wade Cooper said, "when love can drive you to kill."

Sydney shook her head. "It wasn't love at all."

"Ms. Bryant? I'm sorry to disturb you . . ."

Sydney looked up from the paper airplane she was folding to see Hannah DeWilde frowning at her from the doorway. "Sorry, what?"

"The computer serviceman insists that Mr. Walker promised him he'd be paid today—"

"That's fine, there's money in the account." A *lot* of money; Wade Cooper had been exceedingly generous in settling her fee.

"Yes, but he's gone—"

"Xavier is? Again?"

"Yes, so I was wondering if you'd sign the check?"

"No problem." She ran her thumbnail along the crease of the airplane, then picked up a pen and waited for Hannah to hand her the check. "And you don't have to call me Ms. Bryant. Sydney will do."

"Are you sure?"

"Absolutely." She signed her name, looked at the amount and whistled. "Maybe I'm in the wrong line of work after all."

Hannah smiled, picking up the check. "I don't think so. You're obviously good at what you do."

"Hmm. But—" she took the airplane between her thumb and index finger "—can I fly?"

"There's only one way to find out."

"Here goes nothing." Sydney sent the plane sailing toward the furthest window, half-expecting it to crash straight to the floor. But it didn't, flying instead in a graceful arc that skirted the glass, and descended into a perfect landing near the door that connected her office to Xavier's.

"Wow," Hannah said.

"No kidding." Sydney got up to retrieve the plane. "Xavier keeps telling me I've got to learn to relax. Maybe there's hope after all."

Mitch had Friday night off as comp for working Sunday and Monday. His Kearny Mesa triple homicide had closed quick and furious; the killings were in retaliation for a soured drug deal, with the shooter too hyped-up to cover his tracks. When they found the guy, he was still wearing clothes stained with his victims' blood.

Dumb sometimes just didn't cover it.

Sydney dressed up for the occasion, wearing a wine-colored sleeveless dress. Admiring the color, she nodded at her reflection; if she couldn't drink it, she'd wear it.

The fit was clingy, and the neckline showed a hint of the black lace she wore beneath it; but she figured what the hell, they were engaged. Sheer black nylons, black high-heeled sandals, and her hair worn up off her neck.

"Ouch," Mitch said when she opened the door. "You sure you want to go out?"

He looked pretty good himself: black shirt, black tie, charcoal gray suit. But she said, "I'm starving, and I'm under strict orders to get a life."

He put his arm around her waist and moved closer. "What you are is gorgeous."

"Flattery isn't going to get you out of taking me to dinner, Lieutenant."

"What about bribery?" He kissed her bare neck, beneath her ear. "Would that do it?"

"Not a chance." Sydney slipped away.

"I forgot," Mitch said, "you're incorruptible."

"Incorruptible?" She turned and leaned against the door. "That's a rotten thing to say."

"Nothing but the truth." He ran a finger along her cheek, then tilted her chin up so she was looking into his hazel eyes.

Sydney smiled faintly. "Maybe I could stand to be corrupted a little bit. Why don't we—"

"Why don't we?"

This time she didn't have an answer.

Prepare Yourself for

PATRICIA WALLACE

LULLABYE   (2917, $3.95/$4.95)
Eight-year-old Bronwyn knew she wasn't like other girls. She didn't
have a mother. At least, not a real one. Her mother had been in a
coma at the hospital for as long as Bronwyn could remember. She
couldn't feel any pain, her father said. But when Bronwyn sat with
her mother, she knew her mother was angry—angry at the nurses and
doctors, and her own helplessness. Soon, she would show them all the
true meaning of suffering . . .

MONDAY'S CHILD   (2760, $3.95/$4.95)
Jill Baker was such a pretty little girl, with long, honey-blond hair
and haunting gray-green eyes. Just one look at her angelic features
could dispel all the nasty rumors that had been spreading around
town. There were all those terrible accidents that had begun to plague
the community, too. But the fact that each accident occurred after
little Jill had been angered had to be coincidence . . .

SEE NO EVIL   (2429, $3.95/$4.95)
For young Caryn Dearborn, the cornea operation enabled her to see
more than light and shadow for the first time. For Todd Reynolds, it
was his chance to run and play like other little boys. For these two
children, the sudden death of another child had been the miracle they
had been waiting for. But with their eyesight came another kind of
vision—of evil, horror, destruction. They could see into other
people's minds, their worst fears and deepest terrors. And they could
see the gruesome deaths that awaited the unwary . . .

THRILL   (3142, $4.50/$5.50)
It was an amusement park like no other in the world. A tri-level mar-
vel of modern technology enhanced by the special effects wizardry of
holograms, lasers, and advanced robotics. Nothing could go wrong—
until it did. As the crowds swarmed through the gates on Opening
Day, they were unprepared for the disaster about to strike. Rich and
poor, young and old would be taken for the ride of their lives, trapped
in a game of epic proportions where only the winners survived . . .